Endpaper design from the wallpaper seen in an 1886 photograph of the front parlor of the Harriet Beecher Stowe House, Hartford, Connecticut. Reproduced exclusively for The Stowe-Day Foundation.

Harriet Beecher Stowe's
New England Novels

POGANUC PEOPLE

POGANUC PEOPLE
Harriet Beecher Stowe

with a new introduction by

Joseph S. Van Why

THE STOWE-DAY FOUNDATION
Hartford, Connecticut
1977

© Copyright 1977 The Stowe-Day Foundation
Library of Congress
Catalogue Card Number 76-56587
ISBN 0-917482-06-9

Stowe, Harriet Elizabeth Beecher, 1811-1896.
   Poganuc people.

   Reprint of the ed. published by Fords, Howard & Hulbert, New York
   I. Title
PZ3.S89Po9   [PS2954]   813'.3   76-56587
ISBN 0-917482-06-9

The Stowe-Day Foundation was established and endowed by the late Katharine Seymour Day, a grandniece of Harriet Beecher Stowe. It is located on Nook Farm, the famous nineteenth-century neighborhood in which Harriet Beecher Stowe, Mark Twain, Isabella Beecher Hooker, Charles Dudley Warner, William Gillette, and other notables lived.

The Stowe-Day Foundation owns and maintains the Harriet Beecher Stowe House, 73 Forest Street, Hartford, Connecticut, and The Stowe-Day Memorial Library, 77 Forest Street. The Library contains over 15,000 volumes, 6,000 pamphlets, and 100,000 manuscript items—all fully catalogued. The basic collections focus upon the architecture, the decorative arts, the history, the literature, and the woman suffrage movement of the nineteenth century.

The publications of The Stowe-Day Foundation reflect the interests of the Library. A recent catalogue is available by writing.

Introduction

POGANUC PEOPLE may be interpreted
on two levels: as an enjoyable novel based
on Harriet Beecher Stowe's childhood in
Litchfield, Connecticut, and as a vehicle for the
expression of her mature social, political and religious philosophy. It is full of local color, vividly
portrayed characters and rich descriptive passages. Scene after scene has the authentic ring of
material which the author had witnessed or experienced. Town meetings, heated political discussions at the local store or over tea in an aristocratic parlor, Fourth of July celebrations with
attendant oratory and daily life in the parsonage
of the village minister dominate the novel.

Harriet Beecher Stowe was a lover of nature.
Her descriptions of the arrival of spring in
Poganuc (see especially pages 181-183) and of
going "a-chestnutting" (Chapter XX) capture
precisely the right details to project lasting images on the reader's mind. She knew also the
social and political structure of a New England
town in the early nineteenth century. Mrs. Stowe
was intimately familiar with the Calvinist theology which so deeply affected the attitudes and
mores of New England life. *Poganuc People*
opens on the eve of 1818, that fateful year which
marked the legal separation of church and state
in Connecticut. This timing provides a reference
and a theme to which Mrs. Stowe addresses some
of her most perceptive observations. She had the
objectivity to perceive the virtues of Puritan
theology and the moral and spiritual values by
which it strove to regulate every facet of com-

munity life. Yet she saw also the weaknesses of a theocracy. She herself basically identified with Jeffersonian democracy, which her father, Lyman Beecher, had seen as a threat to the foundation of Calvinist theocracy.

Dr. Cushing, the Congregational minister of Poganuc, and his daughter, Dolly, two of the principal characters, are in many ways thin disguises of Lyman and Harriet Beecher. The gamut of Poganuc society is portrayed with skill. Colonel Davenport, Judge Belcher and Judge Gridley provide models of the aristocratic Federalists, certain that the severance of church and state foretold "... the ruin of the state ...the triumph of the lower classes. ..." The yeoman class and the independent farmers are richly delineated in the characters of Nabby, the Cushings' housekeeper, jovial Hiel Jones and flinty, obstinate Zeph Higgins. Harriet Beecher Stowe is sensitive to the feelings and struggles of the ordinary citizens of Poganuc. She relishes the wit and humor of their behavior. Chapter XI illustrates her insight into the "two distinct circles of people" in the little Connecticut town.

> There was the *haute noblesse*—very affably disposed, and perfectly willing to *condescend;* and there was the proud democracy, prouder than the noblesse, who wouldn't be condescended to, and insisted on having their way and their say, on the literal, actual standpoint of the original equality of human beings.

1. First Congregational Church, Litchfield, Connecticut, 1830.

The Litchfield Historical Society

Mrs. Stowe uses humor with consummate deftness. She narrates the episode of Zeph Higgins' decision to take into his own hands the issue of relocating the village schoolhouse. Zeph's fellow citizens were of a mind to approve the moving of the schoolhouse at the next town meeting, but so cantankerous was Zeph in his support of the proposal that he drove people to the opposite side of the issue! The Friday before the crucial town meeting, however, Zeph determined to move the schoolhouse on his own. After announcing his intention to his family, Zeph "took the family Bible, and, in a high-pitched and determined voice, read the account of Sampson carrying off the gates of Gaza, repeated his evening prayer, ordered all hands to bed, raked up the fire, . . and stepped into bed. . . . ."

Local scenery plays an important role in *Poganuc People,* for Mrs. Stowe had the eye of both a naturalist and an artist. She also unfolds to the reader scenes of everyday life, be they preparations for high tea or the process of candle making, which are remarkable for their detail and offer a fund of information about early New England life.

As an expression of Mrs. Stowe's mature philosophy, *Poganuc People* shares much in common with the first of her New England novels, *The Minister's Wooing.* The question of salvation and the Calvinist doctrines of regeneration, or spiritual rebirth, predestination and the elect are central to both novels. *The Minister's Wooing,* which first appeared as a serial in *The At-*

2. A wood cutting on the Litchfield, Connecticut, Town Green, c. 1850.

The Litchfield Historical Society

lantic Monthly during 1858, was written less than a year after Mrs. Stowe's son, Henry, had drowned while swimming the Connecticut River with some of his Dartmouth College classmates. Young Henry had not experienced regeneration and, according to Lyman Beecher's interpretation of Calvinist doctrine, he was doomed to eternal damnation. The tragedy of Henry's death must have graphically recalled the earlier crisis of Mrs. Stowe's sister, Catharine Beecher, whose fiancé, Alexander Metcalf Fisher, was lost at sea in 1822 while sailing to England. Fisher, too, had not experienced regeneration. Catharine Beecher's subsequent rejection of Calvinist dogma, so staunchly defended by Lyman Beecher, had left an indelible impression upon the eleven-year-old Harriet Beecher.

Long before writing *The Minister's Wooing,* therefore, Mrs. Stowe had evolved a religious philosophy which emphasized Christ's love and compassion. In a letter to Lady Byron she wrote in 1859:

> Certain ideas once prevalent certainly must be thrown off. An endless infliction for past sins was once the doctrine that we now generally reject. . . . Of one thing I am sure, — probation does not end with this life, and the number of the redeemed may therefore be infinitely greater than the world's history leads us to suppose.

If Mrs. Stowe had already rejected the harsh doctrines of Calvinism, why does she then develop the plot of *The Minister's Wooing* in such a way

3. Winter scene on Litchfield, Connecticut, Town Green, late 19th century.

The Litchfield Historical Society

that the principles of Calvinism are upheld? Why have James Marvyn, its young hero, supposedly lost at sea in an unregenerated spiritual state, miraculously returned, only to report that he *had* experienced regeneration? While the simple, optimistic view of Christianity expressed by Candace, the black housekeeper, reflects Mrs. Stowe's views, *The Minister's Wooing* seems essentially to be working everything out in terms of Calvinist doctrine. This novel, perhaps, was a type of psychological therapy.

With the loss of her son, Henry, the whole series of doctrinal questions must have recurred to Mrs. Stowe. Through the influence of her brothers, Edward and Henry Ward, and of her theologian-husband, Calvin Stowe, Harriet Beecher Stowe had arrived, intellectually, at conclusions far removed from the doctrines of her father, Lyman Beecher. Under the strain of Henry's loss, Mrs. Stowe must have experienced deep-seated emotional challenges to her mature religious viewpoint. It is one thing to progress on an intellectual plane to viewpoints contrary to the moral and religious upbringing of one's youth. But it is quite another matter to escape emotionally from such early influences. Considering the strong influence which Lyman Beecher had upon all his children, and how much his daughter idolized him, it seems reasonable to conclude that Mrs. Stowe underwent a spiritual crisis with Henry's death and entertained haunting questions as to whether her mature religious viewpoint was certain and sound.

Published in 1878, *Poganuc People,* the last and most autobiographical of Mrs. Stowe's New England novels, reflects a more assured religious viewpoint. To be sure, in this novel most of the principal characters adhere to Calvinism or, if they stray, return to the fold through Dr. Cushing's revival services. Dolly herself, however, moves away, actually and symbolically, from Calvinism towards a more liberal, more optimistic religious attitude. In the last chapter, after Dolly marries a distant cousin, Alfred Dunbar, Mrs. Stowe reflectively summarizes: "And so our Dolly goes to her new life, and, save in memories of her childhood, is to be no longer one of the good people of Poganuc."

In time the people of Poganuc whom Dolly had known all pass away. The old religious and political order of Dr. Cushing and the Federalists becomes a thing of the past. Dolly, or if one will, Mrs. Stowe, has left these behind as well and married an Episcopalian, discovering in the liturgy of the Episcopal service spiritual uplift and comfort. Symbolically, it seems, Harriet Beecher Stowe had now resolved, intellectually and emotionally, those issues of religious and political doctrine which had so deeply impressed her — and the lives of all the good Poganuc people.

Joseph S. Van Why

POGANUC PEOPLE.

MRS. STOWE'S RECENT BOOKS.

THE PARSON'S DAUGHTER.

" Oh, Nabby, Nabby! do tell me what they are doing up at your
church. I've seen 'em all day carrying armfulls and arm-
fulls—ever so much—of spruce and pine up that way."—p. 8.

Poganuc People:

THEIR LOVES AND LIVES.

By Harriet Beecher Stowe.

Author of "Uncle Tom's Cabin," "My Wife and I," "We and Our Neighbors," etc.

With Illustrations.

NEW YORK:

FORDS, HOWARD, & HULBERT.

CONTENTS.

Illustrations.

POGANUC PEOPLE.

CHAPTER I.

DISSOLVING VIEWS.

THE scene is a large, roomy, clean New England kitchen of some sixty years ago. There was the great wide fireplace, with its crane and array of pothooks; there was the tall black clock in the corner, ticking in response to the chirp of the crickets around the broad, flat stone hearth. The scoured tin and pewter on the dresser caught flickering gleams of brightness from the western sunbeams that shone through the network of elm-boughs, rattling and tapping as the wind blew them against the window. It was not quite half-past four o'clock, yet the December sun hung low and red in the western horizon, telling that the time of the shortest winter days was come. Everything in the ample room shone with whiteness and neatness; everything was ranged, put up, and in order, as if work were some past and bygone affair, hardly to be remembered. The only living figure in this picture of still life was that of a strapping, buxom Yankee maiden, with plump arms stripped to the elbow and hands plunged deep in the white, elastic cushion of puffy dough, which rose under them as she kneaded.

Apparently pleasant thoughts were her company in her solitude, for her round, brown eyes twinkled with a pleased sparkle, and every now and then she broke into fragments of psalmody, which she practiced over and over, and then nodded her head contentedly, as if satisfied that she had caught the tune.

Suddenly the outside door flew open and little Dolly Cushing burst into the kitchen, panting and breathless, her cheeks glowing with exercise in face of the keen winter wind.

In she came, noisy and busy, dropping her knitting-work and spelling-book in her eagerness, shutting the door behind her with a cheerful bang, and opening conversation without stopping to get her breath :

" Oh, Nabby, Nabby! do tell me what they are doing up at your church. I've seen 'em all day carrying armfulls and armfulls—ever so much—spruce and pine up that way, and Jim Brace and Tom Peters told me they were going to have a 'lumination there, and when I asked what a 'lumination was they only laughed at me and called me a Presbyterian. Don't you think it's a shame, Nabby, that the big boys will laugh at me so and call me names and won't tell me anything?"

"Oh, land o' Goshen, Dolly, what do you mind them boys for?" said Nabby; "boys is mostly hateful when girls is little; but we take our turn by and by," she said with a complacent twinkle of her brown eyes. "I make them stand around, I bet ye, and you will when you get older."

"But, Nabby, what is a 'lumination?"

"Well now, Dolly, you jest pick up your book, and put up your knittin' work, and sweep out that snow you've tracked in, and hang up your bonnet and cloak, and I'll tell you all about it," said Nabby, taking up her whole cushion of dough and letting it down the other side with a great bound and beginning kneading again.

The little maiden speedily complied with all her requisitions and came and stood, eager and breathless, by the bread bowl.

And a very pretty picture she made there, with her rosy mouth just parted to show her little white teeth, and the afternoon sunshine glinting through the window brightness to go to the brown curls that hung over her round, white forehead, her dark blue eyes kindling with eagerness and curiosity.

"Well, you see," said Nabby, "to-morrow's

Christmas; and they've been dressin' the church with ground pine and spruce boughs, and made it just as beautiful as can be, and they're goin' to have a great gold star over the chancel. General Lewis sent clear to Boston to get the things to make it of, and Miss Ida Lewis she made it; and to-night they're going to 'luminate. They put a candle in every single pane of glass in that air church, and it 'll be all just as light as day. When they get 'em all lighted up you can see that air church clear down to North Poganuc."

Now this sentence was a perfect labyrinth of mystery to Dolly; for she did not know what Christmas was, she did not know what the chancel was, she never saw anything dressed with pine, and she was wholly in the dark what it was all about; and yet her bosom heaved, her breath grew short, her color came and went, and she trembled with excitement. Something bright, beautiful, glorious, must be coming into her life, and oh, if she could only see it!

"Oh, Nabby, are you going?" she said, with quivering eagerness.

"Yes, I'm goin' with Jim Sawin. I belong to the singers, and I'm agoin' early to practice on the anthem."

"Oh, Nabby, won't you take me? Do, Nabby!" said Dolly, piteously.

"Oh, land o' Goshen! no, child; you mustn't think on 't. I couldn't do that noways. Your pa never would hear of it, nor Mis' Cushing neither. You see, your pa don't b'lieve in Christmas."

"What is Christmas, Nabby?"

"Why, it's the day Christ was born—that's Christmas."

"Why, my papa believes Christ was born," said Dolly, with an injured air; "you needn't tell me that he don't. I've heard him read all about it in the Testament."

"I didn't say he didn't, did I?" said Nabby; "but your papa ain't a 'Piscopal, and he don't believe in keeping none of them air prayer-book days—Christmas, nor Easter, nor nothin'," said Nabby, with a generous profusion of negatives. "Up to the 'Piscopal church they keep Christmas, and they don't keep it down to your meetin' house; that's the long and short on 't," and Nabby turned her batch of dough over with a final flounce, as if to emphasize the statement, and, giving one last poke in the middle of the fair, white cushion, she proceeded to rub the paste from her hands and to cover her completed batch with a clean white towel and then with a neat comforter of quilted cotton. Then, establishing it in the warmest corner of the fireplace, she proceeded to wash her hands and look at

the clock and make other movements to show
that the conversation had come to an end.

Poor little Dolly stood still, looking wistful
and bewildered. The tangle of brown and golden
curls on the outside of her little head was not
more snarled than the conflicting ideas in the
inside. This great and wonderful idea of Christmas, and all this confusion of images, of gold
stars and green wreaths and illuminated windows
and singing and music—all done because Christ
was born, and yet something that her papa did
not approve of—it was a hopeless puzzle. After
standing thinking for a minute or two she resumed:

"But, Nabby, *why* don't my papa like it? and
why don't we have a 'lumination in our meeting-
house?"

"Bless your heart, child, they never does them
things to Presbyterian meetin's. Folks' ways is
different, and them air is 'Piscopal ways. For
my part I'm glad father signed off to the 'Piscopalians, for it's a great deal jollier."

"Oh, dear! my papa won't ever sign off,"
said Dolly, mournfully.

"To be sure he won't. Why, what nonsense
that is!" said Nabby, with that briskness with
which grown people shake off the griefs of children. "Of course *he* won't when he's a minister, so what's the use of worryin'? You jest

shet up now, for I've got to hurry and get tea; 'cause your pa and ma are goin' over to the lecture to-night in North Poganuc school-house and they'll want their supper early."

Dolly still hung about wishfully.

"Nabby, if I should ask papa, and he *should* say I might go, would you take me?" said Dolly.

Now, Nabby was a good-natured soul enough and in a general way fond of children; she encouraged Miss Dolly's prattling visits to the kitchen, let her stand about surveying her in various domestic processes, and encouraged that free expression of opinion in conversation which in those days was entirely repressed on the part of juveniles in the presence of their elders. She was, in fact, fond of Dolly in a certain way, but not fond enough of her to interfere with the serious avocations of life; and Nabby was projecting very serious and delicate movements of diplomacy that night. She was going to the church with Jim Sawin, who was on the very verge of a declared admiration, not in the least because her heart inclined toward Jim, but as a means of bringing Ike Peters to capitulation in a quarrel of some weeks' standing. Jim Sawin's "folks," as she would have phrased it, were "meetin'ers," while Ike Peters was a leading member of the Episcopal choir, and it was designed expressly to aggravate him that she was to come in exhibiting her captive in triumph. To have "a child 'round under her feet," while engaged in conducting affairs of such delicacy, was manifestly impossible—so impossible that she thought stern repression of any such idea the very best policy.

"Now, Dolly Cushing, you jest shet up—for 'tain't no use talkin'. Your pa nor your ma wouldn't hear on't; and besides, little girls like you must go to bed early. They can't be up 'night-hawkin',' and goin' round in the cold. You might catch cold and die like little Julia Cavers. Little girls must be in bed and asleep by eight o'clock."

Dolly stood still with a lowering brow. Just then the world looked very dark. Her little rose-leaf of an under lip rolled out and quivered, and large bright drops began falling one by one over her cheeks.

Nabby had a soft spot in her heart, and felt these signs of affliction; but she stood firm.

"Now, Dolly, I'm sorry; but you can't go. So you jest be a good girl and not say no more about it, and don't cry, and I'll tell you what I'll do: I'll buy you a sugar dog down to the store, and I'll tell you all about it to-morrow."

Dolly had seen these sugar dogs in the window of the store, resplendent with their blue backs and yellow ears and pink tails—designed probably to represent dogs as they exist at the end of the rainbow. Her heart had burned within her with hopeless desire to call one of these beauties her own; and Nabby's promise brought out a gleaming smile through the showery atmosphere of her little face. A sugar dog might reconcile her to life.

" Now, you must promise me ' certain true as black is blue,' " said Nabby, adjuring by an apparently irrational form of conjuration in vogue among the children in those times. " You must promise you won't say a word about this 'ere thing to your pa or ma; for they wouldn't hear of your goin', and if they would I shouldn't take you. I really couldn't. It would be very inconvenient."

Dolly heaved a great sigh, but thought of the sugar dog, and calmed down the tempest that seemed struggling to rise in her little breast. A rainbow of hope rose over the cloud of disappointment, and a sugar dog with yellow ears and pink tail gleamed consolingly through it.

CHAPTER II.

DOLLY.

OUR little Dolly was a late autumn chicken, the youngest of ten children, the nursing, rearing and caring for whom had straitened the limited salary of Parson Cushing, of Poganuc Center, and sorely worn on the nerves and strength of the good wife who plied the laboring oar in these performances.

It was Dolly's lot to enter the family at a period when babies were no longer a novelty, when the house was full of the wants and clamors of older children, and the mother at her very wits' end with a confusion of jackets and trowsers, soap, candles and groceries, and the endless harassments of making both ends meet which pertain to the lot of a poor country minister's wife. Consequently Dolly was disposed of as she grew up in all those short-hand methods by which children were taught to be the least possible trouble to their elders. She was taught to come when called, and do as she was bid without a question or argument, to be quenched in bed at the earliest possible hour at night, and to speak only when

16

spoken to in the presence of her elders. All this was a dismal repression to Dolly, for she was by nature a lively, excitable little thing, bursting with questions that she longed to ask, and with comments and remarks that she burned to make, and so she escaped gladly to the kitchen where Nabby, the one hired girl, who was much in the same situation of repressed communicativeness, encouraged her conversational powers.

On the whole, although it never distinctly occurred to Dolly to murmur at her lot in life yet at times she sighed over the dreadful insignificance of being only a little girl in a great family of grown up people. For even Dolly's brothers nearest her own age were studying in the academy and spouting scraps of superior Latin at her to make her stare and wonder at their learning. They were tearing, noisy, tempestuous boys, good natured enough and willing to pet her at intervals, but prompt to suggest that it was "time for Dolly to go to bed" when her questions or her gambols interfered with their evening pleasures.

Dolly was a robust, healthy little creature, never ailing in any way, and consequently received none of the petting which a more delicate child might have claimed, and the general course of her experience impressed her with the mournful conviction that she was always liable to be in the

way—as she commonly was, with her childish curiosity, her burning desire to see and hear and
know all that interested the grown people above
her. Dolly sometimes felt her littleness and insignificance as quite a burden, and longed to be
one of the grown-up people. *They* got civil answers when they asked questions, instead of being
told not to talk, and they were not sent to bed
the minute it was dark, no matter what pleasant
things were going on about them. Once Dolly
remembered to have had sore throat with fever.
The doctor was sent for. Her mother put away
all her work and held her in her arms. Her
father came down out of his study and sat up
rocking her nearly all night, and her noisy, rois-
tering brothers came softly to her door and
inquired how she was, and Dolly was only sorry
that the cold passed off so soon, and she found
herself healthy and insignificant as ever. Being
gifted with an active fancy, she sometimes imagined a scene when she should be sick and die,
and her father and mother and everybody would
cry over her, and there would be a funeral for
her as there was for a little Julia Cavers, one of
her playmates. She could see no drawback to
the interest of the scene except that she could
not be there to enjoy her own funeral and see
how much she was appreciated; so on the whole
she turned her visions in another direction and

fancied the time when she should be a grown woman and at liberty to do just as she pleased.

It must not be imagined, however, that Dolly had an unhappy childhood. Indeed it may be questioned whether, if she had lived in our day when the parents often seem to be sitting at the feet of their children and humbly inquiring after their sovereign will and pleasure, she would have been much happier than she was. She could not have all she wanted, and the most petted child on earth cannot. She had learned to do without what she could not get, and to bear what she did not like; two sources of happiness and peace which we should judge to be unknown to many modern darlings. For the most part Dolly had learned to sail her own little boat wisely among the bigger and bustling crafts of the older generation.

There were no amusements then specially provided for children. There were no children's books; there were no Sunday-schools to teach bright little songs and to give children picnics and presents. It was a grown people's world, and not a child's world, that existed in those days. Even children's toys of the period were so poor and so few that, in comparison with our modern profusion, they could scarcely be said to exist.

Dolly, however, had her playthings, as every

child of lively fancy will. Childhood is poetic
and creative, and can make to itself toys out of
nothing. Dolly had the range of the great wood-
pile in the back yard, where, at the yearly "wood-
spell," the farmers deposited the fuel needed for
the long, terrible winters, and that woodpile was
a world of treasure to her. She skipped, and
sung, and climbed among its intricacies and found
there treasures of wonder. Green velvet mosses,
little white trees of lichen that seemed to her to
have tiny apples upon them, long grey-bearded
mosses and fine scarlet cups and fairy caps she
collected and treasured. She arranged landscapes
of these, where green mosses made the fields,
and little sprigs of spruce and ground-pine the
trees, and bits of broken glass imitated rivers
and lakes, reflecting the overshadowing banks.
She had, too, hoards of chestnuts and walnuts
which a squirrel might have envied, picked up
with her own hands from under the yellow
autumn leaves; and she had—chief treasure of
all—a wooden doll, with staring glass eyes, that
had been sent her by her grandmother in Boston,
which doll was the central point in all her arrangements. To her she showed the chestnuts
and walnuts; she gave to her the jay's feathers
and the bluebird's wing which the boys had
given to her; she made her a bed of divers colors
and she made her a set of tea-cups out of the

backbone of a codfish. She brushed and curled her hair till she took all the curl out of it, and washed all the paint off her cheeks in the zeal of motherly ablutions.

In fact nobody suspected that Dolly was not the happiest of children, as she certainly was one of the busiest and healthiest, and when that evening her two brothers came in from the Academy, noisy and breezy, and tossed her up in their long arms, her laugh rung gay and loud, as if there were no such thing as disappointment in the world.

She pursed her mouth very tight for fear that she should let out something on the forbidden subject at the supper-table. But it was evident that nothing could be farther from the mind of her papa, who, at intervals, was expounding to his wife the difference between natural and moral inability as drawn out in a pamphlet he was preparing to read at the next ministers' meeting —remarks somewhat interrupted by reproof to the boys for giggling at table and surreptitiously feeding Spring, the dog, in contravention of family rules.

It is not to be supposed that Will and Tom Cushing, though they were minister's boys, were not *au courant* in all that was going on noteworthy in the parish. In fact, they were fully versed in all the details of the projected cere-

monies at the church and resolved to be in at
the show, but maintained a judicious reticence
as to their intentions lest, haply, they might be
cut short by a positive interdict.

The Episcopal church at Poganuc Center was
of recent origin. It was a small, insignificant
building compared with the great square three-
decker of a meeting-house which occupied con-
spicuously the green in Poganuc Center. The
minister was not a man particularly gifted in any
of those points of pulpit excellence which Dr.
Cushing would be likely to appreciate, and the
Doctor had considered it hitherto too small and
unimportant an affair to be worth even a combative notice; hence his ignorance and indifference
to what was going on there. He had heard inci-
dentally that they were dressing the church with
pines and going to have a Christmas service, but
he only murmured something about "*tolerabiles
ineptiæ*" to the officious deacon who had called
his attention to the fact. The remark, being in
Latin, impressed the Deacon with a sense of
profound and hidden wisdom. The people of
Poganuc Center paid a man a salary for knowing
more than they did, and they liked to have a
scrap of Latin now and then to remind them
of this fact. So the Deacon solemnly informed
all comers into the store who discussed recent
movements that the Doctor had his eyes open;

he knew all about these doings and they should hear from him yet; the Doctor had expressed his mind to him.

The Doctor, in fact, was far more occupied with a certain Dr. Pyncheon, whose views of moral inability he expected entirely to confound by the aforesaid treatise which he had been preparing.

So after supper the boys officiously harnessed and brought up the horse and sleigh destined to take their parents to North Poganuc school house, and saw them set off—listening to the last jingle of the sleigh bells with undisguised satisfaction.

" Good! Now, Tom, let's go up to the church and get the best places to see," exclaimed Bill.

"Oh, boys, are you going?" cried Dolly, in a piteous voice. "Oh, do take me! Nabby's going, and everybody, and I want to go."

"Oh, you mustn't go; you're a little girl and it's your bed-time," said Tom and Bill, as with Spring barking at their heels they burst in a windy swoop of noise out of the house, boys and dog about equally intelligent as to what it was all about.

CHAPTER III.

EFORE going farther in our story we
pause to give a brief answer to the
queries that have risen in the minds of
some who remember the old times in
New England: How came there to be any Episcopalians or Episcopal church in a small Puritan
town like Poganuc?

The Episcopal Church in New England in the
early days was emphatically a root out of dry
ground, with as little foothold in popular sympathy as one of those storm-driven junipers, that
the east wind blows all aslant, has in the rocky
ledges of Cape Cod. The soil, the climate, the
atmosphere, the genius, and the history of the
people were all against it. Its forms and ceremonies were all associated with the persecution
which drove the Puritans out of England and
left them no refuge but the rock-bound shores
of America. It is true that in the time of Governor Winthrop the colony of Massachusetts
appealed with affectionate professions to their
Mother, the Church of England, and sought her

24

sympathy and her prayers; but it is also unfortunately true that the forms of the Church of England were cultivated and maintained in New England by the very party whose intolerance and tyranny brought on the Revolutionary war.

All the oppressive governors of the colonies were Episcopalians, and in the Revolutionary struggle the Episcopal Church was very generally on the Tory side; hence, the New Englanders came to have an aversion to its graceful and beautiful ritual and forms for the same reason that the free party in Spain and Italy now loathe the beauties of the Romish Church, as signs and symbols of tyranny and oppression.

Congregationalism—or, as it was then called by the common people, Presbyterianism—was the religion established by law in New England. It was the State Church. Even in Boston in its colonial days, the King's Chapel and Old North were only dissenting churches, unrecognized by the State, but upheld by the patronage of the colonial governors who were sent over to them from England. For a long time after the Revolutionary war the old *régime* of the State Church held undisputed sway in New England. There was the one meeting-house, the one minister, in every village. Every householder was taxed for the support of public worship, and stringent law and custom demanded of every one a personal attendance on Sunday at both services. If any defaulter failed to put in an appearance it was the minister's duty to call promptly on Monday and know the reason why. There was no place for differences of religious opinion. All that individualism which now raises a crop of various little churches in every country village was sternly suppressed. For many years only members of churches could be eligible to public offices; Sabbath-keeping was enforced with more than Mosaic strictness, and New England justified the sarcasm which said that they had left the Lords-Bishops to be under the Lords-Brethren. In those days if a sectarian meeting of Methodists or Baptists, or an unseemly gathering of any kind, seemed impending, the minister had only to put on his cocked hat, take his gold-headed cane and march down the village street, leaving his prohibition at every house, and the thing was so done even as he commanded.

In the very nature of things such a state of society could not endure. The shock that separated the nation from a king and monarchy, the sense of freedom and independence, the hardihood of thought which led to the founding of a new civil republic, were fatal to all religious constraint. Even before the Revolutionary war there were independent spirits that chafed under the constraint of clerical supervision, and Ethan Allen advertised his farm and stock for sale, expressing his determination at any cost to get out of "this old holy State of Connecticut."

It was but a little while after the close of the war that established American independence that the revolution came which broke up the State Church and gave to every man the liberty of "signing off," as it was called, to any denomination that pleased him. Hence arose through New England churches of all names. The nucleus of the Episcopal Church in any place was generally some two or three old families of ancestral traditions in its favor, who gladly welcomed to their fold any who, for various causes, were discontented with the standing order of things. Then, too, there came to them gentle spirits, cut and bleeding by the sharp crystals of doctrinal statement, and courting the balm of devotional liturgy and the cool shadowy indefiniteness of more æsthetic forms of worship. Also, any one that for any cause had a controversy with the dominant church took comfort in the power of "signing off" to another. In those days, to belong to no church was not respectable, but to sign off to the Episcopal Church was often a compromise that both gratified self-will and saved one's dignity; and, having signed off, the new convert was obliged, for consistency's sake, to

justify the step he had taken by doing his best
to uphold the doctrine and worship of his chosen
church.

The little edifice at Poganuc had been trimmed
and arranged with taste and skill. For that matter, it would seem as if the wild woods of New
England were filled with garlands and decorations already made and only waiting to be used
in this graceful service. Under the tall spruces
the ground was all ruffled with the pretty wreaths
of ground-pine; the arbor vitæ, the spruce,
the cedar and juniper, with their balsamic breath,
filled the aisles with a spicy fragrance. It was
a cheaply built little church, in gothic forms,
with pointed windows and an arch over the
chancel; and every arch was wreathed with
green, and above the chancel glittered a great
gold star, manufactured by Miss Ida Lewis out
of pasteboard and gilt paper ordered in Boston.
It was not gold, but it glittered, and the people
that looked on it were not *blasé*, as everybody
in our days is, with sight seeing. The innocent rustic life of Poganuc had no pageants, no
sights, no shows, except the eternal blazonry of
nature; and therefore the people were prepared
to be dazzled and delighted with a star cut out
of gilt paper. There was bustling activity of
boys and men in lighting the windows, and a

general rush of the populace to get the best seats.

"Wal, now, this beats all!" said Hiel Jones the stage driver, who had secured one of the best perches in the little gallery.

Hiel Jones, in virtue of his place on the high seat of the daily stage that drove through Poganuc Center on the Boston turnpike, felt himself invested with a sort of grandeur as occupying a predominant position in society from whence he could look down on all its movements and interests. Everybody bowed to Hiel. Every housekeeper charged him with her bundle or commissioned him with her errand. Bright-eyed damsels smiled at him from windows as he drove up to house-doors, and of all that was going on in Poganuc Center, or any of the villages for twenty miles around, Hiel considered himself as a competent judge and critic. Therefore he came at an early hour and assumed a seat where he could not only survey the gathering congregation but throw out from time to time a few suggestions on the lighting up and arrangements.

"Putty wal got up, this 'ere, for Poganuc Center," he said to Job Peters, a rather heavy lad who had secured the place beside him.

"Putty wal, considerin'! Take care there, Siah Beers, ye'll set them air spruce boughs afire ef you ain't careful lightin' your candles; spruce

boughs go like all natur ef ye once start 'em.
These 'ere things takes jedgment, Siah. Tell Ike
Bissel there to h'ist his pole a leetle higher; he
don't reach them air top candles; what's the
feller thinkin' of? Look out, Jimmy! Ef ye let
down that top winder it flares the candles, and
they'll gutter like thunder; better put it up."

When the church was satisfactorily lighted
Hiel began his comments on the assembling
audience:

"There goes Squire Lewis and Mis' Lewis
and old lady Lewis and Idy Lewis and the
Lewis boys. On time, they be. Heads down
—sayin' prayers, I s'pose! Folks don't do so
t' our meetin'; but folks' ways is different. Bless
my soul, ef there ain't old Zeph Higgins, lookin'
like a last year's mullen-stalk! I swow, ef the
old critter hain't act'ally hitched up and come
down with his hull team—wife and boys and
yaller dog and all."

"Why, Zeph Higgins ain't 'Piscopal, is he?"
said Job, who was less versed than Hiel in
the gossip of the day.

"Lordy massy, yis! Hain't ye heard that
Zeph's signed off two months ago, and goin' in
strong for the 'Piscopals?"

"Wal, that air beats all," said his auditor.
"Zeph is about the last timber I'd expect to
make a 'Piscopal of."

"Oh, lands! he ain't no more 'Piscopal than
I be, Zeph Higgins ain't; he's nothin' but a mad
Presbyterian, like a good many o' the rest on
'em," said Hiel.

"Why, what's he mad about?"

"Laws, it's nothin' but that air old business
about them potatoes that Zeph traded to Deacon
Dickenson a year ago. Come to settle up, there
was about five and sixpence that they couldn't
'gree 'bout. Zeph, he said the deacon cheated
him, and the deacon stood to it he was right;
and they had it back and forth, and the deacon
wouldn't give in, and Zeph wouldn't. And
there they stood with their horns locked like
two bulls in a pastur' lot. Wal, they had
'em up 'fore the church, and they was labored
with—both sides. The deacon said, finally, he'd
pay the money for peace' sake, if Zeph would
take back what he said 'bout his bein' a cheat
and a liar; and Zeph he said he wouldn't take
nothin' back; and then the church they suspended Zeph; and Zeph he signed off to the
'Piscopals."

"I want to know, now," said Job, with a satisfied air of dawning comprehension.

"Yis, sir, that air's the hull on't. But I tell
you, Zeph's led the old deacon a dance. Zeph,
ye see, is one o' them ropy, stringy fellers, jest
like touch-wood—once get 'em a burnin' and

they keep on a burnin' night and day. Zeph really sot up nights a hatin' the deacon, and contrivin' what he could do agin him. Finally, it come into his head that the deacon got his water from a spring on one of Zeph's high pastur' lots. The deacon had laid pipes himself and brought it 'cross lots down to his house. Wal, wat does Zeph do, without sayin' a word to the deacon, but he takes up all the deacon's logs that carried the water 'cross his lot, and throw'd 'em over the fence; and, fust the deacon's wife knowed, she hadn't a drop o' water to wash or cook with, or drink, nor nothin'. Deacon had to get all his water carted in barrels. Wal, they went to law 'bout it and 'tain't settled yit; but Zeph he took Squire Lewis for his lawyer. Squire Lewis, ye see, he's the gret man to the 'Piscopal Church. Folks say he putty much built this 'ere church."

" Wal, now," said Job, after an interval of meditation, " I shouldn't think the 'Piscopals wouldn't get no gret advantage from them sort o' fellers."

" That air's jest what I was a tellin' on 'em over to the store," said Hiel, briskly. " Deacon Peasley, he was a mournin' about it. Lordy massy, deacon, says I, don't you worry. If them 'Piscopalians has got Zeph Higgins in their camp—why, they've bit off more 'n they can chaw, that's all. They'll find it out one o' these days—see if they don't."

"Wal, but Zeph's folks is putty nice folks, now," said Job.

"O—wal, yis—they be; don't say nothin' agin his folks. Mis' Higgins is a meek, marciful old body, kind o' heart-broken at leavin' Parson Cushing and her meetin'. Then there's Nabby, and the boys. Wal, they sort o' like it—young folks goes in for new things. There's Nabby over there now, come in with Jim Sawin. I believe she's makin' a fool o' that 'ere fellow. Harnsom gal, Nabby is—knows it too—and sarves out the fellers. Maybe she'll go through the wood and pick up a crooked stick 'fore she knows it. I've sot up with Nabby myself; but laws, she ain't the only gal in the world—plenty on 'em all 'round the lot."

"Why," exclaimed his neighbor, "if there ain't the minister's boys down there in that front slip!"

"Sartin; you may bet on Bill and Tom for bein' into the best seat whatever's goin' on. Likely boys; wide awake they be! Bill there could drive stage as well as I can, only if I didn't hold on to him he'd have us all to the darnation in five minutes. There's the makin' of suthin' in that Bill. He'll go strong to the Lord or to the devil one o' these days."

"Wal, what's his father think of his bein' here?"

"Parson Cushing! Lordy massy, he don't know nothin' where they be. Met him and Mis' Cushing jinglin' over to the Friday evenin' prayer-meetin' to North Poganuc."

"Wal, now," said his neighbor, "ef there ain't Lucius Jenks down there and Mis' Jenks, and all his folks."

"Yis—yis, jes' so. They say Lucius is thinkin' of signin' off to the 'Piscopals to get the trade. He's jest sot up store, and Deacon Dickenson's got all the ground; but there's the Lewises and the Copleys and the Danforths goes to the 'Piscopals, and they's folks that lives well and uses lots of groceries. I shouldn't wonder ef Lucius should make a good thing on 't. Jenks ain't one that cares much which church he goes to, and, like enough, it don't make much difference to some folks."

"You know this 'ere minister they've got here?" asked Job.

"Know him? Guess so!" said Hiel, with a superior smile. "I've known Sim Coan ever since he wore short jackets. Sim comes from over by East Poganuc. His gran'ther was old Gineral Coan, a gret Tory he was, in the war times. Sim's ben to college, and he's putty smart and chipper. Come to heft him, tho', he

don't weigh much 'longside o' Parson Cushing.
He's got a good voice, and reads well; but come
to a *sermon*—wal, ain't no gret heft in't."

" Want to know," said his auditor.

" Yis," said Hiel, "but Sim's almighty plucky.
You'd think now, comin' into this 'ere little bit of
a church, right opposite Parson Cushing's great
meetin'-house, and with the biggest part of folks
goin' to meetin', that he'd sing small at fust; but
he don't. Lordy massy, no! He comes right out
with it that Parson Cushing ain't no minister,
and hain't got no right to preach, nor administer
sacraments, nor nothin'—nor nobody else but him
and his 'Piscopal folks, that's been ordained by
bishops. He gives it to 'em, hip and thigh, I tell
you."

" That air don't look reasonable," said Job, after
a few minutes of profound reflection.

" Wal, Sim says this 'ere thing has come
right stret down from the 'Postles—one ordainin'
another in a steady string all the way down till it
come to him. And Parson Cushing, he's out in
the cold, 'cause there hain't no bishop ordained
him."

" Wal, I declare!" said the other. " I think that
air 's cheek."

" Ain't it now?" said Hiel. " Now, for my
part, I go for the man that does his work best.
Here's all our ministers round a savin' sinners and

convartin' souls, whether the 'Postles ordained
'em or not—that's what ministers is *fur*. I'll set
Parson Cushing 'longside any minister—preachin'
and teachin' and holdin' meetin's in Poganuc
Center, and North and South Poganuc, and
gatherin' church members, and seein' to the
schools, and keepin' every thing agoin'. That
air kind o' minister 's good enough for *me*."

"Then you've no thoughts of signing off?"

"Not a bit on't. My old mother, she thinks
every thing o' Parson Cushing. She's a gret deal
better jedge than I be o' this 'ere sort o' thing. I
shall go to meetin' with Mother."

"It's sort o' takin' and pretty, though, this 'ere
dressing up the church and all," said his neighbor.

"Wal, yis, *'t is* putty," said Hiel, looking
around with an air of candid allowance, "but
who 's going to pay for it all? These 'ere sort
of things chalk up, ye know. All these 'ere taller
candles ain't burnt out for nothing—somebody's
got to foot the bills."

"Wal, I like the orgin," said Job. "I wish we
had an orgin to our meetin'."

"Dunno," said Hiel, loth to admit any superiority. "Wal, they wouldn't a hed none ef it
hadn't been for Uncle Sol Peters. You know he's
kind o' crazy to sing, and he hain't got no ear, and
no more voice 'n a saw-mill, and they wouldn't
hev 'im in our singer seats, and so he went off to

the 'Piscopals. And he bought an orgin right out and out, and paid for it, and put it in this church so that they'd let him be in the singin'. You know they can make noise enough with an orgin to drown his voice."

" Wal, it was considerable for Uncle Sol to do —wa'n't it?" said Job.

" Laws, he's an old bachelor, hain't got no wife and children to support, so I s'pose he may as well spend his money that way as any. Uncle Sol never could get any gal to hev him. There he is now, tryin' to get 'longside o' Nabby Higgins; but you'll see he won't do it. She knows what she's about. Now, for my part, I like our singin' up to the meetin'-house full as wal as this 'ere. I like good old-fashioned psalm tunes, with Ben Davis to lead—that's the sort *I* like."

It will have been remarked that Hiel was one of that common class of Yankees who felt provided with a ready-made opinion of everything and every subject that could possibly be started, from stage-driving to apostolic succession, with a most comfortable opinion of the importance of his approbation and patronage.

When the house was filled and the evening service begun Hiel looked down critically as the audience rose or sat down or bowed in the Creed. The tones of the small organ, leading the choral chant and somewhat covering the uncult-

ured roughness of the voices in the choir, rose
and filled the green arches with a solemn and
plaintive sound, affecting many a heart that scarce
could give a reason why. It was in truth a very
sweet and beautiful service, and one calculated to
make a thoughtful person regret that the Church
of England had ever expelled the Puritan leaders
from an inheritance of such lovely possibilities.
When the minister's sermon appeared, however,
it proved to be a spirited discourse on the obliga-
tion of keeping Christmas, to which Hiel listened with pricked-up ears, evidently bristling
with combativeness.

"Parson Cushing could knock that air all to
flinders; you see if he can't," said Hiel, the moment the concluding services allowed him space
to speak his mind. "Wal, did ye see old Zeph
a-gettin' up and a-settin' down in the wrong place,
and tryin' to manage his prayer-book?" he said.
"It's worse than the militia drill—he never hits
right. I hed to laugh to see him. Hulloa! if
there ain't little Dolly down there in the corner,
under them cedars. How come she out this time
o' night? Guess Parson Cushing 'll hev to look
out for this 'ere!"

CHAPTER IV.

ND, after all, Dolly was there! Yes, she was. Human nature, which runs wild with the oldest of us at times, was too strong for poor little Dolly.

Can any of us look back to the earlier days of our mortal pilgrimage and remember the helpless sense of desolation and loneliness caused by being forced to go off to the stillness and darkness of a solitary bed far from all the beloved voices and employments and sights of life? Can we remember lying, hearing distant voices, and laughs of more fortunate, older people, and the opening and shutting of distant doors, that told of scenes of animation and interest from which we were excluded? How doleful sounded the tick of the clock, and how dismal was the darkness as sunshine faded from the window, leaving only a square of dusky dimness in place of daylight!

All who remember these will sympathize with Dolly, who was hustled off to bed by Nabby

39

the minute supper was over, that she might
have the decks clear for action.

"Now be a good girl; shut your eyes, and
say your prayers, and go right to sleep," had
been Nabby's parting injunction as she went
out, closing the door after her.

The little head sunk into the pillow and Dolly
recited her usual liturgy of "Our Father who
art in Heaven," and "I pray God to bless my
dear father and mother and all my dear friends
and relations, and make me a good girl;" and
ending with

" 'Now I lay me down to sleep.' "

But sleep she could not. The wide, bright,
wistful blue eyes lay shining like two stars
towards the fading light in the window, and the
little ears were strained to catch every sound. She
heard the shouts of Tom and Bill and the loud
barking of Spring as they swept out of the door;
and the sound went to her heart. Spring—her
faithful attendant, the most loving and sympathetic
of dogs, her friend and confidential counsellor
in many a solitary ramble—Spring had gone with
the boys to see the sight, and left her alone.
She began to pity herself and cry softly on her
pillow. For awhile she could hear Nabby's energetic movements below, washing up dishes,
setting back chairs, and giving energetic thumps

and bangs here and there, as her way was of
producing order. But by and by that was all
over, and she heard the loud shutting of the
kitchen door and Nabby's voice chatting with
her attendant as she went off to the scene of
gaiety.

In those simple, innocent days in New England
villages nobody thought of locking house doors
at night. There was in those times no idea either
of tramps or burglars, and many a night in summer had Dolly lain awake and heard the voices of
tree-toads and whippoorwills mingling with the
whisper of leaves and the swaying of elm boughs,
while the great outside door of the house lay
broad open in the moonlight. But then this was
when everybody was in the house and asleep,
when the door of her parents' room stood open
on the front hall, and she knew she could run to
the paternal bed in a minute for protection.
Now, however, she knew the house was empty.
Everybody had gone out of it; and there is something fearful to a little lonely body in the possibilities of a great, empty house. She got up and
opened her door, and the "tick-tock" of the old
kitchen clock for a moment seemed like company;
but pretty soon its ticking began to strike louder
and louder with a nervous insistancy on her ear,
till the nerves quivered and vibrated, and she
couldn't go to sleep. She lay and listened to all

the noises outside. It was a still, clear, freezing
night, when the least sound clinked with a me-
tallic resonance.   She heard the runners of
sleighs squeaking and crunching over the frozen
road, and the lively jingle of bells. They would
come nearer, nearer, pass by the house, and go
off in the distance. Those were the happy folks
going to see the gold star and the Christmas
greens in the church. The gold star, the Christmas greens, had all the more attraction from their
vagueness. Dolly was a fanciful little creature,
and the clear air and romantic scenery of a mountain town had fed her imagination. Stories she
had never read, except those in the Bible and the
Pilgrim's Progress, but her very soul had vibrated
with the descriptions of the celestial city—something vague, bright, glorious, lying beyond some
dark river ; and Nabby's rude account of what
was going on in the church suggested those
images.

Finally a bright thought popped into her little
head. She could see the church from the front
windows of the house ; she would go there and
look. In haste she sprang out of bed and dressed
herself. It was sharp and freezing in the fire-
less chamber, but Dolly's blood had a racing,
healthy tingle to it ; she didn't mind cold. She
wrapped her cloak around her and tied on her
hood and ran to the front windows. There it

was, to be sure—the little church with its sharp-pointed windows every pane of which was sending streams of light across the glittering snow. There was a crowd around the door, and men and boys looking in at the windows. Dolly's soul was fired. But the elm-boughs a little obstructed her vision; she thought she would go down and look at it from the yard. So down stairs she ran, but as she opened the door the sound of the chant rolled out into the darkness with a sweet and solemn sound:

"*Glory be to God on high; and on earth peace, good will towards men.*"

Dolly's soul was all aglow—her nerves tingled and vibrated; she thought of the bells ringing in the celestial city; she could no longer contain herself, but faster and faster the little hooded form scudded across the snowy plain and pushed in among the dark cluster of spectators at the door. All made way for the child, and in a moment, whether in the body or out she could not tell, Dolly was sitting in a little nook under a bower of spruce, gazing at the star and listening to the voices:

"*We praise Thee, we bless Thee, we worship Thee, we glorify Thee, we give thanks to thee for thy great glory, O Lord God, Heavenly King, God, the Father Almighty.*"

Her heart throbbed and beat; she trembled

with a strange happiness and sat as one entranced
till the music was over. Then came reading,
the rustle and murmur of people kneeling, and
then they all rose and there was the solemn
buzz of voices repeating the Creed with a curious
lulling sound to her ear. There was old Mr.
Danforth with his spectacles on, reading with a
pompous tone, as if to witness a good confession
for the church; and there was Squire Lewis
and old Ma'am Lewis; and there was one place
where they all bowed their heads and all the
ladies made courtesies—all of which entertained
her mightily.

When the sermon began Dolly got fast asleep
and slept as quietly as a pet lamb in a meadow,
lying in a little warm roll back under the
shadows of the spruces. She was so tired and
so sound asleep that she did not wake when the
service ended, lying serenely curled up, and having perhaps pleasant dreams. She might have
had the fortunes of little Goody Two-Shoes,
whose history was detailed in one of the few
children's books then printed, had not two friends
united to find her out.

Spring, who had got into the slip with the
boys, and been an equally attentive and edified
listener, after service began a tour of investiga-
tion, dog-fashion, with his nose; for how could
a minister's dog form a suitable judgment of any

new procedure if he was repressed from the use of his own leading faculty? So, Spring went round the church conscientiously, smelling at pew-doors, smelling of the greens, smelling at the heels of gentlemen and ladies, till he came near the door of the church, when he suddenly smelt something which called for immediate attention, and he made a side dart into the thicket where Dolly was sleeping, and began licking her face and hands and pulling her dress, giving short barks occasionally, as if to say, "Come, Dolly, wake up!" At the same instant Hiel, who had seen her from the gallery, came down just as the little one was sitting up with a dazed, bewildered air.

"Why, Dolly, how came you out o' bed this time o' night! Don't ye know the nine o'clock bell's jest rung?"

Dolly knew Hiel well enough—what child in the village did not! She reached up her little hands saying in an apologetic fashion,

"They were all gone away, and I was so lonesome!"

Hiel took her up in his long arms and carried her home, and was just entering the house-door with her as the sleigh drove up with Parson Cushing and his wife.

"Wal, Parson, your folks has all ben to the 'lumination—Nabby and Bill and Tom and Dolly here; found her all rolled up in a heap like a rabbit under the cedars."

"Why, Dolly Cushing!" exclaimed her mother. "What upon earth got you out of bed this time of night? You'll catch your death o' cold."

"I was all alone," said Dolly, with a piteous bleat.

"Oh, there, there, wife; don't say a word," put in the Parson. "Get her off to bed. Never mind, Dolly, don't you cry;" for Parson Cushing was a soft-hearted gentleman and couldn't bear the sight of Dolly's quivering under lip. So Dolly told her little story, how she had been promised a sugar dog by Nabby if she'd be a good girl and go to sleep, and how she couldn't go to sleep, and how she just went down to look from the yard, and how the music drew her right over.

"There, there," said Parson Cushing, "go to bed, Dolly; and if Nabby don't give you a sugar dog, I will.

"This Christmas dressing is all nonsense," he added, "but the child 's not to blame—it was natural."

"After all," he said to his wife the last thing after they were settled for the night, "our little Dolly is an unusual child. There were not many little girls that would have dared to do that. I shall preach a sermon right away that will set all this

Christmas matter straight," said the doctor. " There is not a shadow of evidence that the first Christians kept Christmas.   It wasn't kept for the first three centuries, nor was Christ born anywhere near the 25th of December."

CHAPTER V.

DOLLY'S FIRST CHRISTMAS DAY.

THE next morning found little Dolly's blue eyes wide open with all the wondering eagerness of a new idea. In those early times the life of childhood was much more in the imagination than now. Children were let alone, to think their own thoughts. There were no kindergartens to train the baby to play philosophically, and infuse a stealthy aroma of geometry and conic sections into the very toys of the nursery. Parents were not anxiously watching every dawning idea of the little mind to set it straight even before it was uttered; and there were then no newspapers or magazines with a special corner for the bright sayings of children.

Not that children were any less beloved, or motherhood a less holy thing. There were many women of deep hearts, who, like the " most blessed among women," kept all the sayings of their darlings and pondered them in their hearts; but it was not deemed edifying or useful to pay

48

much apparent attention to these utterances and
actions of the youthful pilgrim.

Children's inquiries were freely put off with
the general answer that Mamma was busy and
they must not talk—that when they were grown
up they would know all about these things, etc.;
and so they lived apart from older people in
their own little child-world of uninvaded ideas.

Dolly, therefore, had her wise thoughts about
Christmas. She had been terribly frightened at
first, when she was brought home from the
church ; but when her papa kissed her and
promised her a sugar dog she was quite sure
that, whatever the unexplained mystery might
be, he did not think the lovely scene of the night
before a wicked one. And when Mrs. Cushing
came and covered the little girl up warmly in
bed, she only said to her, " Dolly, you must never
get out of bed again at night after you are put
there ; you might have caught a dreadful cold
and been sick and died, and then we should have
lost our little Dolly." So Dolly promised quite
readily to be good and lie still ever after, no
matter what attractions might be on foot in the
community.

Much was gained, however, and it was all clear
gain; and forthwith the little fanciful head proceeded to make the most of it, thinking over
every feature of the wonder. The child had a

vibrating, musical organization, and the sway and
rush of the chanting still sounded in her ears
and reminded her of that wonderful story in the
" Pilgrim's Progress," where the gate of the
celestial city swung open, and there were voices
that sung, " Blessing and honor and glory and
power be unto Him who sitteth on the throne."
And then that wonderful star, that shone just
as if it were a real star—how could it be! For
Miss Ida Lewis, being a young lady of native
artistic genius, had cut a little hole in the center
of her gilt paper star, behind which was placed
a candle, so that it gave real light, in a way most
astonishing to untaught eyes.   In Dolly's simple
view it verged on the supernatural—perhaps it
was *the* very real star read about in the gospel
story.   Why not?   Dolly was at the happy age
when anything bright and heavenly seemed cred-
ible, and had the child-faith to which all things
were possible.   She had even seriously pondered
at times the feasibility of walking some day to
the end of the rainbow to look for the pot of
gold which Nabby had credibly assured her was
to be found there; and if at any time in her
ramblings through the wood a wolf had met her
and opened a conversation, as in the case of
little Red Riding Hood, she would have been
no way surprised, but kept up her part of the
interview with becoming spirit.

"I wish, my dear," said Mrs. Cushing, after they were retired to their room for the night, "that to-morrow morning you would read the account of the birth of Christ in St. Matthew, and give the children some good advice upon the proper way of keeping Christmas."

"Well, but you know we don't *keep* Christmas; nobody knows anything about Christmas," said the Doctor.

"You know what I mean, my dear," replied his wife. "You know that my mother and her family *do* keep Christmas. I always heard of it when I was a child; and even now, though I have been out of the way of it so long, I cannot help a sort of kindly feeling towards these ways. I am not surprised at all that the children got drawn over last night to the service. I think it's the most natural thing in the world, and I know by experience just how attractive such things are. I shouldn't wonder if this Episcopal church should draw very seriously on your congregation; but I don't want it to begin by taking away our own children. Dolly is an inquisitive child; a child that thinks a good deal, and she'll be asking all sorts of questions about the why and wherefore of what she saw last night."

"Oh, yes, Dolly is a bright one. Dolly's an uncommon child," said the Doctor, who had a pardonable pride in his children—they being, in fact, the only worldly treasure that he was at all rich in.

"And as to that little dress-up affair over there," he continued, "I don't think any real harm has been done as yet. I have my eyes open. I know all about it, and I shall straighten out this whole matter next Sunday," he said, with the comfortable certainty of a man in the habit of carrying his points.

"I don't feel so very sure of that," said his wife; "at the same time I shouldn't want anything like an open attack on the Episcopalians. There are sincere good people of that way of thinking—my mother, for instance, is a saint on earth, and so is good old Madam Lewis. So pray be careful what you say."

"My dear, I haven't the least objection to their dressing their church and having a good Christian service any day in the year if they want to, but our people may just as well understand our own ground. I know that the Democrats are behind this new move, and they are just using this church to carry their own party purposes—to break up the standing order and put down all the laws that are left to protect religion and morals. They want to upset everything that our fathers came to New England to establish. But I'm going to head this thing off in Poganuc. I shall write a sermon to-morrow, and settle matters."

Now, there is no religious organization in the world in its genius and history less likely to assimilate with a democratic movement than the Episcopal Church. It is essentially aristocratic in form, and, in New England, as we have already noticed, had always been on the side of monarchical institutions.

But, just at this point in the history of New England affairs, all the minor denominations were ready to join any party that promised to break the supremacy of the State Church and give them a foothold.

It was the "Democratic party" of that day that broke up the exclusive laws in favor of the Congregational Church and consequently gained large accessions to their own standard. To use a brief phrase, all the *outs* were Democrats, and all the *ins* Federalists. But the Democratic party had, as always, its radical train. Not satisfied with wresting the scepter from the hands of the Congregational clergyman, and giving equal rights and a fair field to other denominations, the cry was now to abolish all laws in any way protective of religious institutions, or restrictive of the fullest personal individualism; in short, the cry was for the liberty of every man to go to church or not, to keep the Sabbath or not, to support a minister or not, as seemed good and proper in his own eyes.

This was in fact the final outcome of things in New England, and experience has demonstrated that this wide and perfect freedom is the best way of preserving religion and morals. But it was not given to a clergyman in the day of Dr. Cushing, who had hitherto felt that a state ought to be like a well-governed school, under the minister for schoolmaster, to look on the movements of the Democratic party otherwise than as tending to destruction and anarchy. This new movement in the Episcopal Church he regarded as but a device by appeals to the senses— by scenic effects, illuminations and music—to draw people off to an unspiritual and superficial form of religion, which, having once been the tool of monarchy and aristocracy, had now fallen into the hands of the far more dangerous democracy; and he determined to set the trumpet to his mouth on the following Sabbath, and warn the watchmen on the walls of Zion.

He rose up early, however, and proceeded to buy a sugar dog at the store of Lucius Jenks, and when Dolly came down to breakfast he called her to him and presented it, saying as he kissed her,

"Papa gives you this, not because it is Christmas, but because he loves his little Dolly."

" But *isn't* it Christmas?" asked Dolly, with a puzzled air.

" No, child; nobody knows when Christ was born, and there is nothing in the Bible to tell us *when* to keep Christmas."

And then in family worship the doctor read the account of the birth of Christ and of the shepherds abiding in the fields who came at the call of the angels, and they sung the old hymn:

"While shepherds watched their flocks by night."

" Now, children," he said when all was over, "you must be good children and go to school. If we are going to keep any day on account of the birth of Christ, the best way to keep it is by doing all our duties on that day better than any other. Your duty is to be good children, go to school and mind your lessons."

Tom and Bill, who had been at the show the evening before and exhausted the capabilities of the scenic effects, were quite ready to fall in with their father's view of the matter. The candles were burnt out, the play over, for them, and forthwith they assumed to look down on the whole with the contempt of superior intelligence. As for Dolly, she put her little tongue advisedly to the back of her sugar dog and found that he was very sweet indeed—a most tempt-

ing little animal. She even went so far as
to nibble off a bit of the green ground he
stood on—yet resolved heroically not to eat
him at once, but to make him last as long as
possible. She wrapped him tenderly in cotton
and took him to the school with her, and when
her confidential friend, Bessie Lewis, displayed
her Christmas gifts, Dolly had something on her
side to show, though she shook her curly head
wisely and informed Bessie in strict confidence
that there wasn't any such thing as Christmas,
her papa had told her so—a heresy which Bessie
forthwith reported when she went home at noon.

"Poor little Presbyterian—and did she say so?"
asked gentle old Grandmamma Lewis. "Well,
dear, you mustn't blame her—she don't know
any better. You bring the little thing in here
to-night and I'll give her a Christmas cookey.
I'm sorry for such children."

And so, after school, Dolly went in to see
dear old Madam Lewis, who sat in her rocking-
chair in the front parlor, where the fire was
snapping behind great tall brass andirons and
all the pictures were overshadowed with boughs
of spruce and pine. Dolly gazed about her with
awe and wonder. Over one of the pictures was
suspended a cross of green with flowers of
white everlasting.

"What is *that* for?" asked Dolly, pointing solemnly with her little forefinger, and speaking under her breath.

"Dear child, that is the picture of my poor boy who died—ever so many years ago. That is my cross—we have all one—to carry."

Dolly did not half understand these words, but she saw tears in the gentle old lady's eyes and was afraid to ask more.

She accepted thankfully and with her nicest and best executed courtesy a Christmas cookey representing a good-sized fish, with fins all spread and pink sugar-plums for eyes, and went home marveling yet more about this mystery of Christmas.

As she was crossing the green to go home the Poganuc stage drove in, with Hiel seated on high, whipping up his horses to make them execute that grand *entrée* which was the glory of his daily existence.

Now that the stage was on runners, and slipped noiselessly over the smooth frozen plain, Hiel cracked his whip more energetically and shouted louder, first to one horse and then to another, to make up for the loss of the rattling wheels; and he generally had the satisfaction of seeing all the women rushing distractedly to doors and windows, and imagined them saying, "There's Hiel; the stage is in!"

"Hulloa, Dolly!" he called out, drawing up

with a suddenness which threw the fore-horses back upon their haunches. "I've got a bundle for your folks. Want to ride? You may jest jump up here by me and I'll take you 'round to your father's door;" and so Dolly reached up her little red-mittened hand, and Hiel drew her up beside him.

"'Xpect ye want a bit of a ride, and I've got a bundle for Widder Badger, down on South Street, so I guess I'll go 'round that way to make it longer. I 'xpect this 'ere bundle is from some of your ma's folks in Boston—'Piscopals they be, and keeps Christmas. Good sized bundle 'tis; reckon it 'll come handy in a good many ways."

So, after finishing his detour, Hiel landed his little charge at the parsonage door.

"Reckon I'll be over when I've put up my hosses," he said to Nabby when he handed down the bundle to her. "I hain't been to see ye much lately, Nabby, and I know you've been a pinin' after me, but fact is—"

"Well, now, Hiel Beers, you jest shet up with your imperence," said Nabby, with flashing eyes; "you jest look out or you'll get suthin."

"I 'xpect to get a kiss when I come round to-night," said Hiel, composedly. "Take care o' that air bundle, now; mebbe there's glass or crockery in 't."

"Hiel Beers," said Nabby, "don't give me none o' your saace, for I won't take it. Jim Sawin said last night you was the brassiest man he ever see. He said there was brass enough in your face to make a kettle of."

"You tell him there's sap enough in his head to fill it, any way," said Hiel. "Good bye, Nabby, I'll come 'round this evenin'," and he drove away at a rattling pace, while Nabby, with flushed cheeks and snapping eyes, soliloquized,

"Well, I hope he will come! I'd jest like a chance to show him how little I care for him."

Meanwhile the bundle was soon opened, and contained a store of treasures: a smart little red dress and a pair of red shoes for Dolly, a half dozen pocket-handkerchiefs for Dr. Cushing, and "Robinson Crusoe" and "Sanford and Merton," handsomely bound, for the boys, and a bonnet trimming for Mrs. Cushing. These were accompanied by a characteristic letter from Aunt Debby Kittery, opening as follows:

"DEAR SISTER:

"Mother worries because she thinks you Presbyterians won't get any Christmas presents. I tell her it serves you right for being out of the true church. However, this comes to give every one of you some of the crumbs which fall from the church's table, and Mother says she wishes you all a pious Christmas, which she thinks is better than a merry one. If I did n't lay violent hands on her she would use all our substance

in riotous giving of Christmas presents to all the beggars
and chimney sweeps in Boston. She is in good health
and talks daily of wanting to see you and the children;
and I hope before long you will bring some of them, and
come and make us a visit.

"Your affectionate sister,

"DEBBY KITTERY."

There was a scene of exultation and clamor
in the parsonage as these presents were pulled
out and discussed; and when all possible joy was
procured from them in the sitting-room, the children rushed in a body into the kitchen and
showed them to Nabby, calling on her to join
their acclamations.

And then in the evening Hiel came in, and
Nabby prosecuted her attacks upon him with
great vigor and severity, actually carrying matters to such a length that she was obliged, as a
matter of pure Christian charity, to "kiss and
make up" with him at the end of the evening.
Of course Hiel took away an accurate inven-
tory of every article in the bundle, for the enlight-
enment of any of his particular female friends
who had a curiosity to know "what Mis' Cushin's
folks sent her in that air bundle from Boston."

On the whole, when Dolly had said her prayers
that night and thought the matter over, she
concluded that her Christmas Day had been
quite a success.

CHAPTER VI.

WE have traced our little Dolly's fortunes, haps and havings through Christmas day, but we should not do justice to the situation did we not throw some light on the views and opinions of the Poganuc people upon this occasion.

The Episcopal church had been newly finished. There was held on this day, for the first time in open daylight, the full Christmas Service. The illumination and services of the evening before had been skillfully designed to make an impression on the popular mind, and to draw in children and young people with all that floating populace who might be desirous of seeing or hearing some new things.

It had been a success. Such an audience had been drawn and such a sensation produced that on Christmas day everybody in the village was talking of the church; and those who did not go ran to the windows to see who did go. A week-day church service other than a fast, and thanksgiving, and "preparatory lecture" was a striking novelty; and when the little bell rang out its peal and the congregation began to assemble it was watched with curious eyes from many a house.

The day was a glorious one. The bright, cold sun made the icicles that adorned the fronts of all the houses glitter like the gems of Aladdin's palace, and a well-dressed company were seen coming up from various points of the village and thronging the portals of the church.

The little choir and their new organ rang out the *Te Deum* with hearty good-will, and many ears for the first time heard that glorious old heroic poem of the early church. The waves of sound rolled across the green and smote on the unresponsive double row of windows of the old meeting-house, which seemed to stare back with a gaze of blank astonishment. The sound even floated into the store of Deacon Dickenson, and caused some of the hard-handed old farmers who were doing their trading there, with their sleds and loads of wood, to stop their discourse on turnips, eggs and apple-sauce, and listen. To them it bore the sound as of a challenge, the battle-cry of an opposing host that was rising up to dispute the ground with them; and so they listened with combative ears.

"Seem to be a hevin' it all their own way

over there, them 'Piscopals. Carryin' all before 'em," said one.

"How they are a gettin' on!" said another.

"Yes," said Deacon Dickenson; "all the Democrats are j'inin' them, and goin' to make a gen'l push next 'lection. They're goin' clean agin everything—Sunday laws and tiding-man and all."

"Wal," said Deacon Peasley, a meek, mournful little man, with a bald top to his head, "the Democrats are goin' to carry the state. I feel sure on 't."

"Good reason," said Tim Hawkins, a stout two-fisted farmer from one of the outlying farms. "The Democrats beat 'cause they're allers up and dressed, and we Fed'lists ain't. Why, look at 'em to town meetin'! Democrats allers on time, every soul on 'em—rag, tag and bobtail—rain or shine don't make no difference with them; but it takes a yoke of oxen to get a Fed'list out, and when you've got him you've got to set down on him to keep him. That's just the diff'rence."

"Wal," said Deacon Peasley in a thin, querulous voice, "all this 'ere comes of extending the suffrage. Why, Father says that when he was a young man there couldn't nobody vote but good church members in regular standin', and couldn't nobody but them be elected to office. Now it's just as you say, 'rag, tag and bobtail' can vote, and you'll see they'll break up all our institutions."

They've got it so now that folks can sign off and go to meetin' anywhere, and next they'll get it so they needn't go nowhere—that's what'll come next. There's a lot of our young folks ben a goin' to this 'ere 'lumination."

"Wal, I told Parson Cushing about that air 'lumination last night," said Deacon Dickenson, "and he didn't seem to mind it. But I tell you he'll hev to mind. Both his boys there, and little Dolly, too, runnin' over there after she was put to bed; he'll hev to do somethin' to head this 'ere off."

"He'll do it, too," said Tim Hawkins. "Parson Cushing knows what he's about, and he'll come out with a sarmon next Sunday, you see if he don't. There's more in Parson Cushing's little finger than there is in that Sim Coan's hull body, if he did come right straight down from the 'Postles.

"I've heard," said Deacon Peasley, "that Mis' Cushing's folks in Boston was 'Piscopal, and some thought mebbe she influenced the children."

"Oh, wal, Mis' Cushing, she did come from a 'Piscopal family," said Deacon Dickenson. "She was a Kittery, and her gran'ther, Israel Kittery, was a tory in the war. Her folks used to go to the old North in Boston, and they didn't like her marryin' Parson Cushing a grain; but when she married him, why, she *did* marry him. She married his work, and married all his pinions. And nobody can say she hain't been a good yoke-fellow; she's kept up her end, Mis' Cushing has. No, there's nobody ought to say nothin' agin Mis' Cushing."

"Wal, I s'pose we shall hear from the doctor next Sunday," said Hawkins. "He'll speak out; his trumpet won't give an unsartin sound."

"I reely want ter know," said Deacon Peasley, "ef Zeph Higgins has reely come down with his folks *to-day*, givin' up a hull day's work! I shouldn't 'a' thought Zeph'd 'a' done that for any meetin'?"

"Oh, laws, yis; Zeph'll do anything he sets his will on, particular if it's suthin' Mis' Higgins don't want to do—then Zeph'll do it, sartin. I kind o' pity that air woman," said Hawkins.

"Oh, yis," said the deacon; "poor Mis' Higgins, she come to my wife reely mournin' when Zeph cut up so about them water-pipes, and says she, 'Mis' Dickenson, I'd rather 'a' worked my fingers to the bone than this 'ere should 'a' happened; but I can't do nothin',' says she; 'he's that sort that the more you say the more sot he gets,' says she. Wal, I don't wish the 'Piscopals no worse luck than to get Zeph Higgins, that's all I've got to say."

"Wal," said Tim Hawkins, "let 'em alone. Guess they'll find out what he is when they

come to pass the hat 'round. I expect keepin'
up that air meetin' 'll be drefful hard sleddin' yit—
and they won't get nothin' out o' Zeph. Zeph's
as tight as the bark of a tree."

"Wonder if that air buildin's paid fer? Hiel
Jones says there's a consid'able debt on't yit,"
said Deacon Peasley, "and Hiel gen'ally knows."

"Don't doubt on't," said Deacon Dickenson.
"Squire Lewis he's in for the biggest part on't,
and he's got money through his wife. She was
one of them rich Winthrops up to Boston. The
squire has gone off now to Lucius Jenks's store,
and so has Colonel Danforth and a lot more of
the biggest on 'em. I told Hiel I didn't mind,
so long as I kep' Colonel Davenport and Judge
Belcher and Judge Peters and Sheriff Dennie.
I have a good many more aristocracy than he
hez."

"For my part I don't care so very much for
these 'ere town-hill aristocracy," said Tim Hawkins. "They live here in their gret houses and
are so proud they think it's a favor to speak to
a farmer in his blue linsey shirt a drivin' his
team. I don't want none on 'em lookin' down
on me. I am as good as they be; and I guess you
make as much in your trade by the farmers
out on the hills as you do by the rich folks here
in town."

"Oh, yis, sartin," said Deacon Dickenson,

CASTE.

"O yis, sartin," said Deacon Dickenson, making haste to pro-
pitiate . . . "I'd rather see your sled a-standin' front o'
my door than the finest carriage any on 'em drives."—p. 67.

making haste to propitiate. " I don't want no better trade than I get out your way, Mr. Hawkins. I 'd rather see your sled a standin' front o' my door than the finest carriage any of 'em drives. I haint forgot Parson Cushing's sarmon to the farmers, ' The king himself is sarved by the field.' "

" I tell you that was a sarmon!" said Hawkins " We folks in our neighborhood all subscribed to get it printed, and I read it over once a month, Sundays. Parson Cushing 's a good farmer himself. He can turn in and plow or hoe or mow, and do as good a day's work as I can, if he does know Latin and Greek; and he and Mis' Cushing they come over and visit 'round 'mong us quite as sociable as with them town-hill folks. I 'm jest a waitin' to hear him give it to them air 'Piscopals next Sunday. He 'll sarve out the Democrats—the doctor will."

" Wal," said Deacon Dickenson, " I don't think the doctor hed reely got waked up when I spoke to him 'bout that 'lumination, but I guess his eyes are open now, and the doctor 's one o' that sort that's *wide* awake when he is awake. He 'll do suthin' o' Sunday."

CHAPTER VII.

THE DOCTOR'S SERMON.

POGANUC was a pretty mountain town in Connecticut. It was a county seat, and therefore of some considerable importance in the vicinity. It boasted its share of public buildings—the great meeting-house that occupied the central position of the village green, the tavern where the weekly stage put up, a court-house, a jail, and other defenses of public morals, besides the recently added Episcopal church.

It was also the residence of some stately and dignified families of comfortable means and traditions of ancestral importance. Of these, as before stated, a few had availed themselves of the loosening of old bonds and founded an Episcopal church; but it must not be supposed that there was any lack of dignified and wealthy old families in the primitive historic church of Poganuc, which had so long borne undisputed sway in the vicinity. There were the fine old residences of Judge Gridley and Judge Belcher adorning the principal streets. Conspicuous in

68

one of the front pews of the meeting-house might be seen every Sunday the stately form of Col. Davenport, who had been a confidential friend of General Washington and an active commander during the revolutionary war, and who inspired awe among the townspeople by his military antecedents. There might be seen, too, the Governor of the State and the High Sheriff of Poganuc County, with one Mr. Israel Deyter, a retired New York merchant, gifted, in popular belief, with great riches. In short, the meeting-house, for a country town, had no small amount of wealth, importance and gentility. Besides these residents, who encamped about the green and on the main street, was an outlying farming population extending for miles around, whose wagons conveying their well-dressed wives, stalwart sons and blooming daughters poured in from all quarters, punctual as a clock to the ringing of the second bell every Sunday morning.

Not the least attentive listeners or shrewd critics were to be found in these hardy yeomanry who scanned severely all that they paid for, whether temporal or spiritual. As may have been noticed from the conversation at Deacon Dickenson's store, Dr. Cushing had rather a delicate rôle to maintain in holding in unity the aristocracy and the democracy of his parish; for in those days people of well-born, well-bred families had a certain

traditional stateliness and punctiliousness which
were apt to be considered as pride by the laboring
democracy, and the doctor, as might be expected,
found it often more difficult to combat pride in
homespun than pride in velvet—perhaps having
no very brilliant success in either case.

The next Sunday was one of high expectation.
Everybody was on tiptoe to hear what "our
minister" would have to say,

The meeting-house of Poganuc was one of
those square, bald, unsentimental structures of
which but few specimens have come down to
us from old times. The pattern of those ancient
edifices was said to be derived from Holland,
where the Puritans were sheltered before they
came to these shores. At all events, they were
a marked departure in every respect from all
particulars which might remind one of the graceful ecclesiastical architecture and customs of the
Church of England. They were wide, roomy,
and of a desolate plainness; hot and sunny in
summer, with their staring rows of windows, and
in winter cold enough in some cases even to
freeze the eucharistic wine at the communion.

It was with great conflict of opinion and much
difficulty that the people of Poganuc had advanced
so far in the ways of modern improvement as to
be willing to have a large box stove set up in
the middle of the broad aisle, with a length of

black pipe extending through the house, whereby the severity of winter sanctuary performances should be somewhat abated. It is on record that, when the proposal was made in town meeting to introduce this luxurious indulgence, the zeal of old Zeph Higgins was aroused, and he rose and gave vent to his feelings in a protest:

"Fire? Fire? A fire in the house o' God? I never heard on't. I never heard o' hevin' fire in a meetin'-house."

Sheriff Dennie here rose, and inquired whether *Mrs.* Higgins did not bring a foot-stove with fire in it into the house of God every Sunday.

It was an undeniable fact not only that Mrs. Higgins but every respectable matron and mother of a family brought her foot-stove to church well filled with good, solid, hickory coals, and that the passing of this little ark of mercy from one frozen pair of feet to another was among the silent motherly ministries which varied the hours of service.

So the precedent of the foot-stove carried the box-stove into the broad aisle of the meeting-house, whereby the air was so moderated that the minister's breath did not freeze into visible clouds of vapor while speaking, and the beards and whiskers of the brethren were no longer coated with frost during service time.

Yet Poganuc was a place where winter stood

for something. The hill, like all hills in our dear
New England, though beautiful for situation in
summer was a howling desolation for about six
months of the year, sealed down under snow and
drifted over by winds that pierced like knives
and seemed to search every fiber of one's gar-
ments, so that the thickest clothing was no protection.

The Sunday in question was one of those many
when the thermometer stood any number of de-
degrees below zero ; the air clear, keen and cutting ; and the bright, blooming faces of the girls
in the singers' seat bore token of the frosty wind
they had encountered. All was animation through
the church, and Mr. Benjamin Davis, the leader
of the singing, had selected old " Denmark " as a
proper tune for opening the parallels between
them and the opposing forces of ritualism. Ben
had a high conceit of his own vocal powers, and
had been heard to express himself contemptuously of the new Episcopal organ. He had been
to Doctor Cushing with suggestions as to the
tunes that the singers wanted, to keep up the
reputation of their " meetin'-house." So after
" Denmark" came old "Majesty," and Ben so
bestirred himself beating time and roaring, first
to treble and then to counter and then to bass,
and all the singers poured forth their voices with
such ringing good-will, that everybody felt sure

they were better than any Episcopal organ in the world.

And as there is a place for all things in this great world of ours, so there was in its time and day a place and a style for Puritan music. If there were pathos and power and solemn splendor in the rhythmic movement of the churchly chants, there was a grand wild freedom, an energy of motion, in the old "fuguing" tunes of that day that well expressed the heart of a people courageous in combat and unshaken in endurance. The church chant is like the measured motion of the mighty sea in calm weather, but those old fuguing tunes were like that same ocean aroused by stormy winds, when deep calleth unto deep in tempestuous confusion, out of which at last is evolved union and harmony. It was a music suggestive of the strife, the commotion, the battle cries of a transition period of society, struggling onward toward dimly-seen ideals of peace and order. Whatever the trained musician might say of such a tune as old "Majesty," no person of imagination and sensibility could ever hear it well rendered by a large choir without deep emotion. And when back and forth from every side of the church came the different parts shouting,

> "On cherubim and seraphim
> Full royally he rode,

> And on the wings of mighty winds
>   Came flying all abroad"—

there went a stir and a thrill through many a stern and hard nature, until the tempest cleared off in the words,

> "He sat serene upon the floods,
>   Their fury to restrain,
>   And he, as sovereign Lord and King,
>   Forever more shall reign."

And when the doctor rose to his sermon the music had done its work on his audience, in exalting their mood to listen with sympathetic ears to whatever he might have to say.

When he spread out his sermon before him there was a rustle all over the house, as of people composing themselves to give the strictest attention.

He announced his text from Galatians iv., 9, 10, 11.

"But now, after that ye have known God, or rather are known of God, how turn ye again to the weak and beggarly elements, whereunto ye desire again to be in bondage? Ye observe days, and months, and times, and years. I am afraid of you, lest I have bestowed on you labor in vain."

The very announcement of the text seemed to bring out upon the listening faces of the audience a sympathetic gleam. Hard, weather-beaten countenances showed it, as when a sunbeam passes over points of rocks.

What was to come of such a text was plain to be seen. The yoke of bondage from which

Puritan New England had escaped across the waters of a stormy sea, the liberty in Christ which they had won in this new untrodden land, made theirs by prayers and toils and tears and sacrifice, for which they had just fought through a tedious and bloody war—there was enough in all these remembrances to evoke a strain of heartfelt eloquence which would awaken a response in every heart.

Then the doctor began his investigations of Christmas; and here his sermon bristled with quotations in good Greek and Latin, which he could not deny himself the pleasure of quoting in the original as well as in the translation. But the triumphant point in his argument was founded on a passage in Clemens Alexandrinus, who, writing at the close of the second century, speaks of the date of Christ's birth as an unimportant and unsettled point. " There are some," says the Father, " who over-curiously assign not only the year but the day of our Saviour's birth, which they say was the 25th of Pachon, or the 20th of May."

The doctor had exulted in the finding of this passage as one that findeth much spoil, and he proceeded to make the most of it in showing that the modern keeping of Christmas was so far unknown in the earliest ages of the church that even the day was a matter of uncertainty.

Now it is true that his audience, more than half of them, did not know who Clement was. Even the judges, men of culture and learning, and the teacher at the Academy, professionally familiar with Greek, had only the vaguest recollection of a Christian Father who had lived some time in the primitive ages; the rest of the congregation, men and women, only knew that their minister was a learned man and were triumphant at this new proof of it.

The doctor used his point so as to make it skillfully exciting to the strong, practical, matter-of-fact element which underlies New England life. "If it had been important for us to keep Christmas," he said, "certainly the date would not have been left in uncertainty. We find no traces in the New Testament of any such observance; we never read of Christmas as kept by the apostles and their followers; and it appears that it was some centuries after Christ before such an observance was heard of at all." In fact the doctor said that the keeping of the 25th of December as Christmas did not obtain till after the fourth century, and then it was appointed to take the place of an old heathen festival, the "*natalis solis invicti*;" and here the doctor rained down names and authorities and quotations establishing conflicting suppositions till the wilderness of learning grew so wild that only the Academy teacher seemed able to follow it through. He indeed sat up and nodded intelligently from point to point, feeling that the eyes of scholars might be upon him, and that it was well never to be caught napping in matters like these.

The last point of the Doctor's sermon consisted in historical statements and quotations concerning the various abuses to which the celebration of the Christmas festival had given rise, from the days of Augustine and Chrysostom down to those of the Charleses and Jameses of England, in all of which he had free course and was glorified; since under that head there are many things more true than edifying that might be recounted.

He alluded to the persecutions which had forced upon our fathers the alternative of conforming to burdensome and unspiritual rites and ceremonies or of flying from their native land and all they held dear; he quoted from St. Paul the passage about false brethren who came in privily to spy out our liberty that we have in Christ Jesus, that they might bring us again into bondage—"to whom" (and here the doctor grew emphatic and thumped the pulpit cushion) " we gave place by subjection *not for an hour.*"

The sermon ended with a stirring appeal to walk in the good old ways, to resist all those, however fair their pretenses, who sought to re-

move the old landmarks and repeal the just laws
and rules that had come down from the fathers.
It was evident from the enkindled faces in every
pew that the doctor carried his audience fully
with him, and when in the closing petition he
prayed to the Lord that "our judges might be
as at the first, and our counsellors as at the beginning," everybody felt sure that he was thinking of the next election, and Tim Hawkins with
difficulty restrained himself from giving a poke
of the elbow to a neighbor in the next pew suspected of Democratic proclivities.

As to Dolly, who as a babe of grace was duly
brought to church every Sunday, her meditations
were of a very confused order. Since the gift
of her red dress and red shoes, and the well remembered delightful scene at the church on
Christmas Eve, Christmas had been an interesting
and beautiful mystery to her mind; a sort of
illuminated mist, now appearing and now dis-
appearing.

Sometimes when her father in his sermon pronounced the word "Christmas" in emphatic
tones, she fixed her great blue eyes seriously
upon him and wondered what he could be saying; but when Greek and Latin quotations began
to rain thick and fast she turned to Spring, who
as a good, well-trained minister's dog was allowed
to go to meeting with his betters, and whose

serious and edified air was a pattern to Dolly and the boys.

When she was cold—a very common experience in those windy pews—she nestled close to Spring and put her arms around his neck, and sometimes dropped asleep on his back. Those sanctuary naps were a generally accorded privilege to the babes of the church, who could not be expected to digest the strong meat of the elders.

Dolly had one comfort of which nothing could deprive her: she had been allowed to wear her new red dress and red shoes. It is true the dress was covered up under a dark, stout little woolen coat, and the red shoes quenched in the shade of a pair of socks designed to protect her feet from freezing; but at intervals Dolly pulled open her little coat and looked at the red dress, and felt warmer for it, and thought whether there was any such day as Christmas or not it was a nice thing for little girls to have aunties and grandmas who believed in it, and sent them pretty things in consequence.

When the audience broke up and the doctor came down from the pulpit he was congratulated on his sermon as a master-piece. Indeed, he had the success that a man has always when he proves to an audience that they are in the right in their previous opinions.

The general opinion, from Colonel Davenport and Sheriff Dennie down to Tim Hawkins and the farmers of the vicinity, was that the doctor's sermon ought to be printed by subscription, and the suggestion was left to be talked over in various circles for the ensuing week.

CHAPTER VIII.

HE doctor's sermon had the usual effect of controversial sermons—it convinced everybody that was convinced before and strengthened those who before were strong. Everybody was talking of it. The farmers as they drove their oxen stepped with a vigorous air, like men that were not going to be brought under any yoke of bondage. Old ladies in their tea-drinkings talked about the danger of making a righteousness of forms and rites and ceremonies, and seemed of opinion that the proceedings at the Episcopal church, however attractive, were only an insidious putting forth of one paw of the Scarlet Beast of Rome, and that if not vigorously opposed the whole quadruped, tooth and claw, would yet be upon their backs.

But it must not be supposed that this side of the question had all the talk to itself. The Rev. Simeon Coan was a youth of bright parts, vigorous combativeness and considerable fluency of speech, and he immediately prepared a sermon on his side of the question, by which, in the

81

opinion of the Lewises, the Danforths, the Copleys and all the rest of his audience, he proved
beyond a doubt that Christmas ought to be kept,
and that the 25th of December was the proper
time for keeping it.   He brought also quotations
from Greek and Latin thick as stars in the skies ;
and as to the quotations of the doctor he ignored
them altogether, and talked about something else.

The doctor had been heard to observe with a
subdued triumph that he really would like to see
how " Coan" would " get round" that passage in
Clement, but he could not have that pleasure,
because " Coan" did not get anywhere near it,
but struck off as far as possible from it into a
region of quotations on his own side ; and as his
audience were not particularly fitted to adjudi-
cate nice points in chronology, and as quotations
from the Church Fathers on all sides of almost
any subject under the sun are plentiful as black-
berries in August, Mr. Coan succeeded in making
his side to the full as irrefragable in the eyes of
his hearers as the doctor's in those of his.

But besides this he reinforced himself by pro-
claiming with vigor the authority of the Church.
" The Church has ordained," " The Church in her
wisdom has directed," " The Church commands,"
and " The Church hath appointed," were phrases
often on his tongue, and the sound rolled
smoothly above the heads of good old families

who had long felt the want of some definite form
of authority to support their religious preferences
in face of the general Congregationalism of the
land.

The *Church*, that mysterious and awful power
that had come down from distant ages, had sur-
vived the dissolution of monarchies and was
to-day the same as of old! The thought was
poetical and exciting, and gave impulse to the
fervor inspired by a liturgy and forms of worship
allowed even by adversaries to be noble and
beautiful; and their minister's confident assertion
that the Church commanded, approved and
backed up all that they were doing was im-
mensely supporting to the little band. The
newly-acquired members, born and brought up
in Congregational discipline, felt all the delight
of a new sense of liberty. It had not always been
possible to go to any other than the dominant
church, and there was a fresh emotion of pleasure
in being able to do as they pleased in the matter; so they readily accepted Mr. Coan's High
Church claims and doctrines. Instead of standing
on the defensive and apologizing for their existence he boldly struck out for the rock of apostolic succession, declared their church *the* true
Apostolic Church, the only real church in the
place, although he admitted with an affable
charity that doubtless good Christian people

among the various sects who departed from this true foundation might at last be saved through the uncovenanted mercies of God.

Imagine the scorn which this doctrine inspired in Puritan people, who had been born in the faith that New England was the vine which God's right hand had planted—who had looked on her church as the Church of God, cast out indeed into the wilderness, but bearing with her "the adoption, and the glory, and the covenants, the giving of the law, and the service of God, and the promises." That faith was woven into the very existence of the New England race. They cast great roots about it as the oaks of the forest grasped and grew out of the eternal rocks of their hard and barren shores. So, when Mr. Simeon Coan, in a white surplice, amid suspicious chantings and bowings and genuflections, announced a doctrine which disfranchised them of the heavenly Jerusalem, and made them aliens from the commonwealth of Israel and strangers to the covenant of promise, there was a grim sense of humor mingled with the indignation which swelled their bosoms.

"Uncovenanted marcies!" said stout Tim Hawkins. "Thet's what they call 'em, do they? Wal, ef thet's what Parson Cushing and all the ministers of our association has got to live and die by—why, it's good enough for me. I don't want

no better; I don't care which kind they be. I
scorn to argue with such folks."

In fact they felt as if they had seen a chip
sparrow flying in the face of an eagle in his
rock-bound eyrie.

But the doctor's sermon had the effect to draw
the lines as to keeping Christmas up to the tight-
est brace. The academy teacher took occasion
on Monday to remark to his scholars how he
had never thought of such a thing as suspend-
ing school for Christmas holidays, and those of
the pupils who, belonging to Episcopal families,
had gone on Christmas Day to church were
informed that marks for absence and non-
performance of lessons would stand against them,
no matter what excuses they might bring from
parents. As to Christmas holidays—the giving
up to amusement a week, from Christmas to New
Year's—he spoke of it as a popish enormity
not to be mentioned or even thought of in God-
fearing New England, which abhorred a holiday
as much as nature abhors a vacuum. Those
parents whose children had been drawn in to
attend these seductive festivities were anxiously
admonished by their elders in homilies from the
text, "Surely, in vain the net is spread in the
sight of any bird."

For example, witness one scene. It is Sunday evening, and the bright snapping fire lights

up the great kitchen chimney where the widow
Jones is sitting by the stand with her great Bible
before her. A thin, weary, kindly old face is
hers, with as many lines in it as Denner's celebrated picture of the old woman. Everything
about her, to her angular figure and her thin
bony hands, bore witness to the unsparing work
that had been laid upon every hour and moment
of her life. Even now the thin hands that rested
on the Bible twitched at times mechanically as
if even in the blessed rest of Sunday evening
she felt the touch of the omnipresent knitting
needles.

On the settle beside the fire, half stretched out,
lounges Hiel, her youngest born son and the
prop of her old age; for all others have gone
hither and thither seeking their future in the
world. Hiel has been comforting her heart by
the heartiest praises of the minister's sermon that
day.

"I tell you what, Mother, them 'Piscopals got
pitched into lively, now; the Doctor pursued 'em
'even unto Shur,' as the Scriptur' says."

"Yis; and, Hiel, I hope you won't be seen
goin' to the 'Piscopal meetings no more. I felt
reely consarned, after I heard the sarmon, to
think of your bein' in to that air 'lumination."

"Oh laws, Mother, I jest *hed* to go to see to
things. Things hez to be seen to; there was

the Doctor's boys right up in the front slips,
and little Dolly there rolled up like a rabbit
down there under them spruces. I had to take
her home. I expect it's what waked up the
Doctor so, what I said to him."

"Wal, Hiel, mebbe it was all fer the best;
but I hope you'll let it alone now. And I heard
you was a settin' up with Nabby Higgins the
other evening; was you?"

A curious expression passed over Hiel's droll
handsome face, and he drew his knife from his
pocket and began reflectively to shave a bit of
shingle.

"Wal, yis, Mother; the fact is, I did stay with
Nabby Christmas evening, as they call it. Nabby
and me's allers ben good friends, you know.
You know, Mother, you think lots of Nabby's
mother, Mis' Higgins, and it ain't her fault nor
Nabby's ef she hez to leave our meetin'. It's
old Zeph that makes 'em."

"O yis. I ha'n't nothin' agin Mis' Higgins.
Polly Higgins is a good woman as is goin'. I
don't want no better; but as to Nabby, why,
she's light and triflin', and she's goin' right into
all these 'ere vanities; and I don't want no son
of mine to get drawn away arter her. You
know how 'twas in old times, it was the Moab-
itish women that allers made mischief."

"Oh land o' Goshen, Mother, jes as ef it would

do any harm for me to set up with Nabby in the minister's own kitchen. Ef she don't pisen the minister's boys and Dolly she won't pisen me; besides, I wanted to see what was in that air bundle Mis' Cushing's folks sent to her from Boston. Of course I knew you'd be a wantin' to know."

"Wal, did you see?" said the widow, snapping at once at the bait so artfully thrown.

"I rather reckon I did. Dolly she got a red frock and red shoes, and she was so tickled nothing would do but she must bring her red frock and red shoes right out to show to Nabby. They think all the world of each other, Nabby and Dolly do."

"Was the dress made up?" said the widow.

"Oh, yis; all made up, ready to put right on."

"Red, did you say?"

"Yes, red as a robin, with little black sprigs in't, and her shoes red morocco. I tell you she put 'em on and squeaked round in 'em lively! Then there was six silk pocket-handkerchers for the Doctor, all hemmed, and his name marked in the corner; and there was a nice book for each o' them boys, and a bonnet-ribbin for Miss Cushing."

"What color was it?" said the widow.

"Wal, I don't know—sort o' sky-blue scarlet," said Hiel, tired of particulars. "I never know what women call their ribbins."

"Wal, reely now, it's a good thing for folks to have rich relations," soliloquized the widow. "I don't grudge Mis' Cushing her prosperity—not a grain."

"Yis, and the doctor's folks was glad enough to get them things, if they *was* Christmas presents. The Christmas didn't pisen 'em, any way; Mis' Cushing's folks up to Boston 's 'Piscopals, but she thinks they're pretty nice folks, if they *be* 'Piscopals.

"Now, Hiel," said the widow, "Nabby Higgins is a nice girl—a girl that's got faculty, and got ambition, and she's handsome. I expect she's prudent and laid by something out of her wages"—and here the widow paused and gazed reflectively at the sparks on the chimney-back.

"Wal, Mother, the upshot on't is that if I and Nabby should want to make a team together there wouldn't be no call for wailin' and gnashin' of teeth. There might wuss things happen; but jes now Nabby and I's good friends—that's all."

And with this settlement the widow Jones, like many another mother, was forced to rest contented, sure that her son, in his own good time, would—do just as he pleased.

CHAPTER IX.

ELECTION DAY IN POGANUC.

THE month of March had dawned over the slippery, snow-clad hills of Poganuc. The custom that enumerates this as among the spring months was in that region the most bitter irony. Other winter months were simple *winter*—cold, sharp and hard enough—but March was winter with a practical application, driven in by winds that pierced through joints and marrow. Not an icicle of all the stalactites which adorned the fronts of houses had so much as thought of thawing; the snow banks still lay in white billows above the tops of the fences; the roads, through which the ox-sleds of the farmers crunched and squeaked their way, were cut deep down through heavy drifts, and there was still the best prospect in the world for future snow-storms; but yet it was called "spring." And the voting day had come; and Zeph Higgins, full of the energy of a sovereign and voter, was up at four o'clock in the morning, bestirring himself with a tempestuous clatter to rouse his household and be by daylight on the way to town to exercise his rights.

The feeble light of a tallow dip seemed to cut but a small circle into the darkness of the great kitchen. The frost sparkled white on the back of the big fire-place, where the last night's coals lay raked up under banks of ashes. An earthquake of tramping cowhide boots shook the rafters and stairs, and the four boys appeared on the scene of action. Backlog and forestick were soon piled and kindlings laid, and the fire roared and snapped and crackled up the ample chimney. Meek, shadowy Mrs. Higgins, with a step like a snow-flake, and resignation and submission in every line of her face, was proceeding to cut off frozen sausages from the strings of the same that garnished the kitchen walls. The tea kettle was hung over the blaze, and Zeph and the boys, with hats crowded down to their eyes, and tippets tied over their ears, plowed their way to the barn to milk and feed the stock.

When they returned, while the tea-kettle was puffing and the sausages frying and sizzling, there was an interval in which Zeph called to family prayers, and began reading the Bible with a voice as loud and harsh as the winds that were blowing out of doors.

Zeph always read the Bible straight along in course, without a moment's thought or inquiry as to the sense of what he was reading, which this morning was from Zechariah xi., as follows: " Open thy doors, O Lebanon, that the fire may devour thy cedars. Howl, fir tree; for the cedar is fallen; because the mighty are spoiled. Howl, O ye oaks of Bashan, for the forest of the vintage is come down. There is a voice of the howling of the shepherds, for their glory is spoiled: a voice of the roaring of young lions, for the pride of Jordan is spoiled." Zeph rendered the whole chapter with his harshest tones, and then, all standing, he enunciated in stentorian voice the morning prayer, whose phrases were an heir-loom that had descended from father to son for generations.

The custom of family worship was one of the most rigid inculcations of the Puritan order of society, and came down from parent to child with the big family Bible, where the births, deaths and marriages of the household stood recorded.

In Zeph's case the custom seemed to be merely an inherited tradition, which had dwindled into a habit purely mechanical. Yet, who shall say?

Of a rugged race, educated in hardness, wringing his substance out of the very teeth and claws of reluctant nature, on a rocky and barren soil, and under a harsh, forbidding sky, who but the All-Seeing could judge him? In that hard soul there may have been thus uncouthly expressed a

loyalty for Something Higher, however dimly
perceived. It was acknowledging that even he
had his master. One thing is certain, the custom
of family prayers, such as it was, was a great
comfort to the meek saint by his side, to whom
any form of prayer, any pause from earthly care
and looking up to a Heavenly Power, was a
blessed rest. In that daily toil, often beyond her
strength, when she never received a word of
sympathy or praise, it was a comfort all day to
her to have had a chapter in the Bible and a
prayer in the morning. Even though the chapter
were one that she could not by possibility understand a word of, yet it put her in mind of things
in that same dear book that she did understand;
things that gave her strength to live and hope
to die by, and it was enough! Her faith in the
Invisible Friend was so strong that she needed
but to touch the hem of his garment. Even a
table of genealogies out of *his* book was a sacred
charm, an amulet of peace.

Four sons—tall, stout and ruddy, in different stages of progression—surrounded the
table and caused sausages, rye and Indian
bread, and pork and beans, rapidly to dis-
appear. Of these sons two only were of the
age to vote. Zeph rigorously exacted of his boys
the full amount of labor which the law allowed
till their majority; but at twenty-one he recog-

nized their legal status, and began giving them the wages of hired men. On this morning he longed to have his way as to their vote; but the boys had enough of his own nature in them to have a purpose and will of their own, and how they were to vote was an impenetrable secret locked up in the rocky fastnesses of their own bosoms.

As soon as there were faint red streaks in the wintry sky, Zeph's sled was on the road, well loaded up with cord-wood to be delivered at Colonel Davenport's door; for Zeph never forgot business nor the opportunity of earning an honest penny. The oxen that drew his sled were sleek, well-fed beasts, the pride of Zeph's heart, and as the red sunlight darted across the snowy hills their breath steamed up, a very luminous cloud of vapor, which in a few moments congealed in sparkling frost lines on their patient eye-winkers and every little projecting hair around their great noses. The sled-runners creaked and grated as Zeph, with loud " Whoa," " Haw," or " Gee," directed the plodding course of his beasts. The cutting March wind was blowing right into his face; his shaggy, grizzled eye-brows and bushy beard were whitening apace; but he was in good spirits—he was going to vote against the Federalists; and as the largest part of the aristocracy of Town Hill were Federalists, he rejoiced all the more. Zeph was a creature born

to oppose, as much as white bears are made to
walk on ice.

And how, we ask, would New England's rocky
soil and icy hills have been made mines of wealth
unless there had been human beings born to
oppose, delighting to combat and wrestle, and
with an unconquerable power of will?

Zeph had taken a thirteen-acre lot so rocky
that a sheep could scarce find a nibble there, had
dug out and blasted and carted the rocks,
wrought them into a circumambient stone fence,
plowed and planted, and raised crop after crop of
good rye thereon. He did it with heat, with
zeal, with dogged determination; he did it all
the more because neighbors said he was a fool for
trying, and that he could never raise anything on
that lot. There was a stern joy in this hand-to-
hand fight with nature. He got his bread as
Sampson did his honeycomb, out of the carcass of
the slain lion. "Out of the eater came forth meat,
and out of the strong came forth sweetness."
Even the sharp March wind did not annoy him.
It was a controversial wind, and that suited him;
it was fighting him all the way, and he enjoyed
beating it. Such a human being has his place
in the Creator's scheme.

Poganuc was, for a still town, pretty well alive
on that day. Farmers in their blue linsey frocks,
with their long cart whips and their sleds hitched

here and there at different doors, formed frequent
objects in the picture. It was the day when they
felt themselves as good as anybody. The court
house was surrounded by groups earnestly discussing the political questions; many of them loafers
who made a sort of holiday, and interspersed
their observations and remarks with visits to the
bar-room of Glazier's tavern, which was doing a
thriving business that morning.

Standing by the side of the distributor of the
Federal votes might be seen a tall, thin man, with
a white head and an air of great activity and
keenness. In his twinkling eye and in every line
and wrinkle of his face might be read the observer
and the humorist; the man who finds something
to amuse him in all the quips and turns and
oddities of human nature. This was Israel
Dennie, High Sheriff of the County, one of the
liveliest and shrewdest of the Federal leaders,
who was, so to speak, crackling with activity, and
entering into the full spirit of the day in all its
phases.

"Here comes one of your party, Adams," he
said with a malicious side twinkle to the distributor of the Democratic votes, as Abe Bowles, a
noted "*mauvais sujet*" of the village, appeared
out of Glazier's bar-room, coming forward with
a rather uncertain step and flushed face.

"Walk up, friend ; here you are."

"I'm a-goin' for toleration," said Abe, with thick utterance. "We've ben tied up too tight by these 'ere ministers, we have. I don't want no priestcraft, I don't. I believe every man's got to do as he darn pleases, I do.

"And go straight to the Devil if he wants to," said Squire Dennie smoothly. "Go ahead, my boy, and put in your vote."

"There comes old Zeph Higgins," he added with alertness; "let us have a bit of fun with him."

"Hulloa, Higgins; step this way; here's Mr. Adams to give you your vote. You're going to vote the Democratic ticket, you know."

"No, I ain't, nuther," said Zeph, from the sheer mechanical instinct of contradiction.

"Not going to vote with the Democrats, Higgins? All right, then you're going to vote the Federal ticket; here 'tis."

"No, I ain't, nuther. You let me alone. I ain't a-goin' to be dictated to. I'm a-goin' to vote jest as I'm a mind ter. I won't vote for nuther, ef I ain't a mind ter, and I'll vote for jest which one I want ter, and no other."

"So you shall, Higgins; so you shall," said Squire Dennie sympathetically, laying his hand on Zeph's shoulder.

"I shan't, nuther; you let me alone," said Zeph, shaking off the Sheriff's hand; and clutching at the Democratic ticket, he pushed up towards the polls.

"There's a fellow, now," said Sheriff Dennie, looking after him with a laugh. "That fellow's so contrary that he hates to do the very thing he wants to, if anybody else wants him to do it. If there was any way of voting that would spite both parties and please nobody, he'd take that. The only way to get that fellow to heaven would be to set out to drive him to hell; then he'd turn and run up the narrow way, full chisel."

It was some comfort to Zeph, however, to work his way up to the polls with Judge Belcher right in front and with Colonel Davenport's aristocratic, powdered head and stately form pushing him along behind, their broadcloth crowded against his homespun carter's frock, and he, Zephaniah, that day just as good as either. He would not have been so well pleased if he knew that his second son, Abner—following not long after him—dropped in the box the Federalist ticket. It was his right as a freeman; but he had no better reason for his preference than the wish to please his mother. He knew that Dr. Cushing was a Federalist, and that his mother was heart and soul for every thing that Dr. Cushing was for, and therefore he dropped this vote for his mother; and thus, as many times

before and since, a woman voted through her
son.

In fact, the political canvass just at this epoch
had many features that might shock the pious
sensibilities of a good house-mother. The union
of all the minor religious denominations to upset
the dominant rule of the Congregationalists had
been reinforced and supplemented by all that
Jacobin and irreligious element which the French
Revolution had introduced into America.

The Poganuc *Banner,* a little weekly paper
published in the village, expended its energies
in coarse and scurrilous attacks upon ministers
in general, and Dr. Cushing in particular. It
ridiculed church-members, churches, Sunday-
keeping, preaching and prayers; in short, every
custom, preference and prejudice which it had
been the work of years to establish in New
England was assailed with vulgar wit and
ribaldry.

Of course, the respectable part of the Democratic party did not exactly patronize these
views; yet they felt for them that tolerance
which even respectable people often feel in a
rude push of society in a direction where they
wish to go. They wanted the control of the
State, and if rabid, drinking, irreligious men
would give it to them, why not use them after
their kind? When the brutes had won the

battle for them, they would take care of the brutes, and get them back into their stalls.

The bar-room of Glazier's Tavern was the scene of the feats and boasts of this class of voters. Long before this time the clergy of Connecticut, alarmed at the progress of intemperance, had begun to use influence in getting stringent laws and restraints upon drinking, and the cry of course was, " Down with the laws."

" Tell ye what," said Mark Merrill; " we've ben tied up so tight we couldn't wink mor'n six times a week, and the parsons want to git it so we can't wink at all; and we won't have it so no longer; we're goin' to have liberty."

" Down with the tithing-man, say I," said Tim Sykes. " Whose business is it what I do Sundays? I ain't goin' to have no tithing-man spying on my liberty. I'll do jest what I'm a mind ter, Sundays. Ef I wan ter go a-fishin' Sundays, I'll go a-fishin'."

"Tell ye what," said Liph Kingsley, as he stirred his third glass of grog. " This 'ere priestcraft's got to go down. Reason's got on her throne, and chains is fallin'. I'm a free man —I be."

" You look like it," said Hiel, who stood with his hands in his pockets contemptuously surveying Liph, while with leering eye and unsteady hand he stirred his drink.

"That air's what you call Reason, is't?" added Hiel. "Wal, she's got on a pretty topplish throne, seems to me. I bet you Reason can't walk a crack now," he said, as Liph, having taken off his glass, fell with a helpless dump upon the settle.

"Sot down like a spoonful of apple-saas," said Hiel, looking him over sarcastically. The laugh now turned against the poor brute, and Hiel added: "Wal, boys, s'pose you like this 'ere sort of thing. Folks is different; for my part I like to kinder keep up a sort o' difference 'tween me and a hog. That air's my taste; but you're welcome to yourn," and Hiel went out to carry his observations elsewhere.

Hiel felt his own importance to the community of Poganuc Center too much to have been out of town on this day, when its affairs needed so much seeing to, therefore he had deputed Ned Bissel, a youth yet wanting some two years of the voting age, to drive his team for him while he gave his undivided attention to public interests; and indeed, as nearly as mortal man can be omnipresent, Hiel had been everywhere and heard everything, and, as the French say, "assisted" generally at the political struggle. Hiel considered himself as the provisional owner and care-taker of the town of Poganuc. It was *our* town, and Dr. Cushing was *our* minister, and the great meeting-house on the green was *our* meeting-house, and the singers' seat therein was *our* singers' seat, and he was ready to bet on any sermon, or action, or opinion of *our* minister. Hiel had not yet, as he phrased it, experienced religion, nor joined the church; but he " calculated he should some of these days." It wasn't Doctor Cushing's fault if he wasn't converted, he was free to affirm. Hiel had been excessively scandalized with the scurrilous attacks of the Poganuc *Banner*, and felt specially called to show his colors on that day. He had assured his mother on going out that morning that she needn't be a mite afeared, for *he* was a-goin' to stand up for the minister through thick and thin, and if any of them Democrats " saassed " him he'd give 'em as good as they sent.

In virtue of his ardent political zeal, he felt himself to-day on equal and speaking terms with all the Federal magnates; he clapped Colonel Davenport on the shoulder assuringly, and talked about "our side," and was familiar with Judge Belcher and Sheriff Dennie—darting hither and thither, observing and reporting with untiring zeal.

But, after all, that day the Democrats beat, and got the State of Connecticut. Sheriff Dennie was the first to carry the news of defeat into the parsonage at eventide.

"Well, Doctor, we're smashed. Democrats beat us all to flinders."

A general groan arose.

"Yes, yes," said the Sheriff. "Everything has voted that could stand on its hind legs, and the hogs are too many for us. It's a bad beat—bad beat."

That night when little Dolly came in to family prayers, she looked around wondering. Her father and mother looked stricken and overcome. There was the sort of heaviness in the air that even a child can feel when deep emotions are aroused. The boys, who knew only in a general way that their father's side had been beaten, looked a little scared at his dejected face.

"Father, what makes you feel so bad?" said Will, with that surprised wonder with which children approach emotions they cannot understand.

"I feel for the Church of God, my child," he said, and then he sung for the evening psalm:

> I love thy kingdom, Lord,
> The house of thine abode;
> The Church our dear Redeemer saved
> With his own precious blood.
>
> For her my tears shall fall,
> For her my prayers ascend;
> To her my cares and toils be given
> Till toils and cares shall end.

In the prayer that followed he pleaded for New England with all the Hebraistic imagery by

which she was identified with God's ancient
people :

"Give ear, O Shepherd of Israel ; thou that
leadest Joseph like a flock ; thou that dwellest
between the cherubims, shine forth. * * Thou
hast brought a vine out of Egypt ; thou didst
cast forth the heathen, and plant it ; thou pre-
paredst room for it and didst cause it to take
deep root, and it filled the land. The hills were
covered with the shadow of it, and the boughs
thereof were like the goodly cedars. Why hast
thou then broken down her hedges so that all
that pass by the way do pluck her? The boar
out of the wood doth waste it ; the wild beast of
the field doth devour it. Return, we beseech
thee, O Lord, and visit this vine and vineyard
that thou has planted and the branch that thou
madest strong for thyself."

It was with a voice tremulous and choking with
emotion that Dr. Cushing thus poured forth the
fears and the sorrows of his heart for the New
England of the Puritans ; the ideal church and
state which they came hither to found.

Little Dolly cried from a strange childish fear,
because of the trouble in her father's voice. The
pleading tones affected her, she knew not why.
The boys felt a martial determination to stand by
their father and a longing to fight for him. All
felt as if something deep and dreadful must have

happened, and after prayers Dolly climbed into her father's lap, and put both arms around his neck, and said: "Papa, there sha'n't anything hurt you. I'll defend you." She was somewhat abashed by the cheerful laugh which followed, but the Doctor kissed her and said: "So you shall, dear; be sure and not let anything catch me," and then he tossed her up in his arms gleefully, and she felt as if the trouble, whatever it was, could not be quite hopeless.

But Dolly marveled in her own soul as she went to bed. She heard the boys without stint reviling the Democrats as the authors of all mischief; and yet Bessie Lewis's father was a Democrat, and he seemed a nice, cheery, good-natured man, who now and then gave her sticks of candy, and there was his mother, dear old Madame Lewis, who gave her the Christmas cookey. How could it be that such good people were Democrats? Poor Dolly hopelessly sighed over the mystery, but dared not ask questions.

But the Rev. Mr. Coan rejoiced in the result of the election. Not that he was by any means friendly to the ideas of the Jacobinical party by whose help it had been carried; but because, as he said, it opened a future for the church—for he too had his idea of "The Church." Meanwhile the true church, invisible to human eyes —one in spirit, though separated by creeds—

was praying and looking upward, in the heart of Puritan and Ritualist, in the heart of old Madame Lewis, of the new Church, and of old Mrs. Higgins, whose soul was with the old meeting-house; of all everywhere who with humble purpose and divine aspiration were praying: "Thy kingdom come; Thy will be done."

That kingdom was coming even then—for its coming is in safer hands than those on either side —and there came a time, years after, when Parson Cushing, looking back on that election and its consequences, could say with another distinguished Connecticut clergyman:

"I suffered more than tongue can tell for the best thing that ever happened to old Connecticut."

CHAPTER X.

DOLLY went to bed that night, her little soul surging and boiling with conjecture. All day scraps of talk about the election had reached her ears; her nerves had been set vibrating by the tones of her father's prayer, some words of which yet rung in her ear—tones of passionate pleading whose purport she could scarcely comprehend. What was this dreadful thing that had happened or was going to happen? She heard her brother Will emphatically laying off the state of the case to Nabby in the kitchen, and declaring that "the Democrats were going to upset the whole State, for father said so."

Exactly what this meant, Dolly could not conceive; but, coupled with her mother's sorrowful face and her father's prayer, it must mean something dreadful. Something of danger to them all might be at hand, and she said her "pray God to bless my dear father and mother" with unusual fervor.

Revolving the matter on her pillow, she had

a great mind, the next time she met General
Lewis with his smiling face, to walk boldly up
to him and remonstrate, and tell him to let her
papa alone and not upset the State!

Dolly had a great store of latent heroism and
felt herself quite capable of making a courageous
defense of her father—and her heart swelled with
a purpose to stand by him to the last gasp, no
matter what came.

But sleep soon came down with her downy
wings, and the great blue eyes were closed, and
Dolly knew not a word more till waked by the
jingling of sleigh bells and the creaking of sleds
at early sunrise.

She sprang up, dressed quickly, and ran to the
window. Evidently the State had *not* been upset
during the night, for the morning was clear,
bright and glorious as heart could desire.

The rosy light of morning filled the air, the
dreary snow wreaths lay sparkling in graceful
lines with tender hues of blue and lilac and pink
in their shadows, and merry sleigh bells were
ringing and the boys were out snow-balling each
other in mere wantonness of boy life, while Spring
was barking frantically, evidently resolved to be
as frisky a boy as any of them.

The fears and apprehensions of last night were
all gone like a cloud, and she hurried down into
the kitchen to find Nabby stirring up her buck-

HIEL IN HIS GLORY.

"And wasn't you running to look at him?" asked Dolly.
"Land o' Goshen, no!" said Nabby. "I jest wanted to see——
well, them horses he's got." . . "Oh," said Dolly.—p. 109.

wheat batter, and running to the window to see Hiel go by on the stage, kissing his hand to her as he passed.

"I declare! the imperence of that cretur," said Nabby.

"What, Hiel?" asked Dolly.

"Yes, Hiel Jones! he's the conceitedest fellow that ever I did see. You can't look out of a window but he thinks your running to look at *him*."

"And wasn't you running to look at him?" asked Dolly.

"Land o' Goshen, no! What should I want to look at *him* for? I jest wanted to see—well, them horses he's got."

"Oh," said Dolly.

Upon reflection she added,

"I thought you liked Hiel, Nabby."

"You thought I liked Hiel?" said Nabby laughing. "What a young 'un! Why, I can't bear the sight of him," and Nabby greased her griddle with combative energy. "He's the saassiest fellow I ever see. *I can't bear him!*"

Dolly reflected on this statement gravely, while Nabby dropped on the first griddleful of cakes; finally she said,

"If you don't like Hiel, Nabby, what made you sit up so late with him Christmas night?"

"Who said I did?" said Nabby, beginning to turn griddle-cakes with velocity.

" Why, Will and Tom; they both say so. They
heard when Hiel went out the kitchen door, and
they counted the clock striking twelve just as he
went. Will says he kissed you, too, Nabby. Did
he?"

" Well, if ever I see such young 'uns!" said
Nabby, flaming carnation color over the fire as
she took off the cakes. " That Bill is saassy
enough to physic a hornbug. I never see the
beat of him!"

" But did Hiel stay so late, Nabby?"

" Well, yes, to be sure he did. I thought I
never should have got him out of the house. If
I hadn't let him kiss me I believe in my soul I'd
a had to set up with him till morning; he said he
wouldn't go without. I've been mad at him ever
since. I told him never to show his face here
again; but I know he'll come. He does it on
purpose to plague me."

" That is dreadful!" said Dolly, meditatively
" I wouldn't let him. I'll tell you what," she
added, with animation, " *I'll* talk to him and tell
him he mustn't come here any more. Sha'n't I,
Nabby?"

But Nabby laughed and said, " No, no; little
girls mustn't talk so. Don't you never say
nothin' to Hiel about it; if you do I won't tell
you no more. Here, carry in this plate o' cakes,
for they're eatin' breakfast. I heard your pa

askin' blessin' just after you came down. You carry these in while I get on the next griddle-ful."

Dolly assumed her seat at table, but there again the trouble met her. Her father and mother were talking together with sad, anxious faces.

" It is a most mysterious dispensation why this is allowed," said her mother.

" Yes, my dear, ' clouds and darkness are round about Him,' but we must have faith."

Here Spring varied the discourse by putting his somber black visage over Dolly's arm and resting his nose familiarly on the table, whereat she couldn't help giving him the half of a griddle-cake.

" How many times must I tell you, Dolly, that Spring is never to be fed at the table?" said her mother. " I love dogs," she added, "but it spoils them to be fed at table."

" Why, papa does it sometimes," pleaded Tom.

Mrs. Cushing was obliged to confess to the truth of this, for the doctor when pursuing the deeper mazes of theology was sometimes so abstracted that his soul took no note of what his body was doing, and he had been more than once detected in giving Spring large rations under the table while expounding some profound mysteries of foreknowledge and free will.

Tom's remark was a home-thrust, but his mother said, reprovingly:

"Your father never means to do it; but he has so much to do and think of that he is sometimes absent-minded."

A conscious twinkle might have been observed playing about the blue eyes of the doctor, and a shrewd observer might have surmised that the offense was not always strictly involuntary, for the doctor, though a most docile and tractable husband, still retained here and there traces of certain wild male instincts and fell at times into singular irregularities. He had been known to upset all Mrs. Cushing's nicely arranged yarn-baskets and stocking-baskets and patch-baskets, pouring the contents in a heap on the floor, and carrying them off bodily to pick up chestnuts in, when starting off with the children on a nutting expedition. He would still persist at intervals in going to hunt eggs in the barn with Dolly, and putting the fruits of the search in his coat-tail pocket, though he had once been known to sit down on a pocketful at a preparatory lecture, the bell for which rung while he was yet on the hay-mow.

On this occasion, therefore, Spring made an opportune diversion in the mournful turn the conversation was taking. The general tone of remark became slightly admonitory on the part of Mrs. Cushing and playfully defensive on the part of the doctor. In their "heart of heart" the boys believed their father sometimes fed Spring when he *did* know what he was about, and this belief caused constant occasional lapses from strict statute law on their part.

That morning, in prayers, their father read: "God is our refuge and strength, a very present help in time of trouble. Therefore will we not fear, though the earth be removed; though the mountains be carried into the midst of the sea;" and at those verses he stopped and said: "There, my dear, there must be our comfort." And then they sung:

> " Our God, our help in ages past,
>   Our hope for years to come,
>   Our shelter from the stormy blast,
>   And our eternal home."

Then in prayer he plead for the Church—the Church of God, the vine of his planting—and said:

"When the enemy cometh in like a flood, may Thy spirit lift up a standard against them;" and again Dolly trembled and wondered. But after prayers Bill suddenly burst back into the house.

"Oh! mamma, there *is* a bluebird! Spring is come!"

"A bluebird! Impossible so early in March. You must be mistaken."

"No. Come to the door; you can hear him just as plain!"

And, sure enough, on the highest top of the great button-ball tree opposite the house sat the little blue angel singing with all his might—a living sapphire dropped down from the walls of the beautiful city above. A most sanguine and imprudent bluebird certainly he must have been, though the day was so lovely and the great icicles on the eaves of the house were actually commencing to drip. But there undoubtedly he was—herald and harbinger of good days to come.

"It is an omen," said the doctor, as he put his arms fondly round his wife. "The Lord liveth, and blessed be our rock!"

And the boys and Dolly ran out, shouting wildly,

"There's been a bluebird. Spring is coming—spring is coming!"

CHAPTER XI.

DOLLY AND NABBY INVITED OUT.

YES. Spring was coming; the little blue herald was right, though he must have chilled his beak and frozen his toes as he sat there. But he came from the great Somewhere, where things are always bright; where life and summer and warmth and flowers are forever going on while we are bound down under ice and snow.

There was a thrill in the hearts of all the children that day, with visions of coming violets, hepaticas and anemones, of green grass and long bright sunny rambles by the side of the Poganuc river.

The boys were so premature in hope as to get out their store of fish-hooks, and talk of trouting. The Doctor looked over his box of garden seeds, and read the labels. "Early Lettuce," "Early Cucumbers," "Summer Squashes" —all this was inspiring reading, and seemed to help him to have faith that a garden was coming round again, though the snow banks yet

lay over the garden-spot deep and high. All day
long it thawed and melted; a warm south wind
blew and the icicles dripped, so that there was
a continual patter.

Two circumstances of importance in Dolly's
horoscope combined on this happy day: Hiel
invited Nabby to an evening sleigh-ride after
supper, and Mrs. Davenport invited her father
and mother to a tea-drinking at the same time.

Notwithstanding her stout words about Hiel,
Nabby in the most brazen and decided manner
declared her intention to accept his invitation,
because (as she remarked) "Hiel had just
bought a bran new sleigh, and Almiry Smith
had said publicly that *she* was going to have
the first ride in that air sleigh, and she would
like to show Almiry that she didn't know every
thing." Nabby had inherited from her father a
fair share of combativeness, which was always
bubbling and boiling within her comely person
at the very idea of imaginary wrongs; and, as
she excitedly wiped her tea-cups, she went on:

"That air Almiry Smith is a stuck-up thing;
always turning up her nose at me, and talking
about my being a hired gal. What's the difference? I live out and work, and she stays to
home and works. I work for the minister's
folks and get my dollar a week, and she works
for her father and don't git nothin' but just her

board and her keep. So, I don't see why she
need take airs over me—and she sha'n't do it!"

But there was a tranquilizing influence breathing over Nabby's soul, and she soon blew off the
little stock of spleen and invited Dolly into her
bed-room to look at her new Leghorn bonnet,
just home from Miss Hinsdale's milliner-shop,
which she declared was too sweet for anything.

Now, Leghorn bonnets were a newly-imported
test of station, grandeur and gentility in Poganuc.
Up to this period the belles of New England had
worn braided straw, abundantly pretty, and often
braided by the fair fingers of the wearers themselves, while they studied their lessons or read
the last novel or poem.

But this year Miss Hetty Davenport, and Miss
Ellen Dennie, and the blooming daughters of the
governor, and the fair Maria Gridley had all
illuminated their respective pews in the meeting-
house with Leghorn flats—large and fine of braid,
and tremulous with the delicacy of their fiber.
Similar wonders appeared on the heads of the
juvenile aristocracy of the Episcopal church; and
the effect was immediate.

Straw bonnets were "no where." To have a
Leghorn was the thing; and Miss Hinsdale imported those of many qualities and prices, to suit
customers. Nabby's was not of so fine a braid as
that of the governor's daughters; still it was a

real Leghorn hat, and her soul was satisfied. She
wanted a female bosom to sympathize with her
in this joy, and Dolly was the chosen one.

Proud of this confidence, Dolly looked, exclaimed, admired, and assisted at the toilette-
trial—yet somewhat wondering at the facility
with which Nabby forgot all her stringent decla-
rations of the morning before.

"You don't suppose he would dare to kiss you
again, Nabby?" Dolly suggested timidly, while
Nabby stood at the glass with her bonnet on,
patting her curls, shaking her head, pulling into
place here a bow and there a flower.

"Why, Dolly Cushing," said Nabby, laughing;
"what a young 'un you are to remember things!
I never saw such a child!"

"But you said "—— cried Dolly,—

"Oh, never mind what I said. Do you suppose
I can't keep that fellow in order? I'd just like to
have him try it again—and see what he'd get!
There now, what do you think of that?" And
Nabby turned round and showed a general
twinkle of nodding flowers, fluttering ribbons,
bright black eyes, and cheeks with laughing
dimples which came and went as she spoke or
laughed.

"Nabby, I do declare, you are splendid," said
Dolly. "Hiel said once you was the handsomest girl in Poganuc."

"He did, did he? Well, I'll let him know a thing or two before I've done with him; and Almiry Smith, too, with her milk-and-water face and stringy curls."

"Did that bonnet cost a great deal?" asked Dolly.

"What do you mean, child?" asked Nabby, turning quickly and looking at her.

"Nothing, only Mrs. Davenport said that hired girls were getting to dress just like ladies."

Nabby flared up and grew taller, and seemed about to rise from the floor in spontaneous combustion.

"I declare!" she said. "That's just like these 'ere stuck-up Town Hill folks. Do they think nobody's to have silk gowns and Leg'orn bonnets but them? Who's a better right, I should like to know? Don't we *work* for our money, and ain't it *ourn?* and ain't we just as good as they be? I'll buy just such clothes as I see fit, and if anybody don't like it why they may lump it, that's all. I've a better right to my bonnet than Hetty Davenport has to hers, for I earned the money to pay for it, and she just lives to do nothing, and be a bill of expense to her folks."

Dolly cowered under this little hurricane; but, Poganuc being a windy town, Dolly had full experience that the best way to meet a sudden

gust is to wait for it to blow itself out, as she
did on the present occasion. In a minute Nabby
laughed and was herself again; it was impossible
to be long uncomfortable with a flower garden
on one's head.

"I shall be lonesome to-night without you,
Nabby," said Dolly; "the boys talk Latin to
me and plague me when I want to play with
them."

"Oh, I heard Mis' Cushing say she was going
to take you to the tea-party, and that 'll be just
as good for you."

Dolly jumped up and down for joy and ran
to her mother only to have the joyful tidings
confirmed. "I shall never leave Dolly alone in
the house again, with nobody but the boys," she
said, "and I shall take her with us. It will be
a lesson in good manners for her."

It may have been perceived by the intimations
of these sketches hitherto that there were in the
town of Poganuc two distinct circles of people,
who mingled in public affairs as citizens and in
church affairs as communicants, but who rarely
or never met on the same social plane.

There was the *haute noblesse*—very affably disposed, and perfectly willing to *condescend;* and
there was the proud democracy, prouder than
the noblesse, who wouldn't be condescended to,
and insisted on having their way and their say,

on the literal, actual standpoint of the original equality of human beings.

The sons and daughters of farmers and mechanics would willingly exchange labor with each other; the daughters would go to a neighboring household where daughters were few, and help in the family work, and the sons likewise would hire themselves out where there was a deficiency of man-power; but they entered the family as full equals, sharing the same table, the same amusements, the same social freedoms, with the family they served.

It was because the Town Hill families wished to hire *servants*, according to the Old-World acceptation of the term, that it became a matter of exceeding difficulty to get any of the free democratic citizens or citizenesses to come to them in that capacity.

Only the absolute need of money reconciled any of them to taking such a place, and then they took it with a secret heart-burning and a jealous care to preserve their own personal dignity.

Nabby had compromised her pride in working for " the minister," for the minister in early New England times was the first gentleman of the parish, and a place in his family was a different thing from one in any other.

Nevertheless, Nabby required to be guided

with a delicate hand and governed with tact and
skill.   There were things that no free-born American girl would do, and Mrs. Cushing had the
grace not to expect those things.   For instance,
no Yankee girl would come at the ringing of a
bell.   To expect this would, as they held it, be to
place them on a level with the negroes still
retained as servants in some old families.   It was
useless to argue the point.   Nabby's cheeks would
flush, and her eyes flash, and the string of her
tongue would be loosed, and she would pour
forth torrents of declamation if one attempted to
show that calling by a bell was no worse than
calling by the voice or sending out one of the
children.   Mrs. Cushing did not try to do it.

Another point was the right to enter the house
by the front door.   Now, as Nabby's work lay
in the kitchen and as her sleeping-room was just
above, it was manifestly an inconvenience to enter
by any other than the kitchen door.   Nevertheless, she had heard the subject discussed among
other girls, and had admired the spirit shown by
her intimate friend, Maria Pratt, when Mrs. Israel
Deyter pointed out to her the propriety of entering by the back door,—" Mrs. Deyter, do you
think there will be a back and a front door to
heaven?"

But Mrs. Cushing avoided the solution of this
theological problem by looking on with a smile

of calm amusement when Nabby very conspicu-
ously and perseveringly persisted in entering by
the front door the first week of her engagement
with the family. As nothing was said and
nothing done about it, Nabby gradually declined
into doing what was most convenient—went the
shortest way to her work and room. Nabby was
in her way and place a person worth making
concessions to, for she was a workwoman not to
be despised. Her mother, Mrs. Higgins, was
one of those almost fabulous wonders of household genius who by early rising, order, system,
neatness and dispatch reduced the seemingly
endless labors of a large family to the very
minimum of possibility. Consequently there was
little occasion for the mistress of a family to
overlook or to teach Nabby. When she entered
the household she surveyed the situation with
trained eyes, took an account of all work to be
done, formed her system and walked through it
daily with energetic ease, always securing to
herself two or three hours of leisure every day in
which to do her own cutting, fitting and sewing.
According to the maxims in which she had been
brought up, a girl that did not "do up her work
in the morning," so as to have this interval of
leisure, was not mistress of her business. On
washing days Nabby's work began somewhere in
the latter part of the night, and daylight saw her

flags of victory waving on the lines in the shape
of renovated linen, and Nabby with great composure getting breakfast as on any other day.

She took all her appointed work as a matter
of course. Strong, young, and healthy, she
scarcely knew what fatigue was. She was cheerful, obliging, and good tempered, as thoroughly
healthy people generally are. There was, to
be sure, a little deposit of gunpowder in Nabby's
nature, and anybody who chose to touch a match
to her self-esteem, her sense of personal dignity
or independence, was likely to see a pretty lively
display of fireworks; but it was always soon
over, and the person making the experiment
did not generally care to repeat it.

But Hiel Jones found this chemical experiment
irresistibly fascinating, and apparently did not
care how often he burned his fingers with it.
Hiel was somewhat *blasé* with easy conquests.

The female sex have had in all ages their spoiled
favorites, who are ungrateful just in proportion
to the favors bestowed upon them; and Hiel
was in his circle as much courted and pursued
with flattering attentions as any spoiled tenor of
the modern opera. For him did Lucinda and
Jane bake surreptitious mountains of sponge cake.
Small tributes of cream, butter, pies of various
name and model, awaited him at different
stopping-places, and were handed him by fair

hands with flattering smiles. The Almira of whom Nabby discoursed with such energetic vehemence had knit Hiel a tippet, worked his name on a pocket-handkerchief with her hair, and even gone so far as to present him with one of the long yellow curls which Nabby was pleased to call "stringy." Nabby's curls certainly could not have merited any such epithet, as every separate one of them had a will and a way of its own, and all were to the full as mutinous as their mistress. Yet Hiel would have given more for one of those rebellious curls than for all Almira's smooth-brushed locks, and although a kiss from Nabby was like a kiss from one on an electric stool, snapping and prickling at every touch, yet somehow the perverse Hiel liked the excitement of the shock.

Hiel's tactics for the subjugation of a female heart were in the spirit of a poet he never heard of:

> " Pique her, and soothe in turns ;
> Soon passion crowns thy hopes."

He instituted a series of regular quarrels with Nabby, varied by flattering attentions, and delighted to provoke her to anger, sure that she would say a vast deal more than she meant, and then, in the reaction which is always sure to follow in the case of hot-tempered, generous people, he should find his advantage.

So, when the stars looked out blinking and winking through a steel-blue sky, Nabby, in the fascinating new bonnet, was handed into the smart new sleigh, tucked in with Hiel under a profusion of buffalo robes, and went jingling away. A supper and a dance awaited them at a village tavern ten miles off, and other sleighs and other swains with their ladies were on the same way, where we take our leave of them to follow our little Dolly into the parlors of the *haute noblesse.*

CHAPTER XII.

HEN Dolly found herself arrayed in her red dress and red shoes, her hair nicely curled, she was so happy that, to speak scripturally, she leaped for joy— flew round and round with her curls flying, like a little mad-cap—till her mother was obliged to apply a sedative exhortation.

"Take care, Dolly; take care. I can't take you, now, unless you are good. If you get so wild as that I shall have to leave you at home. Come here, and let me talk to you."

And Dolly came and stood, grave and serious, at her mother's knee, who, while she made over and arranged some of the tumbled curls, proceeded to fortify her mind for the coming emergency with suitable precepts.

"It's a great thing for a little girl like you, Dolly, to be allowed to sit up with grown people till nine o'clock, and to go out with your mamma, and I want you to be very careful and behave as a good little girl should. I take you, so that you may learn good manners. Now, remember, Dolly,

127

you mustn't speak to any of them unless you are spoken to."

Dolly reflected on this precept gravely, and then said:

"Don't they speak to any one except when they are spoken to?"

"Yes, my dear, because they are grown-up people, and know when to speak and what is proper to be said. Little girls do not; so they must be silent. Little girls should be seen and not heard."

Dolly knew this maxim by heart already, and she no more questioned the propriety of it than of any of the great laws of nature.

After an interval of serious reflection, she asked:

"But, if any of them should talk to me, then I may talk to them; may I?"

"Yes, my dear; if any body talks to you, you must answer, but be careful not to talk too long."

"Do you think, Mamma, that Judge Gridley will be there?"

"Yes, my dear, I presume so."

"Because I am acquainted with him," remarked Dolly gravely; "he always talks to me. He meets me sometimes coming home from school and talks to me. I am glad he will be there."

Mrs. Cushing smiled aside to her husband as she was tying on Dolly's little hood, and then her father took her up in his arms and they started.

Tea parties in the highest circles of Poganuc
began at six and ended at nine, and so when
Dolly and her father and mother arrived they
found a room full of people. Col. Davenport was
a tall, elegant man, with an upright, soldierly
carriage, his hair powdered white, and tied in a
queue down his back; his eyes of a clear, piercing
blue, looking out each side of a well-defined
aquiline nose; his voice deep and musical, with
a sort of resonance which spoke of one used to
command. The Colonel was one of the most
active members of the church;—the one who in
the absence of the pastor officiated as lay-reader,
and rendered the sermon and made the prayers,
in the same sonorous, military voice that suggested the field and the commander. Mrs.
Davenport, a lady of delicate and refined appearance, with a certain high-bred manner toned
down to a kind of motherly sweetness, received
the Doctor and Mrs. Cushing with effusion,
kissed and patted Dolly on the cheek, and remarked what a nice little girl she was getting
to be; and the Colonel stooped down and took
her hand, like an affable eagle making court to a
little humming-bird, and hoped she was quite
well, to which Dolly, quite overcome with awe,
answered huskily: "Very well, I thank you, sir."

Then kind Mrs. Davenport busied herself in
ordering to the front a certain little chair that

had a family history. This was duly brought and placed for Dolly by old Cato, an ancient negro servitor of the Colonel's, who had once served as his waiter in the army, and had never recovered from the sense of exaltation and dignity conferred by this experience. Dolly sat down, and began employing her eyes about the high and dainty graces of the apartment. The walls were hung with paper imported from France and ornamented with family portraits by Copley. In the fire place, the high brass andirons sustained a magnificent fire, snapping and sparkling and blazing in a manner gorgeous to behold. Soon Cato came in with the tea on a waiter, followed by Venus, his wife, who, with a high white turban on her head and a clear-starched white apron in front, bore after him a tray laden with delicate rolls, sandwiches, and multiplied and tempting varities of cake. Dolly spread her handkerchief in her little lap, and comported herself as nearly as possible as she saw the grand ladies doing, who, in satin and velvet and point lace, were making themselves agreeable, and taking their tea with elegant ease.

The tea parties of Poganuc were not wanting in subjects for conversation. It was in rule to discuss the current literature of the day, which at that time came from across the water—the last articles in the *Edinburgh Review*, the latest Waverley novel, the poetry of Moore, Byron, Southey, and Wordsworth—all came under review and had place of consideration.

In those days, when newspapers were few and scanty, when places were isolated and travel was tedious and uncertain, the intellectual life of cultivated people was intense. A book was an event in Poganuc. It was heard of first across the ocean, and watched for, as one watches for the rising of a new planet. While the English packet was slowly laboring over, bearing it to our shores, expectation was rising, and when the book was to be found in the city book stores an early copy generally found its way to the élite circle of Poganuc.

Never in this day—generation of jaded and sated literary appetite—will any one know the fresh and eager joy, the vivid sensation of delight with which a poem like "The Lady of the Lake," a novel like "Ivanhoe," was received in lonely mountain towns by a people eager for a new mental excitement. The young folks called the rocks and glens and rivers of their romantic region by names borrowed from Scott; they clambered among the crags of Benvenue and sailed on the bosom of Loch Katrine.

The students in the law offices and the young ladies of the first families had their reading circles and their literary partialities—some being partisans of Byron, some of Scott, etc.—and there was much innocent spouting of poetry. There were promising youths who tied their open shirt collars with a black ribbon, and professed disgust at the hollow state of human happiness in general, and there were compassionate young ladies who considered the said young men all the more interesting for this state of mysterious desolation, and often succeeded in the work of consoling them. It must be remarked, however, that the present gathering was a married people's party, and the number of young men and maidens was limited to the immediate family connections. The young people had their parties, with the same general decorum, where the conversation was led by them. In the elderly circles all these literary and social topics came under discussion. Occasionally Judge Belcher, who was an authority in literary criticism, would hold the ear of the drawing-room while he ran a parallel between the dramatic handling of Scott's characters as compared with those of Shakespeare, or gave an analysis of the principles of the Lake School of Poetry. The Judge was an admirable talker, and people in general liked to hear him quite as well as he liked to hear himself, and so his monologues proceeded *nem. con.*

On this particular evening, however, liter-

ature was forgotten in the eagerness of politics.
The news from the state elections was not in
those days spread by telegraph, it lumbered up
in stages, and was recorded at most in weekly
papers; but enough had come to light to make
the Poganuc citizens aware that the State of
Connecticut had at last been revolutionized, and
gone from the Federalists to the Democrats.

Judge Belcher declaimed upon the subject in
language which made the very hair rise upon
Dolly's head.

" Yes, sir," he said, addressing Dr. Cushing; " I
consider this as the ruin of the State of Connecticut! It's the triumph of the lower orders;
the reign of 'sans culotte-ism' begun. In my
opinion, sir, we are over a volcano; I should
not be suprised, sir, at an explosion that will
blow up all our institutions!"

Dolly's eyes grew larger and larger, although
she was a little comforted to observe the Judge
carefully selecting a particular variety of cake that
he was fond of, and helping himself to a third cup
of tea in the very midst of these shocking prog-
nostications.

Dolly had not then learned the ease and suavity
of mind with which both then and ever since
people at tea drinkings and other social recrea-
tions declare their conviction that the country is
going to ruin. It never appears to have any im-

mediate effect upon the appetite. Dolly looked at her father, and thought he assented with somewhat of a saddened air; and Mrs. Davenport looked concerned; and Mrs. Judge Gridley said it ·was a very dark providence why such things were permitted, but a little while after was commending the delicacy of the cake, and saying she must inquire of Venus about her peculiar mode of confection.

Judge Gridley — a white-haired, lively old gentleman with bright eyes, who wore the old-fashioned small-clothes, knee-buckles, silk stockings and low shoes—had fixed his eyes upon Dolly for some time, and now crossing the room drew her with him into a corner, saying: "Come, now, Miss Dolly, you and I are old friends, you know. What do you think of all these things?"

"Oh, I'm so glad you came," said Dolly, with a long sigh of relief. "I hoped you would, because mamma said I mustn't talk unless somebody spoke to me, and I do so want to know all about those dreadful things. What is a volcano? Please tell me!"

"Why, my little Puss," he said, lifting her in his lap and twining her curls round his finger, "what do you want to know that for?"

"Because I heard Judge Belcher say that we were all over a volcano and it would blow us all up some day. Is it like powder?"

" You dear little soul! don't you trouble your head about what Judge Belcher says. He uses strong language. He only means that the Demo- crats will govern the state."

"And are they so dreadfully wicked?" asked Dolly. " I want to tell you something"—and Dolly whispered, " Bessie Lewis's father is a Democrat, and yet they don't seem like wicked people."

" No, my dear; when you grow up you will learn that there are good people in every party."

" Then you don't think Bessie's father is a bad man?" said Dolly. " I'm so glad!"

" No; he's a good man in a bad party; that is what I think."

"I wish you'd talk to him and tell him not to do all these dreadful things, and upset the state," said Dolly. " I thought the other night *I* would; but I'm only a little girl, you know; he wouldn't mind me. If I was a grown-up woman I would," she said, with her cheeks flushing and her eyes kindling.

Judge Gridley laughed softly to himself and stroked her head.

" When you are a grown-up woman I don't doubt you can make men do almost anything you please, but I don't think it would do any good for *me* to talk to General Lewis; and now, little Curly-wurly, don't bother your pretty head about politics. Neither party will turn the world upside down. There's a good God above us all, my little girl, that takes care of our country, and he will bring good out of evil. So now don't you worry."

"I'm afraid, Judge Gridley, that Dolly is troubling you," said Mrs. Cushing, coming up.

"Oh, dear me! madame, no; Miss Dolly and I are old acquaintances. We have the best possible understanding."

But just then, resounding clear and loud through the windy March air, came the pealing notes of the nine o'clock bell, and an immediate rustle of dresses, and rising, and shaking of hands, and cutting short of stories, and uttering last words followed.

For though not exactly backed by the arbitrary power which enforced the celebrated curfew, yet the nine o'clock bell was one of the authoritative institutions of New England; and at its sound all obediently set their faces homeward, to rake up house-fires, put out candles, and say their prayers before going to rest.

Old Captain Skeggs, a worn-out revolutionary soldier, no longer good for hard service, had this commanding post in Poganuc, and no matter how high blew the wind, how fiercely raged the storm, the captain in his white woolen great coat, with three little capes to it, stamped his

way through the snow, pulled valiantly on the
rope, and let all the hills and valleys of Poganuc
know that the hour of rest had come. Then,
if it were a young people's party, each young
man chose out his maiden and asked the pleasure
of seeing her home; and in the clear frosty night
and under the silent stars many a word was said
that could not be said by candle-light indoors:—
whereof in time came life-long results.

CHAPTER XIII.

FEW days after the tea-party, Colonel and Mrs. Davenport came to take tea at the parsonage. It was an engagement of long standing, and eagerly looked forward to by the children, who with one accord begged that they might be allowed to sit up and hear the Colonel's stories.

For, stories of the war it was known the Colonel could tell; the fame of them hovered in vague traditions on the hills and valleys of Poganuc, and whenever he was to be in the circle it was always in the programme of hope that he might be stimulated and drawn out to tell of some of the stirring scenes of his camp-life.

In a general way, too, the children were always glad to have company. The preparations had a festive and joyous air to their minds. Mrs. Cushing then took possession of the kitchen in person, and various appetizing and suggestive dainties and condiments stood about in startling profusion.

138

Dolly and the boys stoned raisins, pounded cinnamon, grated nutmegs and beat eggs with enthusiasm, while Nabby heated the oven and performed
the part of assistant priestess in high and solemn
mysteries. Among her many virtues and graces,
Mrs. Cushing had one recommendation for a
country minister's wife which commanded universal respect: she could make cake. Yea, more,
she could make *such* cake as nobody else could
make—not even Colonel Davenport's Venus.

So the children had stoned raisins, without eat-
ing more than the natural tribute to be expected
in such cases; they had been allowed in per-
quisites a stick of cinnamon apiece; and the
pound-cake, the sponge-cake, the fruit-cake and the
tea-rusks were each in their kind a perfect success.

During tea-time every word uttered by the
Colonel was eagerly watched by attentive and
much-desiring ears; but as yet no story came.
The vivacity imparted by two or three cups of
the best tea was all spent in denunciations of the
Democrats, their schemes, designs and dangers to
the country, when the Colonel and Dr. Cushing
seemed to vie with each other in the vigor and
intensity of their prognostigations of evil.

But after tea there came the genial hour of the
social sit-down in front of the andirons, when the
candles were duly snuffed, and the big fore-stick had
burned down to glowing coals, and the shadows

played in uncertain flashes up and down the walls
of the fire-lighted room; and then the Colonel's
mind began traveling a road hopeful to his listening auditors.

From Democracy to Jefferson, from Jefferson
to France and the French Revolution, the conversation led by easy gradations, and thence to the
superior success of our own Revolution—from
La Fayette to Washington.

Now, the feeling of the Doctor and of his
whole family for General Washington was to the
full as intense as that of the ancient Israelites for
Moses. They were never tired of hearing the
smallest particular about him—how he looked;
how he walked; what he wore; the exact shade
of his eyes; the least word that ever dropped
from his lips.

"You have no doubt whatever that the General
was a religious man?" said the Doctor, pro-
pounding what was ever his most anxious inquiry
with regard to one who had entered on the Invisible Verities.

"Not a doubt, sir," was the Colonel's reply, in
those ringing and decisive tones which were
characteristic of him.

"I have always heard," pursued the Doctor,
"that he was eminently a man of prayer."

"Eminently so," said the Colonel. "The General, sir, was a communicant in the Episcopal

Church, a firm believer in Christianity, and I think he was sustained in all the trying emergencies of the war by his faith in his God. That, sir, I have not a doubt of."

"That has always been my belief," said the Doctor; "but I am glad to hear you say so."

"Yes, sir," added the Colonel with energy; "his influence in the army was openly and decidedly that of a Christian. You recollect his general order at one time, excusing soldiers and sailors from fatigue-duty on Sunday, that they might have time to attend religious service, and his remarks upon the custom of profane swearing in the army; how he reminded both officers and men that 'We could have but little hope of the blessing of Heaven upon our arms, if we insult it by impiety.'"

"Yes, I remember all that," said the Doctor. "Nothing could have been better worded. It must have had an immense influence. But does it not seem astonishing that a military man, going through the terrible scenes that he did, should never have been tempted to profanity? I declare," said the Doctor, musingly, "I would not answer for myself. There were times in that history when without preventing grace I am quite sure *I* could not have held myself in."

"Well, sir, since you speak on that subject," said the Colonel, "I am free to say that, on one occasion I saw our General carried beyond himself. I have often thought I would like to tell you the circumstances, Doctor."

There was a little edging towards the Colonel, both of the Doctor and Mrs. Cushing, as the Colonel, looking dreamily far into the hickory coals, said :

"Yes, sir ; that was one of those critical times in our war, when it turned on the events of a few hours whether we had been the nation we are now, or trodden down under the British heel ; whether Washington had been made President of the United States, or hanged for treason. It was at the time of the Long Island retreat."

"And you were there?" asked Dr. Cushing. The Doctor knew very well that the Colonel was there, and was eager to draw him out.

"There? Sir, indeed I was," answered the Colonel. "I shall never forget it to my dying day. We had been fighting all day at terrible odds, our men falling all around us like leaves, and the British pressing close upon us ; so close, that when it grew dark we could hear every movement in their camp, every sound of pick, or shovel, or gun. Our men had got behind their intrenchments, and there the enemy stopped pursuing. What a night that was ! We were deadly tired—dispirited as only fellows can be that have seen their friends shot down about them ; no tents, no shelter, and the sentries of the victorious enemy only a quarter of a mile from our lines. Nearly two thousand, out of the five thousand men we had in the fight, were killed, wounded, or missing. Well, it was a terribly anxious night for Washington; for what had we to expect, next day? He went round at four o'clock in the morning to see to us and speak a word of cheer here and there. It was a cold, drizzling, gloomy, rainy morning, but we could see through the fog a large encampment; and they were intrenching themselves, though' the rain drove them into their tents. The day advanced, continuing rainy and stormy, and they made no move to attack us. Our scouts, that were out watching the motions of the enemy down at Red Hook, got a peep at the shipping at Staten Island and saw at once that there was a movement and bustle there, as if there were something on foot; and they got the idea that the enemy were planning at turn of tide to come up behind us in the East River, and cut us off from the army in New York. Sir, that was just what they were meaning to do; and, if they had, we should have been caught there like rats in a trap, the war would have been ended, and Washington hanged. The party hurried back to tell the General. A council of war was held, and it was decided that we all must cross to New York that very night. There it was; nine thousand men, with all our baggage and artillery, to steal away in the night from that great army, and they so near that we could hear every dog that barked or man that whistled among them."

"How wide was the place to be crossed?" asked the Doctor.

"Full three-quarters of a mile, sir, and with a rapid tide sweeping through. As the Lord's providence would have it, Colonel Glover had just come in that day with his Marblehead regiment—thirteen hundred fishermen and sailors, such as the world cannot equal."

"Glorious!" exclaimed the Doctor. "God bless the Marblehead boys!"

"Yes, they saved us, under God and the General; we never could have crossed without them.

"Well, the General sent to the Quartermaster to impress all the boats and transports of every kind that could be got, and have them ready by evening. By eight o'clock they were all at Brooklyn, and under the management of the Marblehead regiment. Word was given out in the army to be prepared for a night attack, and the poor fellows, tired as they were, were all up and ready to move on order.

"Then Washington ordered Gen. Mifflin's brigade, including what remained of our regiment, to stay and keep the intrenchments with guards and patrols and sentinels posted, to make the enemy believe we were there, while the rest all moved down to the water and embarked.

"Now I tell you, sir, it was a good deal harder to stand there than to be moving just then. We were wide awake and we counted the minutes. It is always longer to those who wait than to those who work. The men were true as steel, but, poor fellows, there is a limit to human endurance, and they got pretty restive and nervous. So, between you and me, did we officers too. Standing still in such a danger is a thousand times worse than fighting.

"Finally the men began to growl and mutter; it was all we could do to hold them; they were sure the army had crossed—word *must* have been sent to them! So, finally, when Washington's aid misunderstood his order and came running to say that we were to move down, we started on the double-quick and got to the shore. There we found that the tide had turned, a strong northeast wind was blowing, the boats had been brought without oars enough to convey the troops, the sail-boats were unable to make head against wind and tide, and full half the army were still on Long Island shore!

"Washington stood there amid the confusion and perplexity—when, in the midst of his troubles, down we all came.

"Sir, I never saw a mortal being look as Gen. Washington looked at us. He ordered us back with a voice like thunder, and I never heard such a terrific volley of curses as he poured out upon us when the men hesitated. Sir, that man was so dreadful that we all turned and ran. We had rather face the judgment-day than face him. Upon my soul, I thought when I turned back that I was going straight into eternity, but I had rather face death than him."

"And he swore?"

"Indeed he did—but it was not profane swearing; it was not taking God's name in vain, for it sent us back as if we had been chased by lightning. It was an awful hour, and he saw it; it was life or death; country or no country."

"Sir," said Dr. Cushing, starting up and pacing the room, "it was the oath of the Lord! It would be profane to call it swearing."

"Yes, sir," said the Colonel, "you remember that one time Moses threw down both tables of the law and broke them, and the Lord did not reprove him."

"Exactly," answered the Doctor; "he saw his nation going to ruin and forgot all else to save them. The Lord knows how to distinguish."

"But, sir," said the Colonel, "I never tell this except to the initiated. No man who saw Washington then dared ever to allude to it afterward.

He was habitually so calm, so collected, so self-contained, that this outburst was the more terrific. Whatever he felt about it was settled between him and his Maker. No man ever took account with him."

Then followed a few moments of silence, when Dolly emerged from a dark corner—her cheeks very much flushed, her eyes very wide and bright—and, pressing up to the Colonel's knee, said eagerly: "But, oh please, sir, what became of you and the men?"

The Colonel looked down and smiled as he lifted Dolly on his knee. "Why, my little girl, here I am, you see; I wasn't killed after all."

"But did you really go clear back?" asked Dolly.

"Yes, my dear, we all went back and staid two or three hours; and when it came morning we made believe to be the whole army. We made our fires and we got our breakfasts and we whistled and talked and made all the stir we could, but as the good Lord would have it there was such a thick fog that you could not see your hand before your face. You see that while the fog hung over the island and covered us, it was all clear down by the river."

"Why, that's just the way it was when they crossed the Red Sea," said Dolly, eagerly; "wasn't it, Papa?"

"Something so, my dear," said her father; but her mother made her a sign not to talk.

"How long did it take to do the whole thing?"

"Well, thanks to those Marblehead boys, by daybreak the greater part of the army were safe on the New York side. A little after daylight we marched off quietly and went down to the ferry. Washington was still there, and we begged him to go in the first boat; but no, he was immovable. He saw us all off, and went himself in the very last boat, after every man was in."

"What a glorious fellow!" said the Doctor.

"Please, sir," said Will, who, with distended eyes, had been listening, "what did the British say when they found out?"

The Colonel laid his head back and gave a hearty laugh.

"They had a message sent them, by a Tory woman down by the ferry, what was going on. She sent her black servant, and he got through our American lines but was stopped by the Hessians, who could not understand his gibberish, and so kept him till long after all was over. Then a British officer overhauled him and was pretty well amazed at his story. He gave the alarm, and General Howe's aid-de-camp, with a body of men, climbed over the intrenchments and found all deserted. They hurried down to the landing just in time to see the rear boats half way across the river."

"Well, that is *almost* like the crossing of the Red Sea," said the Doctor.

"Oh, weren't the British furious!" cried Bill.

"Yes, they did fire away at the boats, and one straggling boat they hit and forced the men to return; but it turned out only three vagabonds that had come to plunder."

It was after the nine o'clock bell had dismissed the Colonel and his lady that the Doctor noticed the wide and radiant eyes of little Dolly and his boys.

"My children," he said, "to use the name of the great God solemnly and earnestly for a great and noble purpose is not to 'swear.' Swearing is taking God's holy name in vain, in a trifling way, for a trivial purpose—a thing which our great and good general never did. But this story I would rather you would never repeat. It might not be understood."

"Certainly," said Bill, with proud gravity; "common boys wouldn't understand—and, Dolly, don't *you* tell."

"Of course I shouldn't," said Dolly. "I never shall tell even Nabby, nor Bessie, nor anybody."

And afterwards, in the family circle, when General Washington was spoken of, the children looked on one another with grave importance, as the trusted depositaries of a state secret.

CHAPTER XIV.

THE PUZZLE OF POGANUC.

NOTWITHSTANDING the apparition of the blue-bird and the sanguine hopes of the boys, the winter yet refused to quit the field. Where these early blue-birds go to, that come to cheer desponding hearts in arctic regions like Poganuc, is more than one can say. Birds' wings are wonderful little affairs, and may carry them many hundred southward miles in a day. Dolly, however, had her own theory about it, and that was that the bird went right up into heaven, and there waited till all the snow-storms were over.

Certain it was that the Poganuc people, after two promising days of thaw, did not fall short of that "six weeks' sledding in March" which has come to be proverbial.

The thaw, which had dripped from icicles and melted from snow-banks, froze stiffer than ever, and then there came a two days' snow-storm—good, big, honest snow-feathers, that fell and fell all day and all night, till all the houses wore great white night-caps, the paths in front of all the house-doors had to be shoveled out again, and the farmers with their sleds turned out to break roads.

The Doctor was planning a tour in his sleigh to fulfill his monthly round of visiting the schools.

Schools there always were in every district, from the time the first log school-house had been erected in the forests, down to the days when, as now, the school-house is a comfortable, well-furnished building.

In the Doctor's day the common schoolhouses were little, mean shanties, built in the cheapest possible manner, consisting of one small room and a vestibule for hanging bonnets, hats, and dinner baskets. In winter, a box-stove, the pipe of which passed through one of the windows, gave warmth. Blackboards were unknown. The teacher's care was simply to hear reading in the Bible and the "Columbian Orator;" to set copies in ruled copy-books; to set "sums" from "Daboll's Arithmetic;" to teach parsing from "Murray's Grammar;" to mend pens, and to ferule and thrash disorderly scholars. In the summer months, when the big boys worked in the fields, a woman generally held sway, and taught knitting and sewing to the girls. On Saturday all recited the "Assembly's Catechism," and once a month the minister, and sometimes his wife, came in to hear and commend the progress of the scholars.

One of the troubles of a minister in those times was so to hold the balance as to keep down neighborhood quarrels;—not an easy matter among a race strong, opinionated, and who, having little variety in life, rather liked the stimulus of disagreements. A good quarrel was a sort of moral whetstone, always on hand for the sharpening of their wits.

Such a quarrel had stood for some two or three years past in regard to the position of the North Poganuc schoolhouse. It had unfortunately been first located on a high, slippery, windy hill, very uncomfortable of access in the winter months, and equally hot and cheerless in summer. Subsequently, the building of several new farmhouses had carried most of the children a considerable distance away, and occasioned increased sense of inconvenience.

The thing had been talked of and discussed in several successive town-meetings, but no vote could be got to change the position of the schoolhouse. Zeph Higgins was one of the most decided in stating what ought to be done and where the school-house ought to stand; but, unfortunately, Zeph's mode of arguing a question was such as to rouse all the existing combativeness in those whom he sought to convince. No more likely mode to ruin a motion in town-meeting than to get Zeph interested to push it. In Poganuc, as elsewhere, there were those in town-meeting that voted on the principle stated by the immortal Bird o' Freedom Sawin:

> " I take the side that isn't took
> By them consarned teetotalers."

In the same manner, Zeph's neighbors were for the most part inclined in town meeting, irrespective of any other consideration, to take the side he didn't take.

Hiel Jones had often been heard to express the opinion that, " Ef Zeph Higgins would jest shet up his gash in town-meetin', that air school-house could be moved fast enough; but the minit that Dr. Cushing had been round, and got folks kind o' slicked down and peaceable, Zeph would git up and stroke 'em all back'ards and git their dander up agin. Folks warn't a-goin' to be druv ; and Zeph was allers fer drivin'."

The subject of an approaching town-meeting was beginning to loom dimly in the discussions of the village. One characteristic of the Yankee mind, as developed in those days, was the slowness and deliberation with which it arrived at any purpose or conclusion. This was not merely in general movements, but in particular ones also. Did the Widow Brown contemplate turning her back buttery into a sink-room, she forthwith went over to the nearest matrons of her vicinity, and announced that she was "talkin' about movin' her sink," and the movement in all its branches and bearings was discussed in private session. That was step No. 1. Then all the women at the next quilting, or tea-drinking, heard that Widow Brown was "talking about changing her sink," and *they* talked about it. Then Seth Chickering, the neighborhood carpenter, was called into consultation, and came and investigated the premises, and reported—first to the widow and second to his wife, who told all the other women what "Seth, he said," etc. The *talking* process continued indefinitely, unless some active Providential dispensation brought it to an end.

The same process was repeated when Mrs. Slocum thought of investing in a new winter cloak; the idea in those days prevailing that a winter cloak was a thing never but once in a life-time to be bought, and after that to endure for all generations, the important article must not be bought lightly or unadvisedly. When Deacon Dickenson proposed to build a new back parlor on his house and to re-shingle the roof, the talking and discussion lasted six months, and threw the whole neighborhood into commotion; carpenters came before daybreak and roosted on the fences, and at odd times as they found leisure, at all hours of the day, gathered together, and Seth Chickering took the opinions of Sam Parmelee and Jake Peters; and all Mrs. Dickenson's female friends talked about it, till every shingle, every shingle-nail and every drop of paint had received a separate consideration, and the bargain was, so to speak, whittled down to the finest possible point.

Imagine the delicacies of discussion, then, that attended the moving of a schoolhouse at the public expense—a schoolhouse in which everybody in the neighborhood had a private and personal claim—and how like the proceedings of a bull in a china shop was the advocacy of a champion like Zeph Higgins, and one may see how infinitely extended in this case might be the area of "talkin' about movin' that air schoolhouse," and how hopelessly distant any decision. The thing had already risen on the horizon of Deacon Dickenson's store, like one of those puzzling stars or fractiously disposed heavenly bodies that seem created to furnish astronomers with something to talk about.

The fateful period was again coming round; the spring town-meeting was at hand, and more than one had been heard to say that "Ef that air schoolhouse hed to be moved, it oughter be done while the sleddin' was good."

In Deacon Dickenson's store a knot of the

talkers were gathered around the stove, having
a final talk and warm-up previous to starting
their sleds homeward to their supper of pork-
and-beans and doughnuts.

Our mournful friend, Deacon Peasley, sat in his
usual drooping attitude on a mackerel-keg placed
conveniently by the stove; and then, like Beattie's
hermit,

> " . . . his plaining begun.
> Tho' mournful his spirit, his soul was resigned."

"I'm sure I hope I don't wanter dictate to the
Lord, nor nothin, but *ef* he should send a turn o'
rheumatism on Zeph Higgins, jest afore town-
meetin' day—why, seems to me 'twould be a
marcy to us all."

"I don't see, fer my part," said Tim Hawkins,
"why folks need to mind what he says; but they
do. He'll do more *agin* a motion talkin' *fer* it,
than I can do talkin' agin it fer a year. I never
see the beat of him—never."

"Aint there nobody," said Deacon Peasley,
caressing his knee, and looking fondly at the stove
door, "that could kind o' go to him, and sort o'
set it in order afore him how he henders the very
thing he's sot on doin'?"

"Guess you don't know him as I do," said
Deacon Dickenson, "or you wouldn't 'a' thought
o' that."

"And now he's gone in with the Democrats,

and agin Parson Cushing and the church, it 'll be worse 'n ever," remarked Tim Hawkins.

" Now, there's Mis' Higgins," said the Deacon; " she can't do nothin' with him; he won't take a word from her; she hez to step round softly arter him, a-settin' things right. Why, Widder Brown, that lives up by the huckleberry pastur'-lot, was a-tellin' my wife, last Sunday, how Zeph's turkeys would come a-trampin' in her mowin', and all she could say and do he wouldn't keep 'em to hum. And then when they stole a nest there, Zeph he took the eggs and carried 'em off, 'cause he said the turkeys was hisn. Mis' Higgins, she jest put on her bonnet, and went right over, that arternoon, and took the turkey eggs back to the widder. Mis' Brown said Mis' Higgins didn't *say* a word, but she *looked* consid'able—her eyes was a-shinin' and her mouth sort o' set, as ef she'd about come to the eend of her patience."

" Wal," said Deacon Peasley, " I rather wonder she durst to do it."

" Wal," said Tim, " my wife sez that there *is* places where Mis' Higgins jest takes her stand, and Zeph has to give in. Ef she gets her back agin a text in the Bible, why, she won't stir from it ef he killed her; and when it comes to that Zeph hez to cave in. Come to standin'—why she kin stand longer 'n he kin. I rather 'xpect he didn't try to git back them turkey eggs. Ef he

did, Mis' Higgins would 'a' stood right in the
road, and he'd 'a' hed to 'a' walked over her. I
'xpect by this time Zeph knows what he kin
make her do and what he can't."

"Wal," said Hiel Jones, who had just dropped
in, "I tell ye Zeph's screwed himself into a
tight place now. That air 'Piscopal parson, he's
gret on orderin' and commandin', and thinks he
didn't come right down from the 'Postles for
nothin'. He puts his new folks through the drills
lively, I tell ye; he's ben at old Zeph 'cause he
don't bow to suit him in the creed—Zeph's back
is stiff as a ramrod, and he jest hates it. Now,
there's Mis' Higgins; *she'll* allers do any thing
to 'blige anybody, and if the minister wants her
to make a curtsey, why she does it the best
she's able, and Nabby and the boys, they take
to it; but it gravels Zeph. Then all this 'ere
gittin' up and sittin' down aggravates him, and
he comes out o' church as cross as a bull in
fly-time."

Of course, the laugh was ready at this picture
of their neighbor's troubles, and Hiram added:

"He'll put it through, though; he won't go
back on his tracks, but it's pikery and worm-
wood to him, I tell ye. I saw him t'other day,
after Parson had been speaking to him, come
out o' church, and give his hoss such a twitch,
and say 'Darn ye!' in a way I knew wa'n't

meant for the *critter*. Zeph don't swear," added Hiel, "but I will say he can make *darn* sound the most like *damn* of any man in Poganuc. He's got lots o' swear in him, that ole feller hez."

"My mother says she remembers when Polly Higgins (that is) was the prettiest gal in all the deestrict," said Deacon Peasley. "She was Polly Adams, from Danbury. She came to keep the deestrict school, and Zeph he sot his eyes on her, and hev her he would; he wouldn't take 'No' for an answer; he didn't give her no peace till he got her."

"Any feller can get a gal that way," said Hiel, with a judicial air. "A gal allers says 'No' at fust—to get time to think on't."

"Is that the way with Nabby?" asked the Deacon, with a wink of superior intelligence. Whereat there came a general laugh, and Hiel pulled up his coat collar, and, looking as if he might say something if delicacy did not forbid, suddenly remembered that "Mother had sent him for a quarter of a pound o' young Hyson."

Definite business at once broke up the session, and every man, looking out his parcels, mounted his sled and wended his way home.

CHAPTER XV.

EPH Higgins had the spirit of a general. He, too, had his vision of an approaching town-meeting, and that evening, sitting in his family circle, gave out his dictum on the subject:

"Wal—they'll hev a town-meetin' afore long, and hev up that air old school'us' bizness," he said, as he sat facing the blaze of the grand kitchen fire.

Mrs. Higgins sat by in her little splint-bottomed rocking-chair, peacefully clicking her knitting-needles. Abner sat at her right hand, poring over a volume of "Rollin's Ancient History." Abel and Jeduthun were playing fox-and-goose with grains of corn in the corner, and Tim was whittling a goose-poke.

All looked up at the announcement of this much-bruited subject.

"They never seem to come to anything on that subject," said Mrs. Higgins. "I wish the school-house was better situated; a great many are kept from the prayer meetings there that would come if it wasn't for that windy, slippery hill. The

160

last time I went, it was all I could do to get up,"
she said ; " and I thought I caught a cold."

" There's not the least doubt on't," said Zeph,
" and the children are allers catchin' colds.
Everybody knows where that air school'us'
ought to be. Confounded fools they be, the hull
lot on 'em ; and, for my part, I'm tired o' this 'ere
quarrelin' and jawin', and I ain't a-goin' to stan'
it no longer. It's a shame and it's a sin to keep
up these 'ere quarrels among neighbors, and I'm
a-goin' to put a stop to it."

It may be imagined that this exordium caused
a sensation in the family circle.

Mrs. Higgins opened her meek blue eyes upon
her husband with a surprised expression; the
two boys sat with their game suspended and their
mouths open, and the goose-poke and " Rollin's
History" were alike abandoned in the pause of
astonishment.

" To-morrow's Saturday," said Zeph; "and Saturday afternoon there won't be no school, and I'll
jest take the boys, both yoke of oxen and the
sleds, and go up and move that air school'us'
down to the place where't orter be. I'll wedge it
up and settle it good and firm, and that'll be the
end on't. Tain't no sort o' use to talk. I'm jest
a-goin' to *do* it."

Zeph looked as if he meant it, and his family
had ceased to think anything impossible that he

took in hand to do. If he had announced his intention of blowing up the neighboring crag of Bluff Head, and building a castle out of the fragments, they would have expected to see it done.

So Zeph took the family Bible, and, in a high-pitched and determined voice, read the account of Samson carrying off the gates of Gaza, repeated his evening prayer, ordered all hands to bed, raked up the fire, had all snug and quiet, and stepped into bed just as the last stroke of the nine o'clock bell was resounding.

At four o'clock the next afternoon, as Hiel Jones was coming in on his high seat on the Poganuc stage, whistling cheerily, a sudden new sensation struck him. Passing over North Poganuc hill, he bethought him of the schoolhouse question, and lifted up his eyes, and lo! no schoolhouse was there. For a moment Hiel felt giddy. What was the matter with his head? He rubbed his eyes, and looked on all the other familiar objects; there was the old pine tree, there the great rock, but the schoolhouse was gone. The place where it had stood was disturbed by tramping of many feet, and a broad, smooth trail led down the hill.

"Wal, somebody hez gone and ben and done it," said Hiel, as he whipped up his horses to carry the news.

Farther on, in a convenient spot at the junction

of three roads, under the shelter of a hill, stood the schoolhouse—serene as if it had grown there; while Zeph Higgins and his son Abner were just coming forward on the road toward Hiel, Zeph triumphantly whipping his oxen and shouting the word of command in an elevated voice.

Hiel drew to one side, and gave a long whistle. "Je-*ru*-salem," he exclaimed, "ef you hain't ben and done it!"

Zeph lifted his head with an air of as much satisfaction as his hard features could assume, and, nodding his head in the direction of the school-house, said:

"Yis—there 'tis!"

Hiel laid his head back, and burst into a loud, prolonged laugh, in which he was joined by Abner and the boys.

"Don't see nothin' to laugh at," said Zeph, with grim satisfaction. "Fact is, I can't hev these 'ere quarrels—and I won't hev 'em. That air's the place for that school us, and it's *got* to stand there, and that's the eend on't. Come, boys, hurry home; mother's beans will be a-gettin cold. Gee—g'lang!" and the black whip cracked over the back of the ox-team.

Hiel was a made man. He had in possession an astounding piece of intelligence, that nobody knew but himself, and he meant to make the most of it.

He hurried first to Deacon Peasley's store, where quite a number were sitting round the stove with their Saturday night purchases. In burst Hiel:

"Wal, that air North Poganuc school'us' is *moved*, and settled down under the hills by the cross-road."

The circle looked for a moment perfectly astounded and stupefied.

"You don't say so!"

"Dew tell!"

"Don't believe ye."

"Wal, ye kin all go and see. I came by, jest half an hour ago, and see it with my own eyes, and Zeph Higgins and his boys a-drivin' off with their sleds and oxen. I tell ye that air thing is jest *done*. I'm a-goin' to tell Dr. Cushing's folks."

Poganuc People had something to talk about now, in good earnest.

Hiel stopped his stage at the parson's door, and Dr. Cushing, expecting some bundle from Boston, came out to the gate.

"Doctor, thought I'd jest stop and tell ye that the North Poganuc school'us' hez ben moved to the cross-roads, down under the hill—thought ye'd like to hear it."

The Doctor's exclamation and uplifted hands brought to the door Mrs. Cushing and Dolly and the two boys, with Nabby. Hiel was in his glory, and recounted all the circumstances with great prolixity, the Doctor and Mrs. Cushing and all his audience laughing at his vigorous narrative.

"Yis," said Hiel, "he said he wa'n't a-goin' to hev no more quarrelin' about it; everybody knew the school'us' ought to be there, and there 'twas. It was all wedged up tight and stiddy, and the stove in it, and the pipe stickin' out o' the winder, all nateral as could be, and he jest goin' off home, as ef nothin' hed happened."

"Well, if that ain't jest like father!" exclaimed Nabby, with an air of pride. "If he wants a thing done he will do it."

"Certainly this time he has done a good thing," said the Doctor; "and for my part I'm obliged to him. I suppose the spirit of the Lord came on him, as it did on Samson."

And for weeks and months thereafter, there was abundance of talking and every variety of opinion expressed as to the propriety of Zeph's *coup d'état*, but nobody, man, woman, or child, ever proposed to move the schoolhouse back again.

CHAPTER XVI.

THE POGANUC PARSONAGE.

THE parsonage was a wide, roomy, windy edifice that seemed to have been built by a succession of after-thoughts. It was at first a model New England house, built around a great brick chimney, which ran up like a light-house in the center of the square roof. Then came, in course of time, a side-wing which had another chimney and another suite of rooms. A kitchen grew out on another side, and out of the kitchen a sink-room, and out of the sink-room a wood-house, and out of the wood-house a carriage-house, and so on with a gradually lessening succession of out-buildings.

New England houses have been said by a shrewd observer to be constructed on the model of a telescope; compartment after compartment, lessening in size, and all under one cover.

But in the climate where the business of one half of the year is to provide fuel for the other half, such a style of domestic architecture becomes convenient. During the long winter

166

months everything was under cover, giving grand scope for the children to play.

When the boys were graciously disposed to Dolly, she had a deal of good fun with them in the long range of the divers sheds. They made themselves houses, castles and fortresses in the wood-pile, and played at giving parties and entertainments, at which Spring and the cat also assisted in silent and subsidiary parts.

Sometimes they held town-meetings or voting-days, in which the Democrats got their dues in speeches that might have struck terror to their souls had they heard them. At other times they held religious meetings, and sung hymns and preached, on which occasions Dolly had been known to fall to exhorting with a degree of fervor and a fluency in reciting texts of Scripture which for the time produced quite an effect on her auditors, and led Nabby, who listened behind the door, to say to Mrs. Cushing that ' that air child was smarter than was good for her; that she'd either die young or else come to suthin' one of these days'—a proposition as to which there could not rationally be any difference of opinion.

The parsonage had also the advantage of three garrets—splendid ground for little people. There was first the garret over the kitchen, the floors of which in the fall were covered with stores of yellow pumpkins, fragrant heaps of quinces, and less fragrant spread of onions. There were bins of shelled corn and of oats, and, as in every other garret in the house, there were also barrels of old sermons and old family papers. But most stimulating to the imagination of all the features of this place was the smoke-house, which was a wide, deep chasm made in the kitchen chimney, where the Parson's hams and dried beef were cured. Its door, which opened into this garret, glistened with condensed creosote, a rumbling sound was heard there, and loud crackling reverberated within. Sometimes Dolly would open the door and peer in fearfully as long as her eyes could bear the smoke, and think with a shudder of a certain passage in John Bunyan, which reads:

"Then I saw in my dream that the shepherds had them to another place, in a bottom, where was a door in the side of a hill; and they opened the door and bid them look in. They looked in, therefore, and saw that within it was dark and smoky; they also thought that they heard a rumbling noise as of fire and a cry of some tormented, and that they smelt the scent of brimstone. Then said Christian, What means this? The shepherds told them, This is a by-way to Hell, a way that hypocrites go in at, namely, such as sell their birthright with Esau; such as sell their

Master with Judas; such as lie and dissemble with Ananias and Sapphira his wife."

Dolly shivered when she thought of this, and was glad when Nabby would come up behind and, with her strong hands, seize and whirl her away, remarking,

"Dolly Cushing, *what* won't you be into next, I want ter know?" And then she would proceed to demonstrate the mundane and earthly character of the receptacle by drawing from it a very terrestrial and substantial ham.

Garret number two was over the central portion of the original house. There were vast heaps of golden corn on the cob, spread upon sheets. There were piles of bed-quilts and comforters, and chests of blankets. There were rows and ranges of old bonnets and old hats, that seemed to nod mysteriously from their nails. There were old spinning-wheels, an old clock, old arm-chairs, and old pictures, snuffy and grim, and more barrels of sermons. There also were the boys' cabinets of mineralogical specimens; for the Academy teacher was strong on geology, and took his boys on long tramps with stone-hammers on their shoulders, and they used to discuss with great unction to Dolly of tourmaline, and hornblende, and mica, and quartz, and feldspar, delighted to exhibit before her their scientific superiority.

This garret was a favorite resort of the children, and the laws of the Parsonage requiring everything to be always in order were conveniently mitigated and abridged in favor of this one spot, where it was so convenient to let the whole noisy brood range when their presence disturbed the order below.

There the boys whittled and made windmills and boats, and rabbit-traps, and whistles with which they whistled grievously at unexpected and startling moments, and this always led to their mother telling them that she was "astonished" at them, or to her asking, How many times she must say whistling was *not* allowed in the house?

Perhaps among other subjects of speculative inquiry it may have occurred to Mrs. Cushing to wonder why nature, having gifted boys in their own proper lungs with such noise-producing power, should also come to their assistance with so many noise-producing instruments. There were all the squash-vines in the garden offering trumpets ready made; there was the elder-bush, growing whistle-wood by the yard; and then the gigantic whistles that could be manufactured from willow, and poplar, and black alder were mysteries distressing to contemplate.

One corner of the garret was reserved safe from the rummaging of the children, and there hung in order the dried herbs, which formed the pharmacopœia of those early days. There were catnip, and boneset, and elder-blow, and hard-hack, and rosemary, and tansy, and pennyroyal, all gathered at the right time of the moon, dried and sorted and tied in bundles, hanging from their different nails—those canonized floral saints, which when living filled the air with odors of health and sweetness, and whose very mortal remains and dry bones were supposed to have healing virtues. Some of Dolly's happiest hours were those long sunny, joyous, Saturday afternoons in which many of these stores were gathered, when she rushed through the lush, long grass, along the borders of mossy old stone fences, and pulled down starry constellations of elder blossoms, and gathered pink spires of hard-hack, till her little arms could scarcely clasp around the bundle. Then she would rush home panting and energetic, with torn dress, her sun-bonnet off on her shoulder, and curls all tangled from the wrestles with blackberry bushes which had disputed the way with her. This corner of the garret always filled Dolly's head with visions and longings for the late, slow-coming spring, which seemed far off as the dream of Heaven.

Then those barrels of sermons and old pamphlets! Dolly had turned and turned them,

upsetting them on the floor, and pawing help-
lessly with her little pink hands and reading their
titles with amazed eyes.   It seemed to her that
there were some thousands of the most unin-
telligible things.   "An Appeal on the Unlawful-
ness of a Man's Marrying his Wife's Sister"
turned up in every barrel she investigated, by
twos or threes or dozens, till her soul despaired
of finding an end.   Then there were Thanksgiving
sermons; Fast-day sermons; sermons that discoursed on the battle of Culloden; on the character of Frederick the Great; a sermon on the
death of George the Second, beginning, " George!
George! George is no more."   This somewhat
dramatic opening caused Dolly to put that one
discourse into her private library.   But oh, joy
and triumph! one rainy day she found at the
bottom of an old barrel a volume of the " Arabian
Nights," and henceforth her fortune was made.
Dolly had no idea of reading like that of our
modern days—to read and to dismiss a book.
No; to read was with her a passion, and a book
once read was read daily; always becoming
dearer and dearer, as an old friend.   The " Arabian Nights" transported her to foreign lands,
gave her a new life of her own; and when things
went astray with her, when the boys went to
play higher than she dared to climb in the barn,
or started on fishing excursions, where they con-

sidered her an incumbrance, then she found a
snug corner, where, curled up in a little, quiet
lair, she could at once sail forth on her bit of
enchanted carpet into fairy land.

One of these resorts was furnished by the third
garret of the house, which had been finished off
into an arched room and occupied by her father
as a study. High above all the noise of the
house, with a window commanding a view of
Poganuc Lake and its girdle of steel-blue pines,
this room had to her the air of a refuge and sanctuary. Its walls were set round from floor to
ceiling with the friendly, quiet faces of books, and
there stood her father's great writing-chair, on
one arm of which lay open always his " Cruden's
Concordance" and his Bible. Here Dolly loved
to retreat and niche herself down in a quiet
corner, with her favorite books around her. She
had a kind of sheltered, satisfied feeling as she
thus sat and watched her father writing, turning
his books, and speaking from time to time to himself in a loud, earnest whisper. She vaguely felt
that he was about some holy and mysterious
work above her little comprehension, and she was
careful never to disturb him by question or
remark.

The books ranged around filled her, too, with a
solemn awe. There on the lower shelves were
great enormous folios, on whose backs she spelled

in black letters, "Lightfooti Opera," a title
whereat she marveled, considering the bulk of
the volumes. And overhead, grouped along in
friendly and sociable rows, were books of all sorts
and sizes and bindings, the titles to which she
had read so often that she knew them by heart.
"Bell's Sermons," "Bonnett's Inquiries," "Bogue's
Essays," "Toplady on Predestination," "Boston's
Fourfold State," "Law's Serious Call," and other
works of that kind she had looked over wistfully,
day after day, without getting even a hope of
something interesting out of them. The thought
that her father could read and could understand
things like these filled her with a vague awe, and
she wondered if ever she should be old enough
to know what it was all about. But there was
one of her father's books which proved a mine
of wealth to her. It was a happy hour when he
brought home and set up in his book-case Cotton
Mather's "Magnalia," in a new edition of two
volumes. What wonderful stories these! and
stories, too, about her own country, stories that
made her feel that the very ground she trod on
was consecrated by some special dealing of God's
providence.

When the good Doctor related how a plague
that had wasted the Indian tribes had prepared
the room for the Pilgrim Fathers to settle undis-
turbed, she felt nowise doubtful of his application

of the text, "He drave out the heathen and planted them."

But who shall describe the large-eyed, breathless wonder with which she read stories of witchcraft, with its weird marvels of mysterious voices heard in lonely places, of awful visitations that had overtaken sinners, and immediate deliverances that had come in answer to the prayers of God's saints? Then, too, the stories of Indian wars and captivities, when the war-whoop had sounded at midnight, and little children like her had awakened to find the house beset with legions of devils, who set fire to the dwellings and carried the people off through dreary snow and ice to Canada. No Jewish maiden ever grew up with a more earnest faith that she belonged to a consecrated race, a people especially called and chosen of God for some great work on earth. Her faith in every word of the marvels related in this book was full as great as the dear old credulous Dr. Cotton Mather could have desired.

But the mysterious areas of the parsonage were not exhausted with its three garrets. Under the whole house in all its divisions spread a great cavernous cellar, where were murky rooms and dark passages explored only by the light of candles. There were rows of bins, in which were stored the apples of every name and race harvested in autumn from the family orchard:

Pearmains, Greenings, Seek-no-furthers, Bristers, Pippins, Golden Sweets, and other forgotten kinds, had each its separate bin, to which the children at all times had free access. There, too, was a long row of cider barrels, from whence, in the hour of their early sweetness, Dolly had delighted to suck the cider through straws for that purpose carefully selected and provided.

Not without a certain awe was her descent into this shadowy Avernus, generally under the protecting wing of Nabby or one of the older boys. Sometimes, with the perverse spirit which moves the male nature to tyrannize over the weaker members, they would agonize her by running beyond her into the darker chambers of the cellar, and sending thence Indian war-whoops and yells which struck terror to her soul, and even mingled their horrors with her dreams.

But there was one class of tenants whose influence and presence in the house must not be omitted—and that was the rats.

They had taken formal possession of the parsonage, grown, bred, and multiplied, and become ancient there, in spite of traps or cats or anything that could be devised against them.

The family cat in Dolly's day, having taken a dispassionate survey of the situation, had given up the matter in despair, and set herself quietly to attending to her own family concerns, as a sensible cat should. She selected the Doctor's pamphlet closet as her special domestic retreat. Here she made her lair in a heap of old sermons, whence, from time to time, she led forth coveys of well-educated, theological kittens, who, like their mother, gazed on the rats with respectful curiosity, and ran no imprudent risks. Consequently, the rats had a glorious time in the old parsonage. Dolly, going up the kitchen stairs into the back garret, as she did on her way bedward, would see them sitting easy and *dégagés* on the corners of boxes and bins, with their tails hanging gracefully down, engaged in making meals on the corn or oats. They ramped all night on the floor of the highest garret over her sleeping room, apparently busy in hopping with ears of corn across the garret and then rolling them down between the beams to their nests below. Sometimes Dolly heard them gnawing and sawing behind the very wainscot of her bed as if they had set up a carpenter's shop there, and she shrunk apprehensively for fear they were coming through into her bed. Then there were battles and skirmishes and squealings and fightings, and at times it would appear as if whole detachments of rats rolled in an avalanche down the walls with the corn they had been stealing. And when the mighty winter winds of Poganuc Mountain were out, and rumbled and thundered, roaring and

tumbling down this chimney, rattling all the
windows and creaking all the doors, while the
beams of the house wrenched and groaned like
a ship at sea, and the house seemed to shake
on its very foundations,—then the uproar among
the rats grew higher and jollier, and, with all
put together, it is not surprising that sometimes Dolly put the bed-clothes over her head in
fear, or ran and jumped into Nabby's warm arms
for protection.

We have dwelt thus long on the old parsonage
because it was a silent influence, every day fash-
ioning the sensitive, imaginative little soul that
was growing up in its own sphere of loneliness
there.

For Mrs. Cushing had, besides Dolly, other
children who engaged her thoughts and care.
The eldest a son, studying for the ministry; the
second a daughter, married and settled in a distant
part of the state; another son working as teacher
to pay his past college expenses; another son in
college, whose bills, clothing, books, and necessary
expenses formed constant items of thought, study,
and correspondence; so that, with the two boys
in the academy and our little Dolly, she had heart
and hands full, and small time to watch all the
fancies and dreams that drifted through that little
head as clouds through summer skies. Satisfied
that the child was healthy, and that there was no

positive danger or harm to be fallen into, she
dismissed her from her thoughts, except in the
way of general supervision.

Yet every day, as the little maiden grew,
some quaint, original touch was put to the forming character by these surroundings.

As to Dolly's father, he was a worthy repre-
sentative of that wise and strong Connecticut
clergy that had the wisdom immediately to face
a change in the growth of society, to lay down
gracefully a species of power they could no longer
wield, and to take up and exercise, and strengthen
themselves in, a kind of power that could
never be taken from them. Privileged orders of
society are often obstructionists, because they do
not know, in the day of it, the things that belong
to their peace.

The Connecticut and New England clergy did
not thus err. When the theocracy had passed
away, they spent no time lamenting it. They let
the cocked hat, gold-headed cane, gown and
bands go down stream; they let all laws protecting their order go by; and addressed themselves simply to the work of leading their
people, as men with men, only by seeking to
be stronger, wiser, and better men. To know
more, to have more faith in the Invisible and
Eternal, to be able to argue more logically to
convince and to persuade—these were now their

ambition.   Dr. Cushing was foremost in this new
crusade of earnestness.   He determined to preach
more and preach better than ever he had done
before, and consequently in his wide parish, which
covered a square of about ten miles, he was every
day preaching, visiting, attending prayer-meetings.   Often his wife was with him, and this gave
Dolly many hours when she was free to follow
her own little pursuits, and to pick up at the
chimney-corner some of the traditionary lore of
the period.

CHAPTER XVII.

SPRING AND SUMMER COME AT LAST.

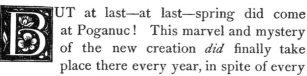UT at last—at last—spring did come at Poganuc! This marvel and mystery of the new creation *did* finally take place there every year, in spite of every appearance to the contrary. Long after the blue-bird that had sung the first promise had gone back into his own celestial ether, the promise that he sang was fulfilled.

Like those sweet, foreseeing spirits, that on high, bare tree-tops of human thought pour forth songs of hope in advance of their age and time, our blue-bird was gifted with the sure spirit of prophecy; and, though the winds were angry and loud, though snows lay piled and deep for long weeks after, though ice and frost and hail armed themselves in embattled forces, yet the sun behind them all kept shining and shining, every day longer and longer, every day drawing nearer and nearer, till the snows passed away like a bad dream, and the brooks woke up and began to laugh and gurgle, and the ice went out of the ponds. Then the pussy-willows threw out their soft catkins, and the ferns came up with their woolly hoods on, like prudent old house mothers, looking to see if it was yet time to unroll their tender greens, and the white blossoms of the shad-blow and the tremulous tags of the birches and alders shook themselves gaily out in the woods. Then under brown rustling leaf-banks came the white waxy shells of the trailing arbutus with its pink buds, fair as a winter's dawn on snow; then the blue and white hepaticas opened their eyes, and cold, sweet white violets starred the moist edges of water courses, and great blue violets opened large eyes in the shadows, and the white and crimson trilliums unfurled under the flickering lace-work shadows of the yet leafless woods; the red columbine waved its bells from the rocks, and great tufts of golden cowslips fringed the borders of the brooks. Then came in flocks the delicate wind-flower family: anemones, starry white, and the crow foot, with its pink outer shell, and the spotted adder's tongue, with its waving yellow bells of blossom. Then, too, the honest, great green leaves of the old skunk cabbage, most refreshing to the eye in its hardy, succulent greenness, though an abomination to the nose of the ill-informed who should be tempted to gather them.

In a few weeks the woods, late so frozen—hope-
lessly-buried in snow drifts—were full of a thousand beauties and delicacies of life and motion,
and flowers bloomed on every hand. " Thou
sendest forth thy spirit, they are created : and
thou renewest the face of the earth."

And, not least, the opening season had set free
the imprisoned children; and Dolly and the
boys, with Spring at their heels, had followed
the courses of the brooks and the rippling brown
shallows of Poganuc River for many a blissful
hour, and the parsonage had every where been
decorated with tumblers and tea-cups holding
floral offerings of things beautiful at the time they
were gathered, but becoming rather a matter of
trial to the eye of exact housekeeping. Yet both
Mrs. Cushing and Nabby had a soft heart tor
Dolly's flowers, sharing themselves the general
sense of joy for the yearly deliverance of which
they were the signs and seals. And so the
work of renewing the face of the earth went on
from step to step. The forest hills around
Poganuc first grew misty with a gentle haze of
pink and lilac, which in time changed to green
and then to greener shades, till at last the full-
clothed hills stood forth in the joy of re-creation,
and, as of old, "all the trees of the field clapped
their hands."

Poganuc in its summer dress was a beautiful

place. Its main street had a row of dignified
white houses, with deep door-yards and large
side-gardens, where the great scarlet peony
flamed forth, where were generous tufts of white
lilies, with tall spires of saintly blossoms, and
yellow lilies with their faint sweet perfume, and
all the good old orthodox flowers of stately family
and valid pretensions. In all the door-yards and
along the grassy streets on either side were overshadowing, long-branching trees, forming a roof
of verdure, a green upper world from whose recesses birds dropped down their songs in lang-
guages unknown to us mortals. Who shall
interpret what is meant by the sweet jargon of
robin and oriole and bobolink, with their endless
reiterations? Something wiser, perhaps, than we
dream of in our lower life here.

Not a bit, however, did Hiel Jones trouble
his head on this subject as he came in on his
high stage seat in lordly style on the evening
of the third of July. Far other cares were in
Hiel's head, for to-morrow was the glorious
Fourth—the only really secular fête known to
the Yankee mind—and a great celebration thereof had been resolved on by the magnates of
Poganuc, and Hiel was captain of the "Poganuc
Rangers"—a flourishing militia company which
was to be the ornament of the forthcoming celebration.

It had been agreed for that time to drop all political distinctions. Federalists and Democrats, Town Hill folk and outside folk, were all of one mind and spirit to make this a celebration worthy of Poganuc Center and the great cause of American Independence. A veritable cannon had been hauled up upon the village green and fired once or twice to relieve the bursting impatience of the boys and men who had helped put it there. The flag with its stars and stripes was already waving from the top of the Court-house, and a platform was being put up in the Meeting-house, and people were running this way and that, and standing in house-doors, and talking with each other over fences, in a way that showed that something was impending.

Hiel sprang from his box, and, after attending to his horses, speedily appeared on the green to see to things—for how could the celebration to-morrow be properly presented without Hiel's counsels?

"Look here, now, boys," he said to the group assembled around the cannon, "don't be a burnin' out yer powder. Keep it for to-morrow. Let her be now; ye don't want to keep bangin' and bangin' afore the time. To-morrow mornin' we'll let 'er rip bright and early, and wake all the folks. Clear out, now, and go home to yer suppers, and don't be a blowin' yerselves up with powder so that ye can't see the show to-morrow."

Hiel then proceeded into the Meeting-house and criticised proceedings there.

" Look here, Jake, you jest stretch that air carpet a leetle forrard; ye see, ye want the most out in front where't shows; back there, why, the chairs and table'll kiver it; it ain't so much matter. Wonder now ef them air boards is firm? Wouldn't do, lettin' on 'em all down into the pews in the midst on't. Look here, Seth Chick-ering, ye need another prop under there; ye hain't calkerlated for the heft o' them fellers — governors and colonels and ministers weighs putty heavy, and there ain't no glory in a gin-eral smash-up, and we're a goin' in for glory to-morrow; we're goin' to sarve it out clear, and no mistake."

Hiel was a general favorite; his word of crit-icism was duly accepted, and things were pretty comfortably adjusted to his mind when he went home to eat his supper and try on his regi-mentals.

The dry, hard, colorless life of a Yankee boy in those days found some relief in the periods called " training-days," when the militia assem-bled in uniform and marched and drilled to the sound of fife and drum. Hiel had expended quite a round sum upon his uniform and was

not insensible to the transformation which it
wrought in his personal appearance.

The widow Jones kept his gold-laced cocked-
hat, his bright gold epaulets, his whole soldier
suit in fact, enveloped in many papers and napkins, and locked away in one of her most sacred
recesses; but it was with pride that she gave
him up the key, and when he came out before
her, all in full array, her soul was inly uplifted.
Her son was a hero in her eyes.

"It's all right, Mother, I believe," said Hiel,
surveying himself first over one shoulder and
then the other, and consulting the looking-glass
fringed with gilt knobs that hung in the widow's
"keeping-room."

"Yes, indeed, Hiel, it's all right. I've kep'
camphor gum with it to keep out the moths, and
wrapped it up to save the gold, and I don't see
that it's a grain altered since it came home new.
It's just as new as ever 'twas."

Hiel may be pardoned for smiling somewhat
complacently on the image in the glass—which
certainly was that of a very comely youth—and
when he reflected that Nabby would to-morrow
see him at the head of his company his heart
swelled with a secret exultation. It is not alone
the privilege of the fair sex to know when things
are becoming to them, and Hiel knew when he
looked well, as surely as if any one had told him.

He gave himself a patronizing wink and whistled a strain of "Yankee Doodle" as he turned away from the glass, perhaps justly confiding in the immemorial power which military trappings have always exercised over the female heart.

It was with reluctance that he laid aside the fascinating costume, and set himself to brightening up here and there a spot upon his sword-hilt or blade that called for an extra touch.

"We must have breakfast early to-morrow, Mother; the boys will be here by sunrise."

"Never you fear," said the widow. "I've got everything ready, and we'll be all through by that time; but it's as well to get to bed now."

And so in a few minutes more the candles were out and only the sound of the frogs and the whippoorwills broke the stillness of the cottage. Long before the nine o'clock bell rung Hiel and his mother were happy in the land of dreams.

In the parsonage, too, there had been an effort of discipline to produce the needed stillness and early hours called for by to-morrow's exactions.

The boys, who had assisted at the dragging in of the cannon and heard its first reverberation, were in a most inflammatory state of patriotism, longing wildly for gunpowder. In those days no fire-crackers or other vents of the kind had been provided for the relief of boys under pressure of excitement, and so they were forced to become explosive material themselves, and the walls of the parsonage rang with the sound. Dolly also was flying wildly around, asking Nabby questions about to-morrow and running away before she got her answer, to listen to some new outburst from the boys.

Nabby, however, had her own very decisive ways of putting things, and settled matters at last by putting her to bed, saying as she did so, " Now, Dolly Cushing, you just shut up. You are crazier than a bobolink, and if you don't be still and go to sleep I won't touch to take you with me to see the trainers to-morrow. Your ma said you might go with me if you'd be good ; so you just shut up and go to sleep ;" and Dolly shut her eyes hard and tried to obey.

We shall not say that there were not some corresponding movements before the glass on the part of Nabby before retiring. It certainly came into her head to try on her bonnet, which had been thriftily re-trimmed and re-arranged for summer use since the time of that sleigh-ride with Hiel. Moreover, she chose out her gown and sorted a knot of ribbons to go with it. " I suppose," she said to herself, " all the girls will be making fools of themselves about Hiel Jones to-morrow, but I ain't a going to." Nevertheless, she thought there was no harm in looking as well as she could.

CHAPTER XVIII.

DOLLY'S "FOURTH."

BANG! went the cannon on the green, just as the first red streak appeared over Poganuc hills, and open flew Dolly's great blue eyes. Every boy in town was out of bed as if he had been fired out of a pop-gun, and into his clothes and out on the green with a celerity scarcely short of the miraculous. Dolly's little toilet took more time; but she, too, was soon out upon the scene with her curls in a wild, unbrushed tangle, her little breast swelling and beating with a great enthusiasm for General Washington and liberty and her country, all of which were somehow to be illustrated and honored that day in Poganuc.

As the first rays of the rising sun struck the stars and stripes floating over the Court-house, and the sound of distant drum and fife announced the coming in of the Poganuc Rangers, Dolly was so excited that she burst into tears.

190

"What in the world are you crying for, Dolly?" said Bill rather impatiently. "I don't see any thing to cry about."

"I can't help it, Will," said Dolly, wiping her eyes, "it's so glorious!"

"If that isn't just like a girl!" said Bill. Contempt could go no farther, and Dolly retreated abashed. She was a girl—there was no help for that; but for this one day she envied the boys—the happy boys who might some day grow up and fight for their country, and do something glorious like General Washington. Meanwhile, from mouth to mouth, every one was giving in advance an idea of what the splendors of the day were to be.

"I tell ye," said Abe Bowles, "this 'ere's goin' to be a reel slam-bang, this 'ere is. Colonel Davenport is a goin' to review the troops, and wear the very same uniform he wore at Long Island.

"Yes," said Liph Kingsley, "and old Cæsar's goin' to wear his uniform and wait on the colonel. Tell ye what, the old snowball is on his high heels this morning—got a suit of the colonel's old uniform. Won't he strut and show his ivories!"

"Hulloa, boys, there's going to be a sham fight; Hiel told me so," said Bob Cushing. "Some are going to be British and some Americans, and the Americans are going to whip the British and make 'em run."

"Tell ye what," said Jake Freeman, "there'll be a bangin' and poppin'! won't there, boys!"

"Oh," said Dolly, who irrepressibly was following her brothers into the throng, "they won't *really* shoot anybody, will they?"

"Oh no, they'll only fire powder, of course," said Bill majestically, "don't you know that?"

Dolly was rebuked and relieved at once.

"I say, boys," said Nabby, appearing suddenly among the throng, "your ma says you must come right home to breakfast this minit; and you, Dolly Cushing, what are you out here for, round among the fellers like a tom-boy? Come right home."

"Why, Nabby, I wanted to see!" pleaded Dolly.

"Oh yes, you're allers up to everything and into everything, and your hair not brushed nor nothin'. You'll see it all in good time—come right away. Don't be a-lookin' at them trainers, now," she added, giving herself, however, a good observing glance to where across the green a knot of the Poganuc Rangers were collecting, and where Hiel, in full glory of his uniform, with his gold epaulets and cocked hat, was as busy and impressive as became the situation.

"Oh, Nabby, do look; there's Hiel," cried Dolly.

"Yes, yes; I see plain enough there's Hiel," said Nabby; "he thinks he's mighty grand, I suppose. He'll be conceiteder'n ever, I expect."

Just as that moment Hiel, recognizing Nabby, took off his gold-laced hat and bowed with a graceful flourish.

Nabby returned a patronizing little nod, and either the morning dawn, or the recent heat of the kitchen fire, or *something*, flushed her cheeks. It was to be remarked in evidence of the presence of mind that distinguishes the female sex that, though she had been sent out on a hurried errand to call the children, yet she had on her best bonnet, and every curl of her hair had evidently been carefully and properly attended to that morning.

"Of course, I wasn't going to look like a fright," she soliloquized. "Not that I care for any of 'em; but looks is looks any time o' day."

At the minister's breakfast-table the approaching solemnities were discussed. The procession was to form at the Court-house at nine o'clock. Democrats and Federalists had united to distribute impartially as possible the honors of the day. As Col. Davenport, the only real live revolutionary officer the county boasted, was an essential element of the show, and as he was a

staunch Federalist, it was necessary to be conciliatory. Then there was the Federal ex-
Governor to sit on the platform with the newly
elected Democratic Governor. The services
were in the Meeting-house, as the largest building in town; and Dr. Cushing was appointed to
make the opening prayer. As a compliment to
the Episcopal Church the Federal members of
the committee allotted a closing prayer to the
Reverend Simeon Coan.

That young man, however, faithful to the
logic of his creed, politely declined joining in
public services where his assisting might be
held to recognize the ordination of an un-
authorized sectarian preacher, and so the Rev.
Dr. Goodman, of Skantic, was appointed in his
place.

Squire Lewis was observed slightly to elevate
his eye-brows and shrug his shoulders as he
communicated to the committee the grounds of
his rector's refusal. He was in fact annoyed,
and a little embarrassed, by the dry, amused expression of Sheriff Dennie's countenance.

"Oh, speak it all out; never fear, Lewis," he
said. " I like to see a man face the music.
Your minister is a logical fellow, and keeps
straight up to what he teaches. You old Episcopalians were getting loose in your ideas; you
needed cording up."

" There's such a thing as cording too tight and breaking a string sometimes," muttered the Squire, who was not well pleased at the scruple that kept his church unrepresented in the exercises.

The domestic arrangements for the parson's family were announced at the breakfast table. The boys were endowed with the magnificent sum of six cents each and turned loose for the day, with the parting admonition to keep clear of powder—a most hopeless and unnecessary charge, since powder was the very heart and essence of all the glory of the day.

At an early hour the bell of the Meeting-house rang out over all the neighboring hills and valleys; the summons was replied to by streams of wagons on the roads leading to Poganuc for a square of ten miles round. Not merely Poganuc—North, South, East, West, and Center— was in motion, but several adjacent towns and villages sent forth their trainers—bands of militia, who rose about midnight and marched till morning to be on time.

By nine o'clock nominally (but far nearer to ten really) the procession started from the Court-house with drum and fife and banners. Dolly had been committed for the day to the charge of Nabby, who should see that she took no harm, and engineer for her the best chances of seeing

all that went on; while Mrs. Cushing, relieved
of this care, took her seat quietly among the
matronage of Poganuc and waited for the entrance of the procession.   But Dolly saw them
start from the Court-house, with beat of drum
and peal of fife; and Dolly saw the banners, and
saw Colonel Davenport with his white hair and
splendid physique, now more splendid in the
blue and gold of his military dress; and they
all marched with majestic tread towards the
meeting-house.   Then Nabby hurried with her
charge and got for her a seat by herself in the
front singers' seat in the gallery, where she could
see them all file in and take their seats on the
platform.   Nabby had been one of the flowers
of this singers' seat before her father's change
of base had transferred her to the Episcopal
Church, and her presence to-day was welcomed
by many old friends— for Nabby had a good,
strong clear voice of her own, and was no small
addition to the choral force.

The services opened by the national Puritan
psalm:

> " Let children hear the mighty deeds
> Which God performed of old,
> Which in our younger years we saw
> And which our fathers told.

> " Our lips shall teach them to our sons,
> And they again to theirs,
> That generations yet unborn
> May teach them to their heirs.

" That they may learn, in God alone
Their hope securely stands ;
That they may ne'er his laws forget,
But practice his commands."

The wild warble of "St. Martin's," the appointed tune whose wings bore these words,
swelled and billowed and reverberated through
the house, carrying with it that indefinable
thrill which always fills a house when deep
emotions are touched—deepest among people
habitually reserved and reticent of outward dem-
onstration. It was this solemn undertone, this
mysterious, throbbing sub-bass of repressed emotion, which gave the power and effect to the
Puritan music. After the singing came Dr. Cushing's prayer—which was a recounting of God's
mercies to New England from the beginning, and
of his deliverances from her enemies, and of
petitions for the glorious future of the United
States of America—that they might be chosen
vessels, commissioned to bear the light of liberty
and religion through all the earth and to bring in
the great millennial day, when wars should cease
and the whole world, released from the thraldom
of evil, should rejoice in the light of the Lord.

The millennium was ever the star of hope in
the eyes of the New England clergy: their faces
were set eastward, towards the dawn of that
day, and the cheerfulness of those anticipations
illuminated the hard tenets of their theology with

a rosy glow. They were children of the morning.
The Doctor, however, did not fail to make use of
his privilege to give some very decided political
hits, and some petitions arose which caused sensation between the different parties. The New
England clergyman on these occasions had his
political antagonists at decided advantage. If he
could not speak at them he could pray at them,
and of course there was no reply to an impeach-
ment in the court of heaven. So when the
Doctor's prayer was over, glances were inter-
changed, showing the satisfaction or dissatisfac-
tion, as might be, of the listeners.

And now rose Colonel Davenport to read the
Declaration of Independence. Standing square
and erect, his head thrown back, he read in
a resonant and emphatic voice that great enuncia-
tion upon which American national existence was
founded.

Dolly had never heard it before, and even now
had but a vague idea of what was meant by some
parts of it; but she gathered enough from the
recital of the abuses and injuries which had
driven her nation to this course to feel herself
swelling with indignation, and ready with all her
little mind and strength to applaud that concluding Declaration of Independence which the
Colonel rendered with resounding majesty. She
was as ready as any of them to pledge her " life,

fortune and sacred honor" for such a cause. The heroic element was strong in Dolly; it had come down by "ordinary generation" from a line of Puritan ancestry, and just now it swelled her little frame and brightened her cheeks and made her long to do something, she scarce knew what; to fight for her country or to make some declaration on her own account.

But now came the oration of the day, pronounced by a lively young Virginia law student in the office of Judge Gridley. It was as ornate and flowery, as full of patriotism and promise, as has been the always approved style of such productions. The bird of our nation received the usual appropriate flourishes, flew upward and sun-ward, waved his pinions, gazed with undaunted eye on the brightness, and did all other things appointed for the American Eagle to do on the Fourth of July. It was a nicely-written classical composition, and eminently satisfactory to the audience; and Dolly, without any very direct conception of its exact meaning, was delighted with it, and so were all the Poganuc People.

Then came the singing of an elaborate anthem, on which the choir had been practicing for a month beforehand and in which the various parts ran, and skipped, and hopped, and chased each other round and round, and performed all sorts

of unheard-of trills and quavers and musical evolutions, with a heartiness of self-satisfaction that
was charming to witness.

Then, when all was over, the procession
marched out—the magnates on the stage to a
dinner, and the Poganuc military to refresh themselves at Glazier's, preparatory to the grand
review in the afternoon.

Dolly spent her six cents for ginger-bread, and
walked unwearyingly the rounds of sight-seeing
with Nabby, her soul inly uplifted with the
grandeur of the occasion.

In the afternoon came the military display;
and Colonel Davenport on his white horse reviewed the troops; and just behind him, also
mounted, was old Cato, with his gold-laced hat
and plume, his buff breeches and long-tailed blue
coat. On the whole, this solemn black attendant
formed a striking and picturesque addition to the
scene. And so there were marching and counter-
marching and military evolutions of all kinds, and
Hiel, with his Poganuc Rangers, figured conspic-
uously in the eyes of all.

It was a dangerous sight for Nabby. She
really could not help feeling a secret awe for
Hiel, as if he had been wafted away from her
into some higher sphere; he looked so very determined and martial that she began to admit
that he might carry any fortress that he set

himself seriously to attack. After the regular
review came the sham fight, which was in fact
but an organized military frolic. Some of the
West Poganuc youth had dressed themselves as
Indians, and other companies, drawn by lot,
were to personate the British, and there was
skirmishing and fighting and running, to the wild
and crazy delight of the boys. A fort, which had
been previously constructed of bushes and trees,
was furiously attacked by British and Indians,
and set on fire; and then the Americans bursting
out scattered both the fire and the forces, and
performed prodigies of valor.

In short, it was a Day of days to Dolly and
the children, and when sober twilight drew on
they came home intoxicated with patriotism and
sight-seeing.

On her way home Dolly was spied out by her
old friend Judge Gridley, who always delighted
to have a gossip with her.

"Ha, my little Dolly, are you out to-day?"

"To be sure, sir," said Dolly; "indeed I'm out.
Oh, hasn't it been glorious! I've never been so
happy in my life. I never heard the Declaration
of Independence before."

"Well, and what do you think of it?" asked
the Judge.

"I never heard anything like it," said Dolly.
"I didn't know before how they did abuse us,

and wasn't it grand that we wouldn't bear it!
I never heard anything so splendid as that last
part."

"You would have made a good soldier."

"If I were a man I would. Only think of it,
Colonel Davenport fought in the war! I'm so
glad we can see one man that did. If we had
lived then, I know my papa and all my brothers
would have fought; we would have had 'liberty
or death.'"

Dolly pronounced these words, which she had
heard in the oration, with a quivering eagerness.
The old Judge gave her cheek a friendly pinch.

"You'll do," he said; "but now you must let
Nabby here get you home and quiet you down,
or you won't sleep all night. Good by, Pussy."

And so went off Dolly's Fourth of July.

But Hiel made an evening call at the parsonage
in his full regimentals; and stayed to a late hour
unreproved. There were occasions when even
the nine o'clock bell did not send a young fellow
home. This appeared to be one of them.

CHAPTER XIX.

SUMMER DAYS IN POGANUC.

O passed Dolly's Fourth of July; a confused dream of glory and patriotism, of wonderful sights and surprises—but, like a dream, it all melted away.

New England life was too practical and laborious to give more than one day to holiday performances, and with the night of the Fourth the whole pageant vanished. Hiel's uniform, with its gold lace and feathers, returned to the obscurity of Mother Jones's pillow-cases and camphorgum, and was locked away in secret places; and Hiel was only a simple stage-driver, going forth on his route as aforetime. So with the trappings of the Poganuc Rangers—who the day before had glittered like so many knights-errant in the front of battle—all were laid by in silent waiting, and the Poganuc Rangers rose at four o'clock and put on their working clothes and cow-hide shoes, and were abroad with their oxen. The shoemaker and the carpenter, who yesterday were transfigured in blue and gold, to-day were hammering shoe-soles and planing boards as if no such thing had happened. In the shadows of the night the cannon had vanished from the village green and gone where it came from; the flag on the Court-house was furled, and the world of Poganuc Center was again the same busy, literal, work-a-day world as ever. Only Liph Kingsbury, who had burned his hand with gunpowder in consequence of carrying too much New England rum in his head, and one or two boys, who had met with a sprain or bruise in the excitement of the day, retained any lasting memorials of the celebration.

It is difficult in this our era of railroads and steam to give any idea of the depths of absolute stillness and repose that brooded in the summer skies over the wooded hills of Poganuc. No daily paper told the news of distant cities. Summer traveling was done in stages, and was long and wearisome, and therefore there was little of that. Everybody staid at home, and expected to stay there the year through. A journey from Poganuc to Boston or New York was more of an undertaking in those days than a journey to Europe is in ours. Now and then some of the great square houses on the street of Poganuc Center received a summer visitor, and then everybody in town knew it and knew all about it. The visitor's family, rank, position in life, probable amount of property, and genealogy to

remote ancestors, were freely discussed and settled, till all Poganuc was fully informed. The
elect circle of Poganuc called on them, and made
stately tea-parties in their honor, and these entertainments pleasantly rippled the placid surface of
society. But life went on there with a sort of
dreamy stillness. The different summer flowers
came out in their successive ranks in the neatly-
kept garden; roses followed peonies, and white
lilies came and went, and crimson and white
phloxes stood ranged in midsummer ranks, and the
yellow tribes of marigolds brought up the autumnal season. And over on the woody hills around
the town the spring tints deepened and grew
dark in summer richness, and then began breaking
here and there into streaks and flecks of gold and
crimson, foretelling autumn. And there were
wonderful golden sunsets, and moonlight nights
when the street of Poganuc seemed overshot
with a silver network of tracery like the arches
of some cathedral. The doors and windows of
the houses stood innocently open all night for the
moon to shine in, and youths and maidens walked
and wandered and sentimentalized up and down
the long, dewy street, and nobody seemed to
know how fast the short, beautiful summer of
those regions was passing away.

As to Dolly, summer was her time of life and
joy; but it was not by any means a joy unmixed.

Dolly's education was conducted on the good old-fashioned principle that everyone must do his little part in the battle of life, and that nobody was pretty enough or good enough to be kept merely for ornamental purposes.

She was no curled darling, to be kept on exhibition in white dresses and broad sashes, and she had been sedulously instructed in the orthodoxy of Dr. Watts, that

> "Satan finds some mischief still
> For idle hands to do."

It was the duty of the good house-mother of those days to be so much in advance of this unpleasant personage that there should be no room for his temptations. Accordingly, any part of the numerous household tasks of the Parsonage that could be trusted to a little pair of hands were turned over to Dolly. In those days were none of the thousand conveniences which now abridge the labors of the housekeeper. Everything came in the rough, and had to be reduced to a usable form in the household.

The delicate, smooth white salt which filled the cellars at the table was prepared by Dolly's manipulation from coarse rock-salt crystals, which she was taught to wash and dry, and pound and sift, till it became of snowy fineness; and quite a long process it was. Then there were spices to be ground, and there was coffee to be browned to the exact and beautiful shade dear to household ideality; and Dolly could do that.

Being a bright, enterprising little body, she did not so much object to these processes, which rather interested her, but her very soul was wearied within her at the drill of the long and varied sewing lessons that were deemed indispensable to her complete education. Pounding salt, or grinding spice, or beating eggs, or roasting coffee, were endurable; but darning stockings and stitching wristbands, and "scratching" gathers, were a weariness unto her spirit. And yet it was only at the price of penances like these, well and truly performed, that Dolly's golden *own* hours of leisure were given.

Most of her household tasks could be performed in the early morning hours before school, and after school Dolly measured the height of the afternoon sun with an avaricious eye. Would there be time enough to explore the woody hills beyond Poganuc River before sundown? and would they let her go?

For oh, those woods! What a world of fairyland, what a world of pure, untold joy was there to Dolly! When she found her face fairly set towards them, with leave to stay till sundown, and with Spring at her heels, Dolly was as blissful, as perfectly happy, as a child can ever be made by any one thing.

The sense of perfect freedom, the wonder, the curiosity, the vague expectation of what she might find or see, made her heart beat with pleasure. First came the race down through the tall, swaying meadow-grass and white-hatted daisies to the Poganuc River—a brown, clear, gurgling stream, wide, shallow, and garrulous, that might be easily crossed on mossy stepping-stones. Here was a world of delight to Dolly. Skipping from stone to stone, or reclining athwart some great rock around which the brown waters rippled, she watched the little fishes come and go, darting hither and thither like flecks of silver. Down under the shade of dark hemlocks the river had worn a deep pool where the translucent water lay dark and still; and Dolly, climbing carefully and quietly to the rocky side, could lean over and watch the slim, straight pickerel, holding themselves so still in the water that the play of their gossamer fins made no ripple,—so still, so apparently unwatchful and drowsy, that Dolly again and again fancied she might slily reach down her little hand and take one out of the water; but the moment the rosy finger-tips touched the wave, with a flash, like a ray of light, the coveted prize was gone. There was no catching a pickerel asleep, however quiet he might appear. Yet, time after time, Dolly tried the experiment, burning with the desire to win glory among the boys by bringing home an actual and veritable pickerel of her own catching.

But there were other beauties, dryad treasures, more accessible. The woods along the moist margin of the river were full of the pink and white azalea, and she gathered besides the fragrant blossoms stores of what were called "honeysuckle apples" that grew upon them—fleshy exudations not particularly nice in flavor, but crisp, cool, and much valued among children. There, too, were crimson wintergreen berries, spicy in their sweetness, and the young, tender leaves of the wintergreen, ranking high as an eatable dainty among little folk. Dolly's basket was sure to fill rapidly when she set herself to gathering these treasures, and the sun would be almost down before she could leave the enchanted shades of the wood and come back to real life again.

But Saturday afternoon was a sort of child's Paradise. No school was kept, and even household disciplinarians recognized a reasonably well-behaved child's right to a Saturday afternoon play-spell.

"Now, Dolly," had Nabby said to her the week before, "you be sure and be a good girl, and do up all your stitching and get the stockings mended afore Saturday comes, and then we'll take Saturday afternoon to go a-huckleberrying up to Pequannock Rock; and we'll stop and see Mis' Persis."

This, let it be known, was a programme to awaken Dolly's ambition. Pequannock Rock was a distance which she never would be permitted to explore alone, and Mis' Persis was to her imagination a most interesting and stimulating personage. She was a widow, and the story ran that her deceased husband had been an Indian—a story which caused Dolly to regard her with a sort of awe, connecting her with Cotton Mather's stories of war-whoops and scalping-knives, and midnight horrors when houses were burned and children carried off to Canada.

Nevertheless, Mis' Persis was an inoffensive and quite useful member of society. She had her little house and garden, which she cultivated with energy and skill. She kept her cow, her pig, her chickens, and contrived always to have something to sell when she needed an extra bit of coin. She was versed in all the Indian lore of roots and herbs, and her preparations of these for medicinal purposes were much in request. Among the farming population around, Mis' Persis was held in respect as a medical authority, and her opinions were quoted with confidence. She was also of considerable repute among the best families of Poganuc as a filler of gaps such as may often occur in household economy. There was nothing wanted to be done that Mis' Persis could not do. She could wash, or iron, or bake, or brew, or nurse the sick, as the case might require. She was, in fact, one of the reserved forces of Poganuc society. She was a member of Dr. Cushing's church, in good and regular standing, and, in her way, quite devoted to her minister and church, and always specially affable and gracious to Dolly.

This particular Saturday afternoon all the constellations were favorable. Dolly was pronounced a good girl, her week's tasks well performed; and never were dinner-dishes more rapidly whirled into place than were Nabby's on that same afternoon; so that before three o'clock the pair were well on their way to the huckleberry-field. There, under the burning August sun, the ground shot up those ardent flower-flames well called fire-lilies, and the wild roses showered their deep pink petals as they pushed through the thickets, and the huckleberry-bushes bent low under the weight of the great sweet berries; and Dolly's cheeks were all a-flame, like the fire-lilies themselves, with heat and enthusiasm as she gathered the purple harvest into her basket. When the baskets were filled and Dolly had gathered fire-lilies and wild roses more than she knew how to carry, it was proposed to stop a little and rest, on the homeward route, at Mis' Persis's cottage.

They found her sitting on her door-step, knitting. A little wiry, swart, thin woman was she, alert in her movements, and quick and decided of speech. Her black eyes had in them a latent fiery gleam that suggested all the while that though pleased and pleasant at the present moment Mis' Persis might be dangerous if roused, and Dolly was always especially conciliatory and polite in her addresses to her.

On the present occasion Mis' Persis was delightfully hospitable. She installed Dolly in a small splint-bottomed rocking-chair at the door, and treated her to a cup of milk and a crisp cooky.

" Why, what a little girl you are to be so far from home!" she said.

" Oh, I don't mind," said Dolly; " I am never tired. I could pick berries all day."

" But, sakes alive! ain't you afraid of snakes?" said Mis' Persis. " Why, my sister got dreadfully bit by a rattlesnake when she wa'n't much older 'n you," and Mis' Persis shook her head weirdly.

" Oh, dear me! Did it kill her?" said Dolly, in horror.

" No; she lived many a year after," said Mis' Persis, with a reticent air, as one who could say more if properly approached.

" Do, do tell us all about it; do, Mis' Persis. I

never saw a rattlesnake. I never heard one. I shouldn't know what it was if I saw one."

" You wouldn't ever forget it if you did," said Mis' Persis, oracularly.

"Oh, please, Mis' Persis, do tell about it," said Dolly, eagerly. " Where were you, and how did it happen?"

" Well," said Mis' Persis, "it was when I was a girl and lived over in Danbury. There's where I come from. My sister Polly and me, we went out to High Ledge one afternoon after huckleberries, and as we was makin' our way through some low bushes we heard the sharpest noise, jest like a locust screechin', right under foot, and jest then Polly she screams out, 'Oh, Sally,' says she, ' somethin's bit me!' and I looked down and saw a great rattlesnake crawlin' off through the bushes—a great big fellow, as big as my wrist.

"'Well,' says I, 'Polly, I must get you home quick as I can;' and we set down our pails and started for home. It was a broilin' hot day, and we hed a'most a mile to walk, and afore we got home I hed to carry her. Her tongue was swelled so that it hung out of her mouth; her neck and throat was all swelled, and spotted like the snake. Oh, it was dreadful! We got her into the house, and on the bed, and sent for the Indian doctor—there ain't nobody knows about them snake-bites but Indians. Well, he come and brought a bag of rattlesnake-weed with him, and he made poultices of it and laid all over her stomach and breast and hands and feet, and he made a tea of it and got some down her throat, and kep' a feedin' on it to her till she got so she could swallow. That's the way she got well."

"Oh, Mis' Persis," said Dolly, after a pause of awe and horror, "what is rattlesnake-weed?"

"Why, it's a worse poison than the snake-bite, and it kills the snake-poison 'cause it's stronger. Wherever the snakes grow, there the rattlesnake-weed grows. The snakes know it themselves, and when they fight and bite each other they go and eat the weed and it cures 'em. Here's some of it," she said, going to the wall of the room which was all hung round with dried bunches of various herbs—"here's some I got over on Poganuc Mountain, if you ever should want any."

"Oh, I hope I never shall," said Dolly. "Nabby, only think! What if there had been a snake in those bushes!"

"Well, you can always know," said Mis' Persis, "if you hear somethin' in the bushes jest like a locust, sharp and sudden—why, you'd better look afore you set your foot down. But we don't hev no rattlesnakes round this way. I've beat all these lots through and never seen tail of one. This 'ere ain't one o' their places; over to Poganuc Mountain, now, a body has to take care how they step."

"Do you suppose, Mis' Persis," said Dolly, after a few moments of grave thought, "do you suppose God made that weed grow on purpose to cure rattlesnake bites?"

"Of course he did," said Mis' Persis, as decidedly as if she had been a trained theologian, "that's what rattlesnake-weed was made fer; any fool can see that."

"It seems to me," said Dolly, "that it would have been better not to have the snakes, and then people wouldn't be bit at all—wouldn't it?"

"Oh, we don't know everything," said Mis' Persis; "come to that, there's a good many things that nobody knows what they's made fer. But the Indians used to say there was some cure grew for every sickness if only our eyes was opened to see it, and I expect it's so."

"Come, Dolly," said Nabby, "the sun is gettin' pretty low; I must hurry home to get supper."

Just then the bell of the distant meeting-house gave three tolling strokes, whereat all the three stopped talking and listened intently.

Of all the old Puritan customs none was more thrillingly impressive than this solemn announcement of a death, and this deliberate tolling out of the years of a finished life.

It was a sound to which every one, whether

alone or in company, at work or in play, stopped
to listen, and listened with a nervous thrill of
sympathy.

"I wonder who that is?" said Nabby.

"Perhaps it's Lyddy Bascom," said Mis' Persis,
"she's been down with typhus fever."

The bell now was rapidly tolling one, two,
three, four, and all the company counted eagerly
up to sixteen, seventeen, when Mis' Persis in-
terposed.

"No, 'taint Lyddy; it's goin' on," and they
counted and counted, and still the bell kept tolling till it had numbered eighty. "It's old Granny
Moss," said Mis' Persis decisively; "she's ben
lyin' low some time. Well, she's in heaven now;
the better for her."

"Ah, I'm glad she's in heaven," said Dolly,
with a shivering sigh; "she's all safe now."

"Oh, yes, she's better off," said Nabby, getting
up and shaking her dress as if to shake off the
very thought of death. A warm, strong, glowing
creature she was, as full of earth-life as the fire-
lilies they had been gathering. She seemed a
creature made for this world and its present uses,
and felt an animal repulsion to the very thought
of death.

"Come, Dolly," she said, briskly, as she counted
the last toll, "we can't wait another minute."

"Well, Dolly," said Mis' Persis, "tell your

mother I'm a comin' this year to make up her
candles for her, and the work sha'n't cost her a
cent. I've been tryin' out a lot o' bayberry wax
to put in 'em and make 'em good and firm."

"I'm sure you are very good," said Dolly, with
instinctive politeness.

"I want to do my part towards supportin' my
minister," said Mis' Persis, "and that's what I
hev to give."

"I'll tell my mother, and I know she'll thank
you," answered Dolly, as they turned homeward.

The sun was falling lower and lower toward
the west. The long shadows of the two danced
before them on the dusty road.

After walking half a mile they came to a stone
culvert, where a little brawling stream crossed
the road. The edges of the brook were fringed
with sweet-flag blades waving in the afternoon
light, and the water gurgled and tinkled pleasantly
among the stones.

"There, Dolly," said Nabby, seating herself on
a flat stone by the brook, "I'm goin' to rest a
minute, and you can find some of them sweet-flag
'graters' if you want." This was the blossom-
bud of the sweet flag, which when young and
tender was reckoned a delicacy among omnivo-
rous children.

"Why, Nabby, I thought you were in such a
hurry to get home," said Dolly, gathering the

blades of sweet-flag and looking for the "graters."

"No need of hurry," said Nabby, "the sun's
an hour and a half high," and she leaned over
the curb of the bridge and looked at herself in
the brook. She took off her sun-bonnet and
fanned herself with it. Then she put a bright
spotted fire-lily in her hair and watched the effect
in the water. It certainly was a brilliant picture,
framed by the brown stones and green rushes of
the brook.

"Oh, Nabby," cried Dolly, "look! There's the
stage and Hiel coming down the hill!"

"Sure e-nough!" said Nabby, in a tone of
proper surprise, as if she had expected anything
else to happen on that road at that time of the
afternoon. "As true as I live and breathe it *is*
Hiel and the stage," she added, "and not a creature in it. Now, we'll get a ride home."

Nabby's sun-bonnet hung on her arm; her hair
fell in a tangle of curls around her flushed cheeks
as she stood waiting for Hiel to come up. Altogether she was a picture.

That young man took in the points of the view
at once and vowed in his heart that Nabby was
the handsomest girl upon his beat.

"Waitin' for me to come along?" he said as
he drew up.

"Well, you're sort o' handy now and then,"

said Nabby. "We've been huckleberrying all the afternoon, and are tired."

Hiel got down and opened the stage door and helped the two to get in with their berries and flowers.

"You owe me *one* for this," said Hiel when he handed in Nabby's things.

"Well, there's one," said Nabby, laughing and striking him across the eyes with her bunch of lilies.

"Never mind, miss. I shall keep the account," said Hiel; and he gathered up the reins, resumed his high seat, made his grand entrance into Poganuc, and drew up at the parson's door.

For a week thereafter it was anxiously discussed in various circles how Nabby and Dolly came to be in that stage. Where had they been? How did it happen? The obscurity of the event kept Hiel on the brain of several damsels who had nothing better to talk about.

And the day closed with a royal supper of huckleberries and milk. So went a specimen number of Dolly's Saturday afternoons.

CHAPTER XX.

THE bright days of summer were a short-lived joy at Poganuc. One hardly had time to say "How beautiful!" before it was past. By September came the frosty nights that turned the hills into rainbow colors and ushered in autumn with her gorgeous robes of golden-rod and purple asters. There was still the best of sport for the children, however; for the frost ripened the shag-bark walnuts and opened the chestnut burrs, and the glossy brown chestnuts dropped down among the rustling yellow leaves and the beds of fringed blue gentians.

One peculiarity of the Puritan New England *régime* is worthy of special notice, and that is the generosity and liberality of its dealing in respect to the spontaneous growths of the soil. The chestnuts, the hickory-nuts, the butternuts—no matter upon whose land they grew—were free to whoever would gather them. The girls and boys roamed at pleasure through the woods and picked, unmolested, wherever they could find

220

the most abundant harvest. In like manner the wild fruits—grapes, strawberries, huckleberries, and cranberries—were for many years free to the earliest comer. This is the more to be remarked in a community where life was peculiarly characterized by minute economy, where everything had its carefully ascertained money-value. Every board, nail, brad, every drop of paint, every shingle, in house or barn, was counted and estimated. In making bargains and conducting domestic economies, there was the minutest consideration of the money-value of time, labor and provision. And yet their rigidly parsimonious habit of life presented this one remarkable exception, of certain quite valuable spontaneous growths left unguarded and unappropriated.

Our Fathers came to New England from a country where the poor man was everywhere shut out from the bounties of nature by game-laws and severe restrictions. Though his children might be dying of hunger he could not catch a fish, or shoot a bird, or snare the wild game of the forest, without liability to arrest as a criminal; he could not gather the wild fruits of the earth without danger of being held a trespasser, and risking fine and imprisonment. When the Fathers took possession of the New England forest it was in the merciful spirit of the Mosaic law, which commanded that something should always be left to be gathered by the poor. From the beginning of the New England life till now there have been poor people, widows and fatherless children, who have eked out their scanty living by the sale of the fruits and nuts which the custom of the country allowed them freely to gather on other people's land.

Within the past fifty years, while this country has been filling up with foreigners of a different day and training, these old customs have been passing away. Various fruits and nuts, once held free, are now appropriated by the holders of the soil and made subject to restriction and cultivation.

In the day we speak of, however, all the forest hills around Poganuc were a free nut-orchard, and one of the chief festive occasions of the year, in the family at the Parsonage, was the autumn gathering of nuts, when Dr. Cushing took the matter in hand and gave his mind to it.

On the present occasion, having just finished four sermons which completely cleared up and reconciled all the difficulties between the doctrines of free agency and the divine decrees, the Doctor was naturally in good spirits. He declared to his wife, " There! my dear, *that* subject is disposed of. I never before succeeded in really clearing it up; but now the matter is done for all time." Having thus wound up the sun and moon, and arranged the courses of the stars in celestial regions, the Doctor was as alert and light-hearted as any boy, in his preparations for the day's enterprise.

"Boys," he said, "we'll drive over to Poganuc Ledge; up there are those big chestnuts that grow right out of the rock; there's no likelihood of anybody's getting them—but I noticed the other day they were hanging full."

"Oh, father, those trees are awful to climb."

"Of course they are. I won't let you boys try to climb them—mind that; but I'll go up myself and shake them, and you pick up underneath."

No Highland follower ever gloried more in the physical prowess of his chief than the boys in that of their father. Was there a tree he could not climb—a chestnut, or walnut, or butternut, however exalted in fastnesses of the rock, that he could not shake down? They were certain there was not. The boys rushed hither and thither, with Spring barking at their heels, leaving open doors and shouting orders to each other concerning the various pails and baskets necessary to contain their future harvest. Mrs. Cushing became alarmed for the stability of her household arrangements.

" Now, father, *please* don't take all my baskets this time," pleaded she, "just let me arrange——"

" Well, my dear, have it all your own way; only be sure to provide things enough."

" Well, surely, they can all pick in pails or cups, and then they can be emptied into a bag," said Mrs. Cushing. " You won't get more than a bushel, certainly."

" Oh yes, we shall—three or four bushels," said Will, triumphantly.

"There's no end of what we shall get when father goes," said Bob. "Why, you've no idea how he rattles 'em down."

Meanwhile Mrs. Cushing and Nabby were packing a hamper with bread-and-butter, and tea-rusks, and unlimited ginger-bread, and dough-nuts crisp and brown, and savory ham, and a bottle of cream, and coffee all ready for boiling in the pot, and tea-cups and spoons—everything, in short, ready for a gipsy encampment, while the parson's horse stood meekly absorbing an extra ration of oats in that contemplative attitude which becomes habitual to good family horses, especially of the ministerial profession. Mrs. Cushing and the Doctor, with Nabby and Dolly, and the hamper and baskets, formed the load of the light wagon, while Will and Bob were both mounted upon " the colt"—a scrawny, ewe-necked beast, who had long outgrown this youthful designation.

The boys, however, had means best known to themselves of rousing his energies and keeping him ahead of the wagon in a convulsive canter, greatly to the amusement of Nabby and Dolly.

Our readers would be happy could they follow the party along the hard, stony roads, up the winding mountain-paths, where the trees, flushing in purple, crimson and gold, seemed to shed light on their paths; where beds of fringed gentian seemed, as the sunlight struck them, to glow like so many sapphires, and every leaf of every plant seemed to be passing from the green of summer into some quaint new tint of autumnal splendor. Here and there groups of pines or tall hemlocks, with their heavy background of solemn green, threw out the flamboyant tracery of the forest in startling distinctness. Here and there, as they passed a bit of low land, the swamp maples seemed really to burn like crimson flames, and the clumps of black alder, with their vivid scarlet berries, exalted the effect of color to the very highest and most daring result. No artist ever has ventured to put on canvas the exact copy of the picture that nature paints for us every year in the autumn months. There are things the Almighty Artist can do that no earthly imitator can more than hopelessly admire.

As to Dolly, she was like a bird held in a

leash, full of exclamations and longings, now to
pick "those leaves," and then to gather "those
gentians," or to get "those lovely red berries;"
but was forced to resign herself to be carried by.

"They would all fade before the day is
through," said her mother; "wait till we come
home at night, and then, if you're not too tired,
you may gather them." Dolly sighed and resigned herself to wait.

We shall not tell the joys of the day: how
the Doctor climbed the trees victoriously, how
the brown, glossy chestnuts flew down in showers
as he shook the limbs, and how fast they were
gathered by busy fingers below. Not merely
chestnuts, but walnuts, and a splendid butternut
tree, that grew in the high cleft of a rocky
ledge, all were made to yield up their treasures
till the bags were swelled to a most auspicious
size.

Then came the nooning, when the boys delighted in making a roaring hot fire, and the coffee
was put on to boil, and Nabby spread the table-
cloth and unpacked the hamper on a broad, flat
rock around which a white foam of moss
formed a soft, elastic seat.

The Doctor was most entertaining, and related
stories of the fishing and hunting excursions of
his youth, of the trout he had caught and the

CHESTNUTTING.

*"How the Doctor climbed the trees victoriously, how the brown,
glossy chestnuts flew down in showers. . . . And Nabby
unpacked the hamper on a broad, flat rock."*—p. 226.

ducks he had shot. The boys listened with ears of emulation, and Dolly sighed to think she never was to be a man and do all these fine things that her brothers were going to do.

But in the midst of all came Abel Moss, a hard-visaged farmer from one of the upland farms, who, seeing the minister's wagon go by, had come to express his mind to him concerning a portion of his last Sunday's sermon; and the Doctor, who but a moment before had thought only of trout and wild ducks, sat down by the side of Abel on a fragment of rock and began explaining to him the difference between the laws of matter and the laws of mind in moral government, and the difference between divine sovereignty as applied to matter and to mind.

The children wandered off during the discussion, which lasted some time; but when the western sunbeams, sloping through the tree-trunks, warned them that it was time to return, the Doctor's wagon might have been seen coming down the rough slope of the mountain.

"There, my dear, I've set Moss right," he said. "There was a block in his wheels that I've taken out. I think he'll go all straight now. Moss has a good head; when he once sees a thing, he does see it,—and I think I've clinched the nail with him to-day."

CHAPTER XXI.

DOLLY'S SECOND CHRISTMAS.

NCE more had Christmas come round in Poganuc; once more the Episcopal church was being dressed with ground-pine and spruce; but this year economy had begun to make its claims felt. An illumination might do very well to open a church, but there were many who said "to what purpose is this waste?" when the proposition was made to renew it yearly. Consequently it was resolved to hold the Christmas Eve service with only that necessary amount of light which would enable the worshipers to read the prayers.

The lines in Poganuc were now drawn. The crowd who flock after a new thing had seen the new thing, and the edge of curiosity was somewhat dulled. Both ministers had delivered their Christmas sermons, to the satisfaction of themselves and their respective flocks, and both congregations had taken the direction of their practical course accordingly.

On this Christmas Eve, therefore, Dolly was

not racked and torn with any violent temptation
to go over to the church, but went to bed at
her usual hour with a resigned and quiet spirit.
She felt herself a year older, and more than a
year wiser, than when Christmas had first dawned
upon her consciousness.

We have seen that the little maiden was a most
intense and sympathetic partisan, and during the
political discussions of the past year she had
imbibed the idea that the Episcopal party were
opposed to her father. Nay, she had heard with
burning indignation that Mr. Simeon Coan had
said that her father was not a regularly ordained
minister, and therefore had no right to preach or
administer ordinances. Dolly had no idea of
patronizing by her presence people who expressed such opinions. Whoever and whatever
in the world might be in error, Dolly was sure
her father never could be in the wrong, and went
to sleep placidly in that belief.

It was not altogether pleasant to Mrs. Cushing
to receive a message from Mis' Persis that she
would come and make up her candles for her on
the 25th of December. In a figurative and
symbolical point of view, the devoting that day
to the creation of the year's stock of light might
have seemed eminently appropriate. But the
making of so many candles involved an amount
of disagreeable particulars hard to conceive in

our days, when gas and kerosene make the
lighting of houses one of the least of cares.

In the times we speak of, candle-making for a
large household was a serious undertaking, and
the day devoted to it was one that any child
would remember as an unlucky one for childish
purposes of enjoyment, seven-fold worse in its
way even than washing-day. Mrs. Cushing still
retained enough of the habits of her early education to have preferred a quiet day for her
Christmas. She would willingly have spent it in
letter-writing, reading and meditation, but when
Mis' Persis *gave* her time and labor it seemed
only fair to allow her to choose her own day.

So, upon this Christmas morning, Mis' Persis
appeared on the ground by day-dawn. A great
kettle was slung over the kitchen fire, in which
cakes of tallow were speedily liquefying; a frame
was placed quite across the kitchen to sustain
candle-rods, with a train of boards underneath to
catch the drippings, and Mis' Persis, with a brow
like one of the Fates, announced: " Now we
can't hev any young 'uns in this kitchen to-day ;"
and Dolly saw that there was no getting any
attention in that quarter.

Mis' Persis, in a gracious Saturday afternoon
mood, sitting in her own tent-door dispensing
hospitalities and cookies, was one thing; but
Mis' Persis in her armor, with her loins girded

and a hard day's work to be conquered, was quite another: she was terrible as Minerva with her helmet on.

Dinner-baskets for all the children were hastily packed, and they were sent off to school with the injunction on no account to show their faces about the premises till night. The Doctor, warned of what was going on, retreated to his study at the top of the house, where, serenely above the lower cares of earth, he sailed off into President Edwards's treatise on the nature of true virtue, concerning which he was preparing a paper to read at the next Association meeting.

That candles were a necessity of life he was well convinced, and by faith he dimly accepted the fact that one day in the year the whole house was to be devoted and given up to this manufacture; and his part of the business, as he understood it, was, clearly, to keep himself out of the way till it was over.

"There won't be much of a dinner at home, anyway," said Nabby to Dolly, as she packed her basket with an extra doughnut or two. "I've got to go to church to-day, 'cause I'm one of the singers, and your ma'll be busy waitin' on *her;* so we shall just have a pick-up dinner, and you be sure not to come home till night; by that time it'll be all over."

Dolly trotted off to school well content with the prospect before her: a nooning, with leave to play with the girls at school, was not an unpleasant idea.

But the first thing that saluted her on her arrival was that Bessie Lewis—her own dear, particular Bessie—was going to have a Christmas party at her house that afternoon, and was around distributing invitations right and left among the scholars with a generous freedom.

" We are going to have nuts, and raisins, and cake, and mottoes," said Bessie, with artless triumph. The news of this bill of fare spread like wildfire through the school.

Never had a party been heard of which contemplated such a liberal entertainment, for the rising generation of Poganuc were by no means *blasé* with indulgence, and raisins and almonds stood for grandeur with them. But these *mottoes*, which consisted of bits of confectionery wrapped up in printed couplets of sentimental poetry, were an unheard-of refinement. Bessie assured them that her papa had sent clear to Boston for them, and whoever got one would have his or her fortune told by it.

The school was a small, select one, comprising the children of all ages from the best families of Poganuc. Both boys and girls, and all with great impartiality, had been invited. Miss Titcome, the teacher, quite readily promised to dismiss at three o'clock that afternoon any scholar who should bring a permission from parents, and the children nothing doubted that such a¹ permission was obtainable.

Dolly alone saw a cloud in the horizon. She had been sent away with strict injunctions not to return till evening, and children in those days never presumed to make any exceptions in obeying an absolute command of their parents.

"But, of course, you will go home at noon and ask your mother, and of course she'll let you: won't she, girls?" said Bessie.

"Oh, certainly; of course she will," said all the older girls, "because you know a party is a thing that don't happen every day, and your mother would think it strange if you *didn't* come and ask her." So too thought Miss Titcome, a most exemplary, precise and proper young lady, who always moved and spoke and thought as became a schoolmistress, so that, although she was in reality only twenty years old, Dolly considered her as a very advanced and ancient person—if anything, a little older than her father and mother.

Even she was of opinion that Dolly might properly go home to lay a case of such importance before her mother; and so Dolly rushed home after the morning school was over, running with all her might and increasing in mental excitement as she ran. Her bonnet blew off upon her shoulders, her curls flew behind her in the wind, and she most inconsiderately used up the little stock of breath that she would want to set her cause in order before her mother.

Just here we must beg any mother and housekeeper to imagine herself in the very midst of the most delicate, perplexing and laborious of household tasks, when interruption is most irksome and perilous, suddenly called to discuss with a child some new and startling proposition to which at the moment she cannot even give a thought.

Mrs. Cushing was sitting in the kitchen with Mis' Persis, by the side of a melted caldron of tallow, kept in a fluid state by the heat of a portable furnace on which it stood. A long train of half-dipped candles hung like so many stalactites from the frames on which the rods rested, and the two were patiently dipping set after set and replacing them again on the frame.

"As sure as I'm alive! if there isn't Dolly Cushing comin' back—runnin' and tearin' like a wild cretur'," said Mis' Persis. "She'll be in here in a minute and knock everything down!"

Mrs. Cushing looked, and with a quick movement stepped to the door.

"Dolly! what are you here for? Didn't I tell you not to come home this noon?"

" Oh, Mamma, there's going to be a party at General Lewis's—Bessie's party—and the girls are all going, and mayn't I go?"

" No, you can't; it's impossible," said her mother. " Your best dress isn't ready to wear, and there's nobody can spend time to get you ready. Go right back to school."

" But, Mamma——"

" Go!" said her mother, in the decisive tone that mothers used in the old days, when arguing with children was not a possibility.

" What's all this about?" asked the Doctor, looking out of the door.

" Why," said Mrs. Cushing, " there's going to be a party at General Lewis's, and Dolly is wild to go. It's just impossible for me to attend to her now."

" Oh, I don't want her intimate at Lewis's; he's a Democrat and an Episcopalian," said the Doctor, and immediately he came out behind his wife.

" There; run away to school, Dolly," he said. " Don't trouble your mother; you don't want to go to parties; why, it's foolish to think of it. Run away now, and don't think any more about it—there's a good girl!"

Dolly turned and went back to school, the tears freezing on her cheek as she went. As for not thinking any more about it—that was impossible.

When three o'clock came, scholar after scholar rose and departed, until at last Dolly was the only one remaining in the school-room.

Miss Titcome made no comments upon the event, but so long as one scholar was left she conscientiously persisted in her duties towards her. She heard Dolly read and spell, and then occupied herself with writing a letter, while Dolly sewed upon her allotted task. Dolly's work was a linen sheet, which was to be turned. It was to be sewed up on one side and ripped out on the other—two processes which seemed especially dreary to Dolly, and more particularly so now, when she was sitting in the deserted school-room. Tears fell and fell on the long, uninteresting seam which seemed to stretch on and on hopelessly before her; and she thought of all the other children playing at "oats, pease, beans and barley grows," of feasting on almonds and raisins, and having their fortunes told by wonderful mottoes bought in Boston. The world looked cold and dark and dreary to Dolly on this her second Christmas. She never felt herself injured; she never even in thought questioned that her parents were doing exactly right by her—she only felt that just here and now the right thing was very disagreeable and very hard to bear.

When Dolly came home that night the coast

was clear, and the candles were finished and put away to harden in a freezing cold room; the kitchen was once more restored, and Nabby bustled about getting supper as if nothing had happened.

"I really feel sorry about poor little Dolly," said Mrs. Cushing to her husband.

"Do you think she cared much?" asked the Doctor, looking as if a new possibility had struck his mind.

"Yes, indeed, poor child, she went away crying; but what could I do about it? I couldn't stop to dress her."

"Wife, we must take her somewhere to make up for it," said the Doctor.

Just then the stage stopped at the door and a bundle from Boston was handed in. Dolly's tears were soon wiped and dried, and her mourning was turned into joy when a large jointed London doll emerged from the bundle, the Christmas gift of her grandmother in Boston.

Dolly's former darling was old and shabby, bnt this was of twice the size, and with cheeks exhibiting a state of the most florid health.

Besides this there was, as usual in Grandmamma's Christmas bundle, something for every member of the family; and so the evening went on festive wings.

Poor little Dolly! only that afternoon she had

watered with her tears the dismal long straight seam, which stretched on before her as life sometimes does to us, bare, disagreeable and cheerless. She had come home crying, little dreaming of the joy just approaching; but before bed-time no cricket in the hearth was cheerier or more noisy. She took the new dolly to bed with her, and could hardly sleep, for the excitement of her company.

Meanwhile, Hiel had brought the Doctor a message to the following effect:

" I was drivin' by Tim Hawkins's, and Mis' Hawkins she comes out and says they're goin' to hev an apple-cuttin' there to-morrow night, and she would like to hev you and Mis' Cushin' and all your folks come—Nabby and all."

The Doctor and his lady of course assented.

" Wal, then, Doctor—ef it's all one to you," continued Hiel, " I'd like to take ye over in my new double sleigh. I've jest got two new strings o' bells up from Boston, and I think we'll sort o' make the snow fly. S'pose there'd be no objections to takin' my mother 'long with ye?"

" Oh, Hiel, we shall be delighted to go in company with your mother, and we're ever so much obliged to you," said Mrs. Cushing.

" Wal, I'll be round by six o'clock," said Hiel.

" Then, wife," said the Doctor, " we'll take Dolly, and make up for the loss of her party."

CHAPTER XXII.

THE APPLE-BEE.

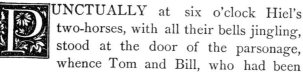UNCTUALLY at six o'clock Hiel's two-horses, with all their bells jingling, stood at the door of the parsonage, whence Tom and Bill, who had been waiting with caps and mittens on for the last half hour, burst forth with irrepressible shouts of welcome.

"Take care now, boys; don't haul them buffalo skins out on t' the snow," said Hiel. "Don't get things in a muss gen'ally; wait for your ma and the Doctor. Got to stow the grown folks in fust; boys kin hang on anywhere."

And so first came Mrs. Cushing and the Doctor, and were installed on the back seat, with Dolly in between. Then hot bricks were handed in to keep feet warm, and the buffalo robe was tucked down securely. Then Nabby took her seat by Hiel in front, and the sleigh drove round for old Mrs. Jones. The Doctor insisted on giving up his place to her and tucking her warmly under the buffalo robe, while he took the middle seat and acted as moderator between the boys, who

239

were in a wild state of hilarity. Spring, with explosive barks, raced first on this and then on that side of the sleigh as it flew swiftly over the smooth frozen road.

The stars blinked white and clear out of a deep blue sky, and the path wound up-hill among cedars and junipers and clumps of mountain laurel, on whose broad green leaves the tufts of snow lay like clusters of white roses. The keen clear air was full of stimulus and vigor ; and so Hiel's proposition to take the longest way met with enthusiastic welcome from all the party. Next to being a bird, and having wings, is the sensation of being borne over the snow by a pair of spirited horses who enjoy the race, apparently, as much as those they carry. Though Hiel contrived to make the ride about eight miles, it yet seemed but a short time before the party drove up to the great red farm-house, whose lighted windows sent streams of radiant welcome far out into the night.

The fire that illuminated the great kitchen of the farm-house was a splendid sight to behold. It is, alas, with us only a vision and memory of the past ; for who in our days can afford to keep up the great fire-place, where the back-logs were cut from the giants of the forest and the fore-stick was as much as a modern man could lift ? And then the glowing fire-palace built thereon! That architectural pile of split and seasoned wood, over which the flames leaped and danced and crackled like rejoicing genii—what a glory it was! The hearty, bright, warm hearth in those days stood instead of fine furniture and handsome pictures. The plainest room becomes beautiful and attractive by fire-light, and when men think of a country and home to be fought for and defended they think of the fireside.

Mr. Timothy Hawkins was a thrifty farmer and prided himself on always having the best, and the fire that was crackling and roaring up the chimney that night was, to use a hackneyed modern expression, a "work of art." The great oak back-log had required the strength of four men to heave it into its place; and above that lay another log scarcely less in size; while the fore-stick was no mean bough of the same tree. A bed of bright solid coals lay stretched beneath, and the lighter blaze of the wood above was constantly sending down contributions to this glowing reservoir.

Of course, on an occasion like this, the "best room" of the house was open, with a bright fire lighting up the tall brass andirons, and revealing the neatly-fitted striped carpet of domestic manufacture, and the braided rugs, immortal monuments of the never-tiring industry of the housewife. Here first the minister and his wife and Dolly were inducted with some ceremony, but all declared their immediate preference of the big kitchen, where the tubs of rosy apples and golden quinces were standing round, and young men, maids, and matrons were taking their places to assist in the apple-bee.

If the Doctor was a welcome guest in the stately circles of Poganuc Center, he was far more at home in these hearty rural gatherings. There was never the smallest room for jealousy, on the part of his plainer people, that he cared more for certain conventional classes of society than for them, because all instinctively felt that in heart he was one of themselves. Like many of the educated men of New England, he had been a farmer's boy in early days, and all his pleasantest early recollections were connected with that simple, wholesome, healthful, rural life. Like many of the New England clergy, too, he was still to some extent a practical farmer, finding respite from brain labor in wholesome out-door work. His best sermons were often thought out at the plow or in the corn-field, and his illustrations and enforcements of truth were those of a man acquainted with real life and able to interpret the significance of common things. His people felt a property in him as their ideal man— the man who every Sunday expressed for them, better than they could, the thoughts and inquiries and aspirations which rose dimly in their own minds.

"I could ha' said all that myself ef I'd only hed the eddication; he puts it so one can see it can't be no other way," was the comment once made on a sermon of the Doctor's by a rough but thoughtful listener; and the Doctor felt more pleased with such applause than even the more cultured approval of Judge Belcher.

In the wide, busy kitchen there was room enough for all sorts of goings on. The Doctor was soon comfortably seated, knee to knee, in a a corner with two or three controversial-looking old farmers, who were attacking some of the conclusions of his last Sunday's sermon. Of the two results, the Doctor always preferred a somewhat combative resistance to a sleepy assent to his preaching, and nothing delighted him more than a fair and square argumentative tilt, showing that the points he made had been taken.

But while the Doctor in his corner discussed theology, the young people around the tubs of apples were having the very best of times.

The apple, from the days of Mother Eve and the times of Paris and Helen, has been a fruit full of suggestion and omen in the meetings of young men and maidens; and it was not less fruitful this evening. Our friend Hiel came to the gathering with a full consciousness of a difficult and delicate

part to be sustained. It is easy to carry on four
or five distinct flirtations when one is a handsome
young stage-driver and the fair objects of attention live at convenient distances along the route.
But when Almiry Ann, and Lucindy Jane, and
Lucretia, and Nabby are all to be encountered
at one time, what is a discreet young man to
do?

Hiel had come to the scene with an armor of
proof in the shape of a new patent apple-peeler
and corer, warranted to take the skin from an
apple with a quickness and completeness hitherto
unimaginable. This immediately gave him a central position and drew an admiring throng about
him. The process of naming an apple for each
girl, and giving her the long ribbon of peel to
be thrown over her head and form fateful initial
letters on the floor, was one that was soon in
vigorous operation, with much shrieking and
laughing and opposing of claims among the young
men, all of whom were forward to claim their
own initials when the peeling was thrown by the
girl of their choice. And Hiel was loud in his
professions of jealousy when by this mode of
divination Almira Smith was claimed to be
secretly favoring Seth Parmelee, and Nabby's
apple-peeling thrown over her head formed a
cabalistic character which was vigorously contended for both by Jim Sawin and Ike Peters.

As the distinction between an I and a J is of a very shadowy nature, the question apparently was likely to remain an open one; and Hiel declared that it was plain that nobody cared for *him*, and that he was evidently destined to be an old bachelor.

It may be imagined that this sprightly circle of young folks were not the ones most particularly efficient in the supposed practical labors of the evening. They did, probably, the usual amount of work done by youths and maids together at sewing societies, church fairs and other like occasions, where by a figure of speech they are supposed to be assisting each other. The real work of the occasion was done by groups of matrons who sat with their bright tin pans in lap, soberly chatting and peeling and cutting, as they compared notes about pies and puddings and custards, and gave each other recipes for certain Eleusinian mysteries of domestic cookery.

Yet, let it not be supposed that all these women thought of nothing but cookery, for in the corner where the minister was talking were silent attentive listeners, thoughtful souls, who had pushed their chairs nearer, and who lost not a word of the discussion on higher themes. Never was there a freer rationalism than in the inquiries which the New England theology tol-

erated and encouraged at every fireside. The
only trouble about them was that they raised
awful questions to which there is no answer, and
when the Doctor supposed he had left a triumphant solution of a difficulty he had often left only
a rankling thorn of doubt.

A marked figure among the Doctor's circle
of listeners is Nabby's mother. A slight figure
in a dress of Quakerlike neatness, a thin old
delicate face, with its aureole of white hair and
its transparent cap-border—the expression of the
face a blending of thoughtful calmness and in-
vincible determination. Her still, patient blue
eyes looked as if they habitually saw beyond
things present to some far off future. She was,
in fact, one of those quiet, resolute women
whose power lay more in doing than in talking. She had passed, through the gate of silence
and self-abnegation, into that summer-land where
it is always peace, where the soul is never more
alone, because God is there.

Now, as she sits quietly by, not a word escapes
her of what her minister is saying; for though
at her husband's command she has left her
church, her heart is still immovably fixed in its
old home.

Her husband had stubbornly refused to join
the social circle, though cordially invited. However, he offered no word of comment or dissent

when his wife departed with all her sons to the gathering. With her boys, Mary Higgins was all-powerful. They obeyed the glance of her eye; they listened to her softest word as they never heeded the stormy imperiousness of their father.

She looks over with satisfaction to where her boys are joining with full heart in the mirth of the young people, and is happy in their happiness. The Doctor comes and sits beside her, and inquires after each one; and the measure of her content is full. She does not need to explain to him why she has left her church; she sees that he understands her position and her motives; but she tells him her heart and her hopes, her ambition for her darling son, Abner, who alone of all her boys has the passion for learning and aspires toward a college education; and the Doctor bids her send her boy to him and he will see what can be done to help him on his way. More talk they have, and more earnest, on things beyond the veil of earth—on the joy that underlies all the sorrows of this life and brightens the life beyond—and the Doctor feels that in the interview he has gained more than he has given.

Long before the evening was through, the task of apple-cutting was accomplished, the tubs and pans cleared away, and the company sat about the fire discussing the nuts, apples and cider which were passed around, reinforced by doughnuts and loaf-cake. Tales of forest life, of exploits in hunting and fishing, were recounted, and the Doctor figured successfully as a *raconteur*, for he was an enthusiast in forest lore, and had had his share of adventure.

In those days there was still a stirring background of wilderness life, of adventures with bears, panthers, and wild Indians, and of witches and wizards and ghostly visitors and haunted houses, to make a stimulating fireside literature; and the nine o'clock bell ringing loudly was the first break in the interest of the circle. All rose at once, and while the last greetings were exchanged, Hiel and the other young men brought their horses to the door, and the whole party were, in their several sleighs, soon flying homeward.

Our little Dolly had had an evening of unmixed bliss. Everybody had petted her, and talked to her, and been delighted with her sayings and doings, and she was carrying home a paper parcel of sweet things which good Mrs. Hawkins had forced into her hand at parting.

As to Hiel and Nabby, they were about on an even footing. If he had been devoted to Lucinda Jane Parsons she had distinguished Jim

Sawin by marks of evident attention, not forgetting at proper intervals to pay some regard to Ike Peters; so that, as she complacently said to herself, 'he didn't get ahead of *her.*'

Of course, on the way home, in the sleigh with Doctor and Mrs. Cushing, there were no advantages for a settling-up quarrel, but Nabby let fly many of those brisk little missiles of sarcasm and innuendo in which her sex have so decided a superiority over the other, and when arrived at the door of the house, announced peremptorily that she was 'going straight to bed and wasn't goin' to burn out candles for nobody *that* night!'

Hiel did not depart broken-hearted, however; and as he reviewed the field mentally, after his return home, congratulated himself that things were going on "'bout as well as they could be."

A misunderstanding to be made up, a quarrel to be settled, was, as he viewed it, a fair stock in trade for a month to come.

CHAPTER XXIII.

SEEKING A DIVINE IMPULSE.

IN the scenes which we have painted we have shown our Dr. Cushing mingling as man with men, living a free, natural, healthy human life. Yet underneath all this he bore always on his spirit a deeper and heavier responsibility.

The ideal of a New England minister's calling was not the mere keeping up of Sunday services, with two regular sermons, the pastoral offices of visiting the sick, performing marriages, and burying the dead. It was not merely the oversight of schools, and catechising of children, and bringing his people into a certain habitual outward routine of religion, though all these were included in it. But, deeper than all these, there was laid upon his soul the yearning desire to bring every one in his flock to a living, conscious union with God; to a life whose source and purposes were above this earth and tending heavenward. In whatever scene of social life he met his people his eye was ever upon them, studying their characters, marking their mental or moral progress, hoping and praying for this final result. Besides the stated services of Sunday, our good Doctor preached three or four evenings in a week in the small district school-houses of the outlying parishes, when the fervor of his zeal drew always a full audience to listen. More especially now, since the late political revolution had swept away the ancient prescriptive defenses of religion and morals, and thrown the whole field open to individual liberty, had the Doctor felt that the clergy must make up in moral influence what had passed away of legal restraints.

With all his soul he was seeking a revival of religion; a deep, pathetic earnestness made itself felt in his preaching and prayers, and the more spiritual of his auditors began to feel themselves sympathetically affected. Of course, all the church members in good standing professed to believe truths which made life a sublime reality, and religion the one absorbing aim. The New Testament gives a glorified ideal of a possible human life, but hard are his labors who tasks himself to keep that ideal uppermost among average human beings.

The coarse, the low, the mean, the vulgar, is ever thrusting itself before the higher and more delicate nature, and claiming, in virtue of its very brute strength, to be the true reality.

New England had been founded as a theocracy. It had come down to Dr. Cushing's time under laws and customs specially made and intended to form a Christian State, and yet how far it was below the teachings of the New Testament none realized so deeply as the minister himself.

He was the confidant of all the conflicts between different neighborhoods, of the small envies, jealousies and rivalries that agitated families and set one part of his parish against another. He was cognizant of all the little unworthy gossip, the low aims, the small ambitions of these would-be Christians, and sometimes his heart sank at the prospect.

Yet the preaching, the prayers, the intense earnestness of the New England religious life had sometimes their hour of being outwardly felt; the sacred altar-flame that was burning in secret in so many hearts threw its light into the darkness, and an upspringing of religious interest was the result.

The quarrel which had separated Zeph Higgins from the church had spread more or less unwholesome influence through the neighborhood, and it was only through some such divine impulse as he sought that the minister could hope to bring back a better state of things. In this labor of love he felt that he had a constant, powerful co-operative force in the silent, prayerful woman, who walked by Zeph's side as a guardian angel. Had it not been tor her peculiar talent for silence and peace the quarrel would have gone much farther and produced wider alienation; but there is nothing that so absolutely quenches the sparks ot contention as silence. Especially is this the case with the silence of a strong, determined nature, that utters itself only to God. For months Zeph had been conscious of a sort of invisible power about his wife—a power that controlled him in spite of himself. It was that mysterious atmosphere created by intense feeling without the help of words.

People often, in looking on this couple, shook their heads and said, "How *could* that woman ever have married that man?"

Such observers forget that the woman may see a side of the man's nature that they never see, and that often the chief reason why a man wins a woman's heart is that she fancies herself to have discerned in him that which no other could discern, an undiscovered realm peculiarly her own. The rough, combative, saturnine man known as Zeph Higgins had had his turn of being young, and his youth's blossoming-time of love, when he had set his heart on this Mary, then an orphan, alone in the world. Like many another woman, she was easily persuaded that the stormy, determined, impetuous passion thus

seeking her could take no denial; was of the
same nature with the kind of love she felt able
to give in return—love faithful, devoted, unseek-
ing of self, and asking only to bless.

But, in time, marriage brought its revelations,
and life lay before her a bare, cold, austere
reality, with the lover changed into the toiling
fellow-laborer or the exacting master.

A late discernment of spirit showed her that
she was married to a man whose love for her
was all demand, who asked everything from her
and had little power of giving in return; that,
while he needed her, and clung to her at times
with a sort of helpless reliance, he had no
power of understanding or sympathizing with
her higher nature, and that her life, in all that
she felt most deeply and keenly, must be a solitary one.

These hours of disillusion come to many,
and are often turning points in the soul's history. Rightly understood, they may prove the
seed-bed where plants of the higher life strike
deepest root. Mary Higgins was one of those
who found in her religion the strength of her
soul. The invisible Friend, whose knock is heard
in every heart-trial, entered in to dwell with
her, bringing the peace which the world cannot
give; and henceforth she was strong in spirit, and
her walk was in green pastures and by still waters.

They greatly mistake the New England religious development who suppose that it was a
mere culture of the head in dry metaphysical
doctrines. As in the rifts of the granite rocks
grow flowers of wonderful beauty and delicacy,
so in the secret recesses of Puritan life, by the
fireside of the farm-house, in the contemplative
silence of austere care and labor, grew up
religious experiences that brought a heavenly
brightness down into the poverty of common-
place existence.

The philosophic pen of President Edwards
has set before us one such inner record, in the
history of the wife whose saintly patience and
unworldly elevation enabled him to bear the
reverses which drove him from a comfortable
parish to encounter the privations of missionary
life among the Indians. And such experiences
were not uncommon among lowly natures, who
lacked the eloquence to set them forth in words.
They lightened the heart, they brightened the
eye, they made the atmosphere of the home
peaceful.

Such was the inner life of her we speak of.
At rest in herself, she asked nothing, yet was
willing to give everything to the husband and
children who were at once her world of duty
and of love. Year in and out, she kept step
in life with a beautiful exactness, so perfect

and complete in every ministry of the household that those she served forgot to thank her, as we forget to thank the daily Giver of air and sunshine. Zeph never had known anything at home but neatness, order, and symmetry, regular hours and perfect service.

His wife had always been on time, and on duty, and it seemed to him like one of the immutable laws of nature that she should do so. He was proud of her housekeeping, proud of her virtues, as something belonging to himself, and, though she had no direct power over his harsher moods of combativeness and self-will, she sometimes came to him as a still small voice after the earthquake and the tempest, and her words then had weight with him, precisely because they were few, and seldom spoken.

She had been silent all through the stormy quarrel that had rent him away from his church. Without an argument where argument would only strengthen opposition, she let his will have its way. She went with him on Sundays to the Episcopal Church, and sat there among her sons, a lowly and conscientious worshiper, carefully following a service which could not fail to bring voices of comfort and help to a devout soul like hers. Nevertheless, the service, to any one coming to it late in life and with no previous training, has its difficulties, which were to her embarrassing, and to him, in spite of his proud self-will, annoying. Zeph had the Spartan contempt for everything æsthetic, the scorn of beauty which characterized certain rough stages of New England life. He not only did not like symbolic forms, but he despised them as effeminate impertinences; and every turn and movement that he was compelled to make in his new ritualistic surroundings was aggravating to his temper. To bend the knee at the name of Jesus, to rise up reverently when the words of Jesus were about to be read in the Gospel of the day, were acts congenial to his wife as they were irksome to him; and, above all, the idea of ecclesiastical authority, whether exercised by rector, bishop or church, woke all the refractory nerves of opposition inherited from five generations of Puritans. So that Zeph was as little comfortable in his new position as his worst enemy could have desired. Nothing but the strength of his obstinate determination not to yield a point once taken kept him even outwardly steady. But to go back to his church, to confess himself in the wrong and make up his old quarrel with the Deacon, would be worse than to stay where he was.

The tenacity and devotion with which some hard natures will cleave to a quarrel which embitters their very life-blood is one of the strange

problems of our human nature. In the heredi-
tary form of family prayer that Zeph Higgins
used every day, there was the customary phrase
"We are miserable sinners;" and yet Zeph, like
many another man who repeats that form in the
general, would rather die than confess a fault in
any particular; and in this respect we must admit that he was not, after all, a very exceptional
character. How often in our experience do we
meet a man brave enough, when once fully committed, to turn a square corner and say "I was
wrong"? If only such have a stone to cast at
Zeph Higgins, the cairn will not be a very high
one.

Zeph never breathed an opposing word when
his wife, every Friday evening, lighted the lan-
tern, and with all her sons about her set off to
the evening prayer-meeting in the little red
school-house, though after his quarrel with the
Deacon he never went himself. Those weekly
meetings, when she heard her minister and joined
in the prayers and praises of her church, were
the brightest hours of her life, and her serene
radiant face, following his words with rapt attention, was a help and inspiration to her pastor.

"There is a revival begun over there," he
said to his wife as they were riding home from
one of his services. "It is begun in the heart
of that good woman. She has long been pray-

ing for a revival, and I am confident that *her* prayers will be answered."

They were answered, but in a way little dreamed of by any one

The prayers we offer for heavenly blessings often come up in our earthly soil as plants of bitter sorrow.

So it proved in this case.

CHAPTER XXIV.

"IN SUCH AN HOUR AS YE THINK NOT."

ONE morning in the latter part of spring Zeph Higgins received a shock which threw his whole soul into confusion.

His wife, on rising to go forth to her wonted morning cares, had fainted dead away and been found lying, apparently lifeless, on the bed, when her husband returned for his breakfast.

Instantly everything was in commotion. The nearest neighbor was sent for, and restoratives applied with such skill as domestic experience could suggest, and one of the boys dispatched in all haste for the doctor, with orders to bring Nabby at once to take her mother's place.

The fainting fit proved of short duration, but was followed by a violent chill and a rise of fever, and when the doctor arrived he reported a congestion of the lungs threatening the gravest results.

Forthwith the household was to be organized for sickness. A fire was kindled in the best bedroom and the patient laid there; Mis' Persis was

sent for and installed as nurse; Nabby became
housekeeper, and to superficial view the usual
order reigned. Zeph went forth to the labors
of the field, struggling with a sort of new
terror; there was an evil threatening his house,
against the very thought and suggestion of which
he fought with all his being. His wife *could* not,
should not, *ought* not to be sick,—and as to dying,
that was not to be thought of! What could he
do without her? What could any of them do
without her? During the morning's work that
was the problem that he kept turning and turning in his mind—what life would be without her.
Yet, when Abner, who was working beside him,
paused over his hoe and stood apparently lost
in thought, he snapped a harsh question at him
with a crack like the sound of a lash.

"What ye doin' there?"

Abner started, looked confused and resumed
his work, only saying, "I was thinking about
Mother."

"Nonsense! Don't make a fool of yourself.
Mother'll come all right."

"The doctor said"— said Abner.

"Don't tell me nothin' what the doctor said;
I don't want to hear on't," said Zeph, in a high
voice; and the two hoes worked on in silence
for a while, till finally Zeph broke out again.

"Wal! what did the doctor say? Out with

it; as good say it 's think it. What *did* the doctor say? Why do n't you speak?"

"He said she was a very sick woman," answered Abner.

"He's a fool. I do n't think nothin' o' that doctor's jedgment. I'll have Dr. Sampson over from East Poganuc. Your mother's got the best constitution of any woman in this neighborhood."

"Yes; but she has n't been well lately, and I've seen it," said Abner.

"That's all croakin'. Do n't believe a word on 't. Mother's been right along, stiddy as a clock; 'taint nothin' but one o' these 'ere pesky spring colds she's got. She'll be up and 'round by to-morrow or next day. I'll have another doctor, and I'll get her wine and bark, and strengthenin' things, and Nabby shall do the work, and she'll come all right enough."

"I'm sure I hope so," said Abner.

"Hope! what d'ye say *hope* for? I ain't a goin' to hope nothin' 'bout it. I *know* so; she's got to git well—ain't no two ways 'bout that."

Yet Zeph hurried home an hour before his usual time and met Nabby at the door.

"Wal, ain't your mother gettin' better?"

There were tears in Nabby's eyes as she answered,

"Oh, dear! she's been a raisin' blood. Doctor

says it's from her lungs. Mis' Persis says it's a bad sign. She's very weak—and she looks so pale!"

"They must give her strengthenin' things," said Zeph. "Do they?"

"They're givin' what the Doctor left. Her fever's beginnin' to rise now. Doctor says we mustn't talk to her, nor let her talk."

"Wal, I'm a goin' up to see her, anyhow. I guess I've got a right to speak to my own wife." And Zeph slipped off his heavy cowhide boots, and went softly up to the door of the room, and opened it without stopping to knock.

The blinds were shut; it seemed fearfully dark and quiet. His wife was lying with her eyes closed, looking white and still; but in the center of each pale cheek was the round, bright, burning spot of the rising hectic.

Mis' Persis was sitting by her with the authoritative air of a nurse who has taken full possession; come to stay and to reign. She was whisking the flies away from her patient with a feather fan, which she waved forbiddingly at Zeph as he approached.

"Mother," said he in an awe-struck tone, bending over his wife, "don't you know me?"

She opened her eyes; saw him; smiled and reached out her hand. It was thin and white, burning with the rising fever.

" Don't you feel a little better?" he asked. There was an imploring eagerness in his tone.

" Oh, yes; I'm better."

" You'll get well soon, won't you?"

" Oh, yes; I shall be well soon," she said, looking at him with that beautiful bright smile.

His heart sank as he looked. The smile was so strangely sweet—and all this quiet, this still- ness, this mystery! She was being separated from him by impalpable shadowy forces that could not be battled with or defied. In his heart a warning voice seemed to say that just so quietly she might fade from his sight—pass away, and be forever gone. The thought struck cold to his heart, and he uttered an involuntary groan.

His wife opened her eyes, moved slightly, and seemed as if she would speak, but Mis' Persis put her hand authoritatively over her mouth. " Don't you say a word," said she.

Then turning with concentrated energy on Zeph, she backed him out of the room and shut the door upon him and herself in the entry before she trusted herself to speak. When she did, it was as one having authority.

"Zephaniah Higgins," she said, " air you crazy? Do you want to kill your wife? Ef ye come round her that way and git her a-talkin' she'll bleed from her lungs agin, and that'll finish her. You've jest got to shet up and submit to the

Lord, Zephaniah Higgins, and that's what you hain't never done yit; you've got to know that the Lord is goin' to do *his* sovereign will and pleasure with your wife, and you've got to be still. That's all. You can't do nothin'. We shall all do the best we can ; but you've jest got to wait the Lord's time and pleasure."

So saying, she went back into the sick-room and closed the door, leaving Zeph standing desolate in the entry.

Zeph, like most church members of his day, had been trained in theology, and had often expressed his firm belief in what was in those days spoken of as the " doctrine of divine sovereignty."

A man's idea of his God is often a reflection of his own nature. The image of an absolute monarch, who could and would always do exactly as he pleased, giving no account to any one of his doings, suited Zeph perfectly as an abstract conception; but when this resistless awful Power was coming right across his path, the doctrine assumed quite another form.

The curt statement made by Mis' Persis had struck him with a sudden terror, as if a flash of lightning had revealed an abyss opening under his feet. That he was utterly helpless in his Sovereign's hands he saw plainly ; but his own will rose in rebellion—a rebellion useless and miserable.

His voice trembled that night as he went through the familiar words of the evening prayer; a rush of choking emotions almost stopped his utterance, and the old words, worn smooth with use, seemed to have no relation to the turbulent tempest of feeling that was raging in his heart.

After prayers he threw down the Bible with an impatient bang, bolted for his room and shut himself in alone.

"Poor Father! he takes it hard," said Nabby, wiping her eyes.

"He takes everything hard," said Abner. "I don't know how we'll get along with him, now Mother isn't round."

"Well, let's hope Mother's goin' to get well," said Nabby. "I can't—I ain't goin' to think anything else."

CHAPTER XXV.

T the Parsonage the illness in Zeph's household brought social revolution.

The whole burden of family ministration, which had rested on Nabby's young and comely shoulders, fell with a sudden weight upon those of Mrs. Cushing. This was all the more unfortunate because the same exigency absorbed the services of Mis' Persis, who otherwise might have been relied on to fill the gap.

But now was Dolly's hour for feeling her own importance and assuming womanly cares. She rushed to the front with enthusiasm and attacked every branch of domestic service, with a zeal not always according to knowledge but making her on the whole quite an efficient assistance. She washed and wiped dishes, and cleared, and cleaned, and dusted, and set away, as she had seen Nabby do; she propped herself on a stool at the ironing-table and plied the irons vigorously; and, resenting the suggestion that she

should confine herself to towels and napkins,
struck out boldly upon the boys' shirts and other
complicated tasks, burning her fingers and heat-
ing her face in the determination to show her
prowess and ability.

"Dolly is really quite a little woman," she
overheard her mother saying to her father; and
her bosom swelled with conscious pride and she
worked all the faster.

"Now, you boys must be very careful not to
make any more trouble than you can help," she
said with an air of dignity as Will and Bob
burst into the kitchen and surprised her at the
ironing-table. "Nabby is gone, and there is
nobody to do the work but me."

"Upon my word, Mrs. Puss!" said Will, stopping short and regarding the little figure with a
serio-comic air. "How long since you've been so
grand? How tall we're getting in our own eyes
—oh my!" and Will seized her off the ironing
stool and, perching her on his shoulder, danced
round the table with her in spite of her indignant
protests.

Dolly resented this invasion of her dignity
with all her little might, and the confusion called
her mother down out of the chamber where she
had been at work.

"Boys, I'm astonished at you," said she. Now
Mrs. Cushing had been "astonished" at these

same boys for about thirteen or fourteen years, so that the sensation could not be quite over-powering at this time.

" Well, Mother," said Will, with brisk assur-ance, setting Dolly down on her stool, " I was only giving Dolly a ride," and he looked up in her face with the confident smile that generally covered all his sins, and brought out an answer-ing smile on the face of his mother.

" Come now, boys," she said, " Nabby has gone home; you must be good, considerate children, make as little trouble as possible and be all the help you can."

"But, Mother, Dolly was taking such grown-up airs, as if she was our mother. I *had* just to give her a lesson, to show her who she was."

" Dolly is a good, helpful little girl, and I don't know what I should do without her," said Mrs. Cushing; "she does act like a grown-up woman, and I am glad of it."

Dolly's face flushed with delight; she felt that at last she had reached the summit of her am-bition: she was properly appreciated!

"And you boys," continued Mrs. Cushing, " must act like grown-up men, and be considerate and helpful."

"All right, Mother; only give the orders. Bob and I can make the fires, and bring in the wood, and fill the tea-kettle, and do lots of things." And, to do the boys justice, they did do their best to lighten the domestic labors of this interregnum.

The exigency would have been far less serious were it not that the minister's house in those days was a sort of authorized hotel, not only for the ministerial brotherhood but for all even remotely connected with the same, and all that miscellaneous drift-wood of hospitality that the eddies of life cast ashore. The minister's table was always a nicely-kept one; the Parsonage was a place where it was pleasant to abide; and so the guest-chamber of the Parsonage was seldom empty. In fact, this very week a certain Brother Waring, an ex-minister from East Poganuc, who wanted to consult the Poganuc Doctor, came, unannounced, with his wife and trunk, and they settled themselves comfortably down.

Such inflictions were in those days received in the literal spirit of the primitive command to "use hospitality without grudging;" but when a week had passed and news came that Mrs. Higgins was going down to the grave in quick consumption, and that Nabby would be wanted at home for an indefinite period, it became necessary to find some one to fill her place at the Parsonage, and Hiel Jones's mother accepted the position temporarily—considering her services in the minister's family as a sort of watch upon the walls of Zion. Not that she was by any means insensible to the opportunity of receiving worldly wages; but she wished it explicitly understood that she was not going out to service. She was "helpin' Mis' Cushing." The help, however, was greatly balanced in this case by certain attendant hindrances such as seem inseparable from the whole class of "lady helps."

Mrs. Jones had indeed a very satisfactory capability in all domestic processes; her bread was of the whitest and finest, her culinary skill above mediocrity, and she was an accomplished laundress. But so much were her spirits affected by the construction that might possibly be put on her position in the family that she required soothing attentions and expressions of satisfaction and confidence every hour of the day to keep her at all comfortable. She had stipulated expressly to be received at the family table, and, further than this, to be brought into the room and introduced to all callers; and, this being done, demeaned herself in a manner so generally abused and melancholy that poor Mrs. Cushing could not but feel that the burden which had been taken off from her muscles had been thrown with double weight upon her nerves.

After a call of any of the "town-hill" aristocracy, Mrs. Jones would be sure to be found weeping in secret places, because 'Mrs. Colonel Davenport had looked down on her,' or the

Governor's lady 'didn't speak to her,' and she 'should like to know what such proud folks was goin' to do when they got to heaven!' Then there was always an implication that if ministers only did their duty all these distinctions of rank would cease, and everybody be just as good as everybody else. The poor body had never even dreamed of a kingdom of heaven where the Highest was "as him that serveth;" and what with Mrs. Jones's moans, and her tears, and her frequent sick headaches, accompanied by abundant use of camphor, Mrs. Cushing, in some desperate moments, felt as if she would rather die doing her own work than wear herself out in the task of conciliating a substitute.

Then, though not a serious evil, it certainly was somewhat disagreeable to observe Mrs. Jones's statistical talents and habits of minute inspection, and to feel that she was taking notes which would put all the parish in possession of precise information as to the condition of Mrs. Cushing's tablecloths, towels, napkins, and all the minutiæ of her housekeeping arrangements. There is, of course, no sin or harm in such particularity; but almost every lady prefers the shades of poetic obscurity to soften the details of her domestic interior. In those days, when the minister was the central object of thought in the parish, it was specially undesirable that all this kind of information should be distributed, since there were many matrons who had opinions all ready made as to the proper manner in which a minister's wife should expend his salary and order his household.

It was therefore with genuine joy that, after a fortnight's care of this kind, a broad-faced, jolly African woman was welcomed by Mrs. Cushing to her kitchen in place of Mrs. Jones. Dinah was picked up in a distant parish, and entered upon her labors with an unctuous satisfaction and exuberance that was a positive relief after the recent tearful episode. It is true she was slow, and somewhat disorderly, but she was unfailingly good-natured, and had no dignity to be looked after; and so there was rest for a while in the Parsonage.

CHAPTER XXVI.

THE VICTORY.

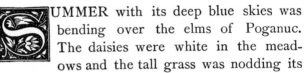UMMER with its deep blue skies was bending over the elms of Poganuc. The daisies were white in the meadows and the tall grass was nodding its feathery sprays of blossom. The windows of the farm houses stood open, with now and then a pillow or a bolster lounging out of them, airing in the sunshine. The hens stepped hither and thither with a drowsy continuous cackle of contentment as they sunned themselves in the warm embracing air.

In the great elm that overhung the roof of Zeph Higgins's farm house was a mixed babble and confusion of sweet bird voices. An oriole from her swinging nest caroled cheerfully, and bobolinks and robins replied, and the sounds blended pleasantly with the whisper and flutter of leaves, as soft summer breezes stirred them.

But over one room in that house rested the shadow of death; there, behind the closed blinds, in darkened stillness days passed by; and watchers came at night to tend and minister; and bottles accumulated on the table; and those who came entered softly and spoke with bated breath; and the doctor was a daily visitor; and it was known that the path of the quiet patient who lay there was steadily going down to the dark river.

Every one in the neighborhood knew it: for, in the first place, everybody in that vicinity, as a matter of course, knew all about everybody else: and then, besides that, Mrs. Higgins had been not only an inoffensive, but a much esteemed and valued neighbor. Her quiet step, her gentle voice, her skillful ministry had been always at hand where there had been sickness or pain to be relieved, and now that her time was come there was a universal sympathy. Nabby's shelves were crowded with delicacies made up and sent in by one or another good wife to tempt the failing appetite. In the laborious, simple life that they were living in those days, there was small physiological knowledge, and the leading idea in most minds in relation to the care of sickness was the importance of getting the patient to *eat;* for this end, dainties that might endanger the health of a well person were often sent in as a tribute to the sick. Then almost every house-mother had her own favorite specific, of sovereign virtue, which she prepared and sent in to increase the army of bottles which always gathered in a sick-room. Mis' Persis, however, while graciously accepting these tributes, had her own mental reservations, and often slyly made away with the medicine in a manner that satisfied the giver and did not harm the patient. Quite often, too, Hiel Jones, returning on his afternoon course, stopped his horses at the farm-house door and descended to hand in some offering of sympathy and good will from friends who lived miles away.

Hiel did not confine himself merely to transmitting the messages of neighbors, but interested himself personally in the work of consolation, going after Nabby wherever she might be found — at the spinning wheel, in the garret, or in the dairy below—and Nabby, in her first real trouble, was so accessible and so confiding that Hiel found voice to say unreproved what the brisk maiden might have flouted at in earlier days.

" I'm sure I don't know what we can do without Mother," Nabby said one day, her long eyelashes wet with tears. " Home won't ever seem home without her."

" Well," answered Hiel, " I know what *I* shall want you to do, Nabby: come to me; and you and I'll have a home all to ourselves."

And Nabby did not gainsay the word, but only laid her head on his shoulder and sobbed, and said he was a real true friend and she should never forget his kindness; and Hiel kissed and comforted her with all sorts of promises of future devotion. Truth to say, he found Nabby in tears and sorrow more attractive than when she sparkled in her gayest spirits.

But other influences emanated from that shadowy room—influences felt through all the little neighborhood. Puritan life had its current expressions significant of the intense earnestness of its faith in the invisible, and among these was the phrase " a triumphant death." There seemed to be in the calm and peaceful descent of this quiet spirit to the grave a peculiar and luminous clearness that fulfilled the meaning of that idea. The " peace that passeth understanding" brightened, in the sunset radiance, into "joy unspeakable and full of glory." Her decline, though rapid and steady, was painless: and it seemed to those who looked upon her and heard her words of joy and trust that the glory so visible to her must be real and near—as if in that sick-chamber a door had in very deed been opened into heaven.

When she became aware that the end was approaching she expressed a wish that her own minister should be sent for, and Dr. Cushing came. The family gathered in her room. She was propped up on pillows, her eyes shining and cheeks glowing with the hectic flush, and an indescribable brightness of expression in her face that seemed almost divine.

The Doctor read from Isaiah the exultant words: "Arise, shine, for thy light is come, and the glory of the Lord is risen upon thee. For behold, darkness shall cover the earth, and gross darkness the people, but the Lord shall arise on thee, and his glory shall be seen on thee. The sun shall no more be thy light by day, neither for brightness shall the moon give light to thee, but the Lord shall be unto thee an everlasting light, and thy God thy glory. Thy sun shall no more go down nor thy moon withdraw itself, for the Lord shall be thy everlasting light, and the days of thy mourning shall be ended." In the prayer that followed he offered thanks that God had given unto our sister the victory, and enabled her to rejoice in hope of the glory of God, while yet remaining with them as a witness of the faithfulness of the promise. He prayed that those dear to her might have grace given them to resign her wholly to the will of God and to rejoice with her in her great joy.

When they rose from prayer, Zeph, who had sat in gloomy silence through all, broke out:

"I can't—I *can't* give her up! It's hard on me. I *can't do it*, and I won't."

She turned her eyes on him, and a wonderful expression of love and sorrow and compassion came into her face. She took his hand, saying, with a gentle gravity and composure:

" I want to see my husband alone."

When all had left the room, he sunk down on his knees by the bed and hid his face. The bed was shaken by his convulsive sobbing. " My dear husband," she said, "you know I love you."

" Yes—yes, and you are the only one that does—the only one that can. I'm hard and cross, and bad as the devil. Nobody *could* love me but you; and I can't—I *won't*—give you up!"

"You needn't give me up; you must come with me. I want you to come where I am; I shall wait for you; you're an old man—it won't be long. But oh, do listen to me now. You can't come to heaven till you've put away all hard feeling out of your heart. You must make up that quarrel with the church. When you know you've been wrong, you must say so. I want you to promise this. Please do!"

There was silence ; and Zeph's form shook with the conflict of his feelings.

But the excitement and energy which had sustained the sick woman thus far had been too much for her; a blood vessel was suddenly ruptured, and her mouth filled with blood. She threw up her hands with a slight cry. Zeph rose and rushed to the door, calling the nurse.

It was evident that the end had come.

CHAPTER XXVII.

THE FUNERAL.

ON that morning, before Dr. Cushing had left the Parsonage to go to the bedside of his dying parishioner, Dolly, always sympathetic in all that absorbed her parents, had listened to the conversation and learned how full of peace and joy were those last days.

When her father was gone, Dolly took her little basket and went out into the adjoining meadow for wild strawberries. The afternoon was calm and lovely; small patches of white cloud were drifting through the intense blue sky, and little flutters of breeze shook the white hats of the daisies as she wandered hither and thither among them looking for the strawberries. Over on the tallest twig of the apple-tree in the corner of the lot a bobolink had seated himself, swinging and fluttering up and down, beating his black and white wings and singing a confused lingo about "sweetmeats and sweetmeats," and "cheer 'em and cheer 'em."

This bobolink was one of Dolly's special acquaintances. She had often seen him perched on this particular twig of the old apple-tree, doubtless because of a nest and family establishment that he had somewhere in that neighborhood, and she had learned to imitate his jargon as she crept about in the tall grass; and so they two sometimes kept up quite a lively conversation.

But this afternoon she was in no mood for chattering with the bobolink, for the strings of a higher nature than his had been set vibrating; she was in a sort of plaintive, dreamy revery— so sorry for poor Nabby, who was going to lose her mother, and so full of awe and wonder at the bright mystery now opening on the soul that was passing away.

Dolly had pondered that 'verse of her catechism which says that "the souls of believers at their death are made perfect in holiness, and do immediately pass into glory," and of what that unknown glory, that celestial splendor, could be she had many thoughts and wonderings.

She had devoured with earnest eyes Bunyan's vivid description of the triumphal ascent to the Celestial City through the River of Death, and sometimes at evening, when the west was piled with glorious clouds which the setting sun changed into battlements and towers of silvered gold, Dolly thought she could fancy it was something like that beautiful land. Now it made her heart thrill to think that one she had known only a little while before—a meek, quiet, patient, good woman—was just going to enter upon such glory and splendor, to wear those wonderful white robes and sing that wonderful song.

She filled her basket and then sat down to think about it. She lay back on the ground and looked up through the white daisies into the deep intense blue of the sky, wondering with a vague yearning, and wishing that she could go there too and see what it was all like. Just then, vibrating through the sunset air, came the plaintive stroke of the old Meeting-house bell. Dolly knew what that sound meant—a soul "made perfect in holiness" had passed into glory; and with a solemn awe she listened as stroke after stroke tolled out the years of that patient earth-life, now forever past.

It was a thrilling mystery to think of where *she* now was. *She* knew all now! she had seen! she had heard! she had entered in! Oh, what joy and wonder!

Dolly asked herself should she too ever be so happy—she, poor little Dolly; if she went up to the beautiful gate, would they let her in? Her father and mother would certainly go there; and they would surely want her too: couldn't she go in with them? So thought Dolly, vaguely dreaming, with the daisy-heads nodding over her, and the bobolink singing, and the bell tolling, while the sun was sinking in the west. At last she heard her father calling her at the fence, and made haste to take up her basket and run to him.

The day but one after this Dolly went with her father and mother to the funeral. Funerals in those old days had no soothing accessories. People had not then learned to fill their houses with flowers, and soften by every outward appliance the deadly severity of the hard central fact of utter separation.

The only leaves ever used about the dead in those days were the tansy and rosemary—bitter herbs of affliction. Every pleasant thing in the house was shrouded in white; every picture and looking-glass in its winding-sheet. The coffin was placed open in the best front room, and the mourners, enveloped in clouds of black crape, sat around. The house on this occasion was crowded; wagons came from far and near; the lower rooms were all open and filled, and Dr. Cushing's voice came faintly and plaintively through the hush of silence.

He spoke tenderly of the departed :—"We have seen our sister for many weeks waiting in the land of Beulah by the River of Death. Angels have been coming across to visit her; we have heard the flutter of their wings. We have seen her rejoicing in full assurance of hope, having laid down every earthly care; we have seen her going down the dark valley, leaning on the Beloved; and now that we have met to pay the last tribute to her memory, shall it be with tears alone? If we love our sister, shall we not rejoice because she has gone to the Father? She has gone where there is no more sickness, no more pain, no more sorrow, no more death, and she shall be ever with the Lord. Let us rejoice, then, and give thanks unto God, who hath given her the victory, and let us strive like her, by patient continuance in well-doing, to seek for glory and honor and immortality."

And then arose the solemn warble of the old funeral hymn:

> " Why should we mourn departing friends
> Or shake at death's alarms?
> 'Tis but the voice that Jesus sends
> To call them to his arms.
>
> " Why should we tremble to convey
> Their bodies to the tomb?
> There the dear form of Jesus lay,
> And scattered all the gloom.
>
> " Thence He arose, ascending high,
> And showed our feet the way;
> Up to the Lord we, too, shall fly
> At the great rising day.

"Then let the last loud trumpet sound,
And bid our kindred rise ;
Awake ! ye nations under ground ;
Ye saints ! ascend the skies !"

The old tune of " China," with its weird arrangement of parts, its mournful yet majestic
movement, was well fitted to express that mysterious defiance of earth's bitterest sorrow, that
solemn assurance of victory over life's deepest
anguish, which breathes in those words. It is
the major key invested with all the mournful
pathos of the minor, yet breathing a grand sustained undertone of triumph—fit voice of that
only religion which bids the human heart rejoice
in sorrow and glory in tribulation.

Then came the prayer, in which the feelings
of the good man, enkindled by sympathy and
faith, seemed to bear up sorrowing souls, as on
mighty wings, into the regions of eternal peace.

In a general way nothing can be more impressive, more pathetic and beautiful, than the Episcopal Church funeral service, but it had been one
of the last requests of the departed that her old
pastor should minister at her funeral; and there
are occasions when an affectionate and devout
man, penetrated with human sympathy, can utter
prayers such as no liturgy can equal. There are
prayers springing heavenward from devout hearts
that are as much superior to all written ones as

living, growing flowers out-bloom the dried treasures of the herbarium.   Not always, not by every one, come these inspirations; too often what is called extemporary prayer is but a form, differing from the liturgy of the church only in being poorer and colder.

But the prayer of Dr. Cushing melted and consoled; it was an uplift from the darkness of earthly sorrow into the grand certainties of the unseen; it had the undertone that can be given only by a faith to which the invisible is even more real than the things that are seen.

After the prayer one and another of the company passed through the room to take the last look at the dead.   Death had touched her gently. As often happens in the case of aged people, there had come back to her face something of the look of youth, something which told of a delicate, lily-like beauty which had long been faded.   There was too that mysterious smile, that expression of rapturous repose, which is the seal of heaven set on the earthly clay.   It seemed as if the softly-closed eyes must be gazing on some ineffable vision of bliss, as if, indeed, the beauty of the Lord her God was upon her.

Among the mourners at the head of the coffin sat Zeph Higgins, like some rugged gray rock— stony, calm and still.   He shed no tear, while his children wept and sobbed aloud; only when

the coffin-lid was put on a convulsive movement
passed across his face. But it was momentary,
and he took his place in the procession to walk
to the grave in grim calmness.

The graveyard was in a lovely spot on the
Poganuc River. No care in those days had been
bestowed to ornament or brighten these last
resting-places, but Nature had taken this in hand
kindly. The blue glitter of the river sparkled
here and there through a belt of pines and hemlocks on one side, and the silent mounds were
sheeted with daisies, brightened now and then
with golden buttercups, which bowed their fair
heads meekly as the funeral train passed over
them.

Arrived at the grave, there followed the usual
sounds, so terrible to the ear of mourners—the
setting down of the coffin, the bustle of preparation, the harsh grating of ropes as the precious
burden was lowered to its last resting-place.
And then, standing around the open grave, they
sang:

> " My flesh shall slumber in the ground
> Till the last trumpet's joyful sound.
> Then burst the chains, with sweet surprise,
> And in my Saviour's image rise."

Then rose the last words of prayer, in which
the whole finished service and all the survivors
were commended to God.

It was customary in those days for the head of

a family to return thanks at the grave to the friends and neighbors who had joined in the last tribute of respect to the departed. There was a moment's pause, and every eye turned on Zeph Higgins. He made a movement and stretched out his hands as if to speak; but his voice failed him, and he stopped. His stern features were convulsed with the vain effort to master his feeling.

Dr. Cushing saw his emotion and said, " In behalf of our brother I return thanks to all the friends who have given us their support and sympathy on this occasion. Let us all pray that the peace of God may rest upon this afflicted family." The gathered friends now turned from the grave and dispersed homeward.

With the instinct of a true soul-physician, who divines mental states at a glance, Dr. Cushing forbore to address even a word to Zeph Higgins; he left him to the inward ministration of a higher Power.

But such tact and reticence belong only to more instructed natures. There are never wanting well-meaning souls who, with the very best intentions, take hold on the sensitive nerves of sorrow with a coarse hand.

Deacon Peaslee was inwardly shocked to see that no special attempt had been made to "improve the dispensation" to Zeph's spiritual state, and therefore felt called on to essay his skill.

"Well, my friend," he said, coming up to him, "I trust this affliction may be sanctified to you."

Zeph glared on him with an impatient movement and turned to walk away; the Deacon, however, followed assiduously by his side, going on with his exhortation.

"You know it's no use contendin' with the Lord."

"Well, who's ben a contendin' with the Lord?" exclaimed Zeph, "I haint."

The tone and manner were not hopeful, but the Deacon persevered.

"We must jest let the Lord do what he will with us and ours."

"I *hev* let him—how was I goin' to help it?"

"We mustn't murmur," continued the Deacon in a feebler voice, as he saw that his exhortation was not hopefully received.

"Who's ben a murmurin? *I* haint!"

"Then you feel resigned, don't you?"

"I can't help myself. I've got to make the best on 't," said Zeph, trying to out-walk him.

"But you know ——"

"Let me alone, can't ye?" cried Zeph in a voice of thunder; and the Deacon, scared and subdued, dropped behind, murmuring, "Drefful state o' mind! poor critter, so unreconciled!— really awful!"

CHAPTER XXVIII.

DOLLY AT THE WICKET GATE.

HE next Sunday rose calm and quiet over the hills of Poganuc.

There was something almost preternatural in the sense of stillness and utter repose which the Sabbath day used to bring with it in those early times. The absolute rest from every earthly employment, the withholding even of conversation from temporal things, marked it off from all other days. To the truly devout the effect was something the same as if the time had been spent in heaven.

On this particular dewy, fresh summer morning it seemed as if Nature herself were hushing her breath to hear the music of a higher sphere. Dolly stood at her open window looking out on the wooded hills opposite, feathered with their varied green, on the waving meadows with their buttercups and daisies, on the old apple tree in the corner of the lot where the bobolink was tilting up and down, chattering and singing with all his might. She was thinking of what she had heard her father saying to her mother at break-

290

fast: how the sickness and death of one good woman had been blessed to all that neighborhood, and how a revival of religion was undoubtedly begun there.

All this made Dolly very serious. She thought a great deal about heaven, and perfectly longed to be quite sure she ever should get there. She often had wished that there were such a thing in reality as a Wicket Gate, and an old Interpreter's house, and a Palace Beautiful, for then she would set right off on her pilgrimage at once, and in time get to the Celestial City. But how to get this spiritual, intangible preparation she knew not. To-day she knew was a sacramental Sunday, and she should see all the good people taking that sacrificial bread and wine, but she should be left out.

And how to get in! There were no Sunday-schools in those days, no hymns or teachings specially adapted to the child; and Dolly remembered to have heard serious elderly people tell of how they were brought "under conviction" and suffered for days and weeks before the strange secret of mercy was revealed to them, and she wondered how she ever should get this conviction of sin. Poor Dolly had often tried to feel very solemn and sad and gloomy, and to think herself a dreadful sinner, but had never succeeded. She was so young and so healthy—the blood raced and tingled so in her young veins; and if she was pensive and sad a little while, yet, the first she knew, she would find herself racing after Spring, or calling to her brothers, or jumping up and down with her skipping rope, and feeling full as airy and gay as the bobolink across in the meadow. This morning she was trying her best to feel her sins and count them up; but the birds and the daisies and the flowers were a sad interruption, and she went to meeting quite dissatisfied.

When she saw the white simple table and the shining cups and snowy bread of the Communion she inly thought that the service could have nothing for her—it would be all for those grown-up, initiated Christians. Nevertheless, when her father began to speak she was drawn to listen to him by a sort of pathetic earnestness in his voice.

The Doctor was feeling very earnestly and deeply, and he had chosen a theme to awaken responsive feeling in his church. His text was the declaration of Jesus: "I call you not servants, but friends;" and his subject was Jesus as the soul-friend offered to every human being. Forgetting his doctrinal subtleties, he spoke with all the simplicity and tenderness of a rich nature concerning the faithful, generous, tender love of Christ, how he cared for the soul's wants, how he was patient with its errors, how he gently led it along the way of right, how he was always with it, teaching its ignorance, guiding its wanderings, comforting its sorrows, with a love unwearied by faults, unchilled by ingratitude, till he brought it through the darkness of earth to the perfection of heaven.

Real, deep, earnest feeling inclines to simplicity of language, and the Doctor spoke in words that even a child could understand. Dolly sat absorbed, her large blue eyes gathering tears as she listened; and when the Doctor said, " Come, then, and trust your soul to this faithful Friend," Dolly's little heart throbbed " I will." And she did. For a moment she was discouraged by the thought that she had not had any conviction of sin; but like a flash came the thought that Jesus could give her that as well as anything else, and that she could trust him for the whole. And so her little earnest child-soul went out to the wonderful Friend. She sat through the sacramental service that followed, with swelling heart and tearful eyes, and walked home filled with a new joy. She went up to her father's study and fell into his arms, saying, " Father, I have given myself to Jesus, and he has taken me."

The Doctor held her silently to his heart a moment, and his tears dropped on her head.

" Is it so?" he said. " Then has a new flower blossomed in the Kingdom this day."

CHAPTER XXIX.

THE CONFLICT.

THERE is one class of luckless mortals in this world of ours whose sorrows, though often more real than those of other people, never bring them any sympathy It is those in whom suffering excites an irritating conflict, which makes them intolerable to themselves and others. The more they suffer the more severe, biting and bitter become their words and actions. The very sympathy they long for, by a strange contrariness of nature they throw back on their friends as an injury. Nobody knows where to have them, or how to handle them, and when everybody steers away from them they are inwardly desolate at their loneliness.

After the funeral train had borne away from the old brown farm-house the silent form of her who was its peace, its light, its comfort, Zeph Higgins wandered like an unquiet spirit from room to room, feeling every silent memorial of her who was no longer there as a stab in the yet throbbing wound. Unlovely people are often cursed with an intense desire to be loved, and the more unlovely they grow the more intense becomes this desire. His love for his wife had been unusually strong in the sense of what is often called loving—that is, he needed her, depended on her, and could not do without her. He was always sure that she loved him; he was always sure of her patient ear to whatever he wished to say, of her wish to do to her utmost whatever he wanted her to do. Then he was not without a certain sense of the beauty and purity of her character, and had a sort of almost superstitious confidence in her prayers and goodness, like what the Italian peasant has in his patron saint. He felt a sort of helplessness and terror at the idea of facing life without her. Besides this, he was tormented by a secret unacknowledged sense of his own unloveliness: he was angry with himself—cursed himself, called himself hard names; and he who quarrels with himself has this disadvantage, that his adversary is inseparably his companion—lies down and rises, eats, drinks and sleeps with him.

What intensified this conflict was the remembrance of his wife's dying words, enjoining on him the relinquishment of the bitter quarrel which had alienated him from his church and his neighbors, and placed her in so false a position.

He knew that he was in the wrong; he knew that she was in the right, and that those words spoken on her death-bed were God's voice to him. But every nerve and fiber in him seemed to rebel and resist; he would not humble himself; he would not confess; he would not take a step toward reconciliation.

The storm that was raging within expressed itself outwardly in an impatience and irritability which tried his children to the utmost. Poor Nabby did her best to assume in the family all her mother's cares, but was met at every turn by vexatious fault-finding.

"There now!" he said, coming out one morning, "where's my stockings? Everything's being neglected—not a pair to put on!"

"Oh yes, Father, I sat up and mended your stockings last night before I went to bed. I didn't go into your room, because I was afraid of waking you; but here they are on my basket."

"Give 'em here, then!" said Zeph harshly. "I want my things where I know where they are. Your mother always had everything ready so I didn't have to ask for it."

"Well, I never shall be as good as Mother if I try till I'm gray," said Nabby, impatiently.

"Don't you be snapping back at me," said Zeph. "But it's jest so everywhere. Nobody won't care for me now. I don't expect it."

"Well, Father, I'm sure I try the best I can, and you keep scolding me all the time It's discouraging."

" Oh, yes, I'm a devil, I suppose. Everybody's right but me. Well, I shall be out of the way one of these days, and nobody'll care. There ain't a critter in the world cares whether I'm alive or dead—not even my own children."

The sparks flashed through the tears in Nabby's eyes. She was cut to the soul by the cruel injustice of these words, and a hot and hasty answer rose to her lips, but was smothered in her throat.

Nabby had become one of the converts of the recently-commenced revival of religion, and had begun to lay the discipline of the Christian life on her temper and her tongue, and found it hard work. As yet she had only attained so far as repression and indignant silence, while the battle raged tempestuously within.

" I'd like just to go off and leave things to take care of themselves," she said to herself, "and then he'd see whether I don't do anything. Try, and try, and try, and not a word said—nothing but scold, scold, scold. It's too bad! Flesh and blood can't stand everything! Mother did, but I ain't Mother. I must try to be like her, though; but it's dreadful hard with Father. How did Mother ever keep so quiet and always be so pleasant? She used—to pray a great deal. Well, I must pray."

Yet if Nabby could have looked in at that moment and seen the misery in her father's soul her indignation would have been lost in pity; for Zeph in his heart knew that Nabby was a good, warm-hearted girl, honestly trying her very best to make her mother's place good. He knew it, and when he was alone and quiet he felt it so that tears came to his eyes; and yet this miserable, irritable demon that possessed him had led him to say these cruel words to her—words that he cursed himself for saying, the hour after. But on this day the internal conflict was raging stronger than ever. The revival in the neighborhood was making itself felt and talked about, and the Friday evening prayer-meeting in the schoolhouse was at hand.

Zeph was debating with himself whether he would take the first step towards reconciliation with his church by going to it. His wife's dying words haunted him, and he thought he might at least go as far as this in the right direction; but the mere suggestion of the first step roused a perfect whirlwind of opposition within him.

Certain moral conditions are alike in all minds, and this stern, gnarled, grizzled old New England farmer had times when he felt exactly as Milton has described a lost archangel as feeling:

> " Oh, then, at last relent !   Is there no place
> Left for repentance ? none for pardon left ?
> None left but by submission, and that word
> Disdain forbids me and my dread of shame."

It is curious that men are not generally ashamed of any form of anger, wrath or malice; but of the first step towards a nobler nature—the confession of a wrong—they are ashamed.

Never had Zeph been more intolerable and unreasonable to his sons in the field-work than on this day.

He was too thoroughly knit up in the habits of a Puritan education to use any form of profane language, but no man knew so well how to produce the startling effect of an oath without swearing; and this day he drove about the field in such a stormy manner that his sons, accustomed as they were to his manners, were alarmed.

" Tell you what," said one of the boys to Abner, "the old man's awful cranky to-day. Reely seems as if he was a little bit sprung.   I don't know but he's going crazy !"

CHAPTER XXX.

THE CRISIS.

T was a warm, soft June evening. The rosy tints of sunset were just merging into brown shadows over the landscape, the frogs peeped and gurgled in the marshes, and the whippoorwills were beginning to answer each other from the thick recesses of the trees, when the old ministerial chaise of Dr. Cushing might have been seen wending its way up the stony road to the North Poganuc school-house.

The Doctor and his wife were talking confidentially, and Dolly, seated between them, entered with eager sympathy into all they were saying.

They were very happy, with a simple, honest, earnest happiness, for they hoped that the great object of his life and labors was now about to be accomplished, that the power of a Divine Influence was descending to elevate and purify and lift the souls of his people to God.

"My dear, I no longer doubt," he said. "The presence of the Lord is evidently with us. If

300

only the church will fully awaken to their duty we may hope for a harvest now."

"What a pity,' answered Mrs. Cushing, "that that old standing quarrel of Zeph Higgins and the church cannot be made up: his children are all deeply interested in religion, but he stands right in their way."

"Why don't you talk to him, Papa?" asked Dolly.

"Nobody can speak to him but God, my child; there's a man that nobody knows how to approach."

Dolly reflected silently on this for some minutes, and then said,

"Papa, do you suppose Christ loves him? Did he die for him?"

"Yes, my child. Christ loved and died for all."

"Do you think *he believes* that?" asked Dolly, earnestly.

"I'm afraid he doesn't think much about it," answered her father.

Here they came in sight of the little school-house. It seemed already crowded. Wagons were tied along the road, and people were standing around the doors and windows.

The Doctor and Mrs. Cushing made their way through the crowd to the seat behind the little pine table. He saw in the throng not merely the ordinary attendance at prayer-meetings, but many of the careless and idle class who seldom were seen inside a church. There were the unusual faces of Abe Bowles and Liph Kingsley and Mark Merrill, who had left the seductions of Glazier's bar-room to come over and see whether there was really any revival at North Poganuc, and not perhaps without a secret internal suggestion that to be converted would be the very best thing for them temporally as well as spiritually. Liph's wife, a poor, discouraged, forsaken-looking woman, had persuaded him to come over with her, and sat there praying, as wives of drunken men often pray, for some help from above to save him, and her, and her children.

Nothing could be rougher and more rustic than the old school-house,—its walls hung with cobwebs; its rude slab benches and desks hacked by many a schoolboy's knife; the plain, ink-stained pine table before the minister, with its two tallow candles, whose dim rays scarcely gave light enough to read the hymns. There was nothing outward to express the real greatness of what was there in reality.

There are surroundings that make us realize objectively the grandeur of the human soul, and the sublimity of the possibilities which Christianity opens to it. The dim cathedral, whose arches seem to ascend to the skies, from whose distant recesses pictured forms of saints and angels look down, whose far-reaching aisles thrill with chants solemn and triumphant, while clouds of incense arise at the holy altar, and white-robed priests and kneeling throngs prostrate themselves before the Invisible Majesty—all this "pomp of dreadful sacrifice" enkindles the ideas of the infinite and the eternal, and makes us feel how great, how glorious, how mysterious and awful is the destiny of man.

But the New England Puritan had put the ocean between him and all such scenic presentations of the religious life. He had renounced every sensuous aid, and tasked himself to bring their souls to face the solemn questions of existence and destiny in their simple nakedness, without drapery or accessories; there were times in the life of an earnest minister when these truths were made so intensely vivid and effective as to overbear all outward disadvantages of surrounding; and to-night the old school-house, though rude and coarse as the manger of Bethlehem, like that seemed hallowed by the presence of a God.

From the moment the Doctor entered he was conscious of a present Power. There was a hush, a stillness, and the words of his prayer seemed to go out into an atmosphere thrilling with emotion and when he rose to speak he saw the countenances of his parishioners with that change upon them which comes from the waking up of the soul to higher things. Hard, weather-beaten faces were enkindled and eager; every eye was fixed upon him; every word he spoke seemed to excite a responsive emotion.

The Doctor read from the Old Testament the story of Achan. He told how the host of the Lord had been turned back because there was one in the camp who had secreted in his tent an accursed thing. He asked, "Can it be now, and here, among us who profess to be Christians, that we are secreting in our hearts some accursed thing that prevents the good Spirit of the Lord from working among us? Is it our pride? Is it our covetousness? Is it our hard feeling against a brother? Is there anything that we know to be wrong that we refuse to make right—anything that we know belongs to God that we are withholding? If we Christians lived as high as we ought, if we lived up to our professions, would there be any sinners unconverted? Let us beware how we stand in the way. If the salt have lost its savor wherewith shall it be salted? Oh, my brethren, let us not hinder the work of God. I look around on this circle and I miss the face of a sister that was always here to help us with her prayers; now she is with the general assembly and church of the first-born, whose names are written in heaven, with the spirits of the just made perfect. But her soul will rejoice with the angels of God if she looks down and sees us all coming up to where we ought to be. God grant that her prayers may be fulfilled in us. Let us examine ourselves, brethren; let us cast out the stumbling-block, that the way of the Lord may be prepared."

The words, simple in themselves, became powerful by the atmosphere of deep feeling into which they were uttered; there were those solemn pauses, that breathless stillness, those repressed breathings, that magnetic sympathy that unites souls under the power of one overshadowing conviction.

When the Doctor sat down suddenly there was a slight movement, and from a dark back seat rose the gaunt form of Zeph Higgins. He was deathly pale, and his form trembled with emotion. Every eye was fixed upon him, and people drew in their breath, with involuntary surprise and suspense.

"Wal, I must speak," he said. "*I'm* a stumbling-block. I've allers ben one. I hain't never ben a Christian—that's jest the truth on't. I never hed oughter 'a' ben in the church. I've ben all wrong—*wrong*—WRONG! I knew I was wrong, but I wouldn't give up. It's ben jest my awful WILL. I've set up my will agin God Almighty. I've set it agin my neighbors—agin the minister and agin the church. And now the Lord's come out agin me; he's struck me down. I know he's got a right—he can do what he pleases—but I ain't resigned—not a grain. I submit 'cause I can't help myself; but my heart's hard and wicked. I expect my day of grace is over. I ain't a Christian, and I can't be, and I shall go to hell at last, and sarve me right!"

And Zeph sat down, grim and stony, and the neighbors looked one on another in a sort of consternation. There was a terrible earnestness in those words that seemed to appall every one and prevent any from uttering the ordinary commonplaces of religious exhortation. For a few moments the circle was silent as the grave, when Dr. Cushing said, "Brethren, let us pray;" and in his prayer he seemed to rise above earth and draw his whole flock, with all their sins and needs and wants, into the presence-chamber of heaven.

He prayed that the light of heaven might shine into the darkened spirit of their brother; that he might give himself up utterly to the will of God; that we might *all* do it, that we might become as little children in the kingdom of heaven. With the wise tact which distinguished his ministry he closed the meeting immediately after the prayer with one or two serious words of exhortation.

He feared lest what had been gained in impression might be talked away did he hold the meeting open to the well-meant, sincere but uninstructed efforts of the brethren to meet a case like that which had been laid open before them.

After the service was over and the throng slowly dispersed, Zeph remained in his place, rigid and still. One or two approached to speak to him; there was in fact a tide of genuine sympathy and brotherly feeling that longed to express itself. He might have been caught up in this powerful current and borne into a haven of peace, had he been one to trust himself to the help of others: but he looked neither to the right nor to the left; his eyes were fixed on the floor; his brown, bony hands held his old straw hat in a crushing grasp; his whole attitude and aspect were repelling and stern to such a degree that none dared address him.

The crowd slowly passed on and out. Zeph sat alone, as he thought; but the minister, his wife, and little Dolly had remained at the upper end of the room. Suddenly, as if sent by an irresistible impulse, Dolly stepped rapidly down the room and with eager gaze laid her pretty little timid hand upon his shoulder, crying, in a voice tremulous at once with fear and with intensity, " O, *why* do you say that you can not be a Christian? Don't you know that Christ loves you?"

Christ loves you! The words thrilled through his soul with a strange, new power; he opened his eyes and looked astonished into the little earnest, pleading face.

"Christ loves you," she repeated; "oh, do believe it!"

"Loves *me!*" he said, slowly. "Why should he?"

"But he does; he loves us all. He died for us. He died for you. Oh, believe it. He'll help you; he'll make you feel right. Only trust him. Please say you will!"

Zeph looked at the little face earnestly, in a softened, wondering way. A tear slowly stole down his hard cheek.

"Thank'e, dear child," he said.

"You will believe it?"

"I'll try."

"You will trust Him?"

Zeph paused a moment, then rose up with a new and different expression in his face, and said, in a subdued and earnest voice, "*I will.*"

"Amen!" said the Doctor, who stood listening; and he silently grasped the old man's hand.

CHAPTER XXXI.

THE JOY OF HARVEST.

HEN Zeph turned from the little red school-house to go home, after the prayer-meeting, he felt that peace which comes after a great interior crisis has passed. He had, for the first time in his life, yielded his will, absolutely and thoroughly. He had humbled himself, in a public confession of wrong-doing, before all his neighbors, before those whom he had felt to be enemies. He had taken the step convulsively, unwillingly, constrained thereto by a mighty overmastering power which wrought within him. He had submitted, without love, to the simple, stern voice of conscience and authority— the submission of a subject to a monarch, not that of a child to a father. Just then and there, when he felt himself crushed, lonely, humbled and despairing, the touch of that child's hand on his, the pleading childish face, the gentle childish voice, had spoken to him of the love of Christ.

There are hard, sinful, unlovely souls, who yet long to be loved, who sigh in their dark prison for that tenderness, that devotion, of which they are consciously unworthy. Love might redeem them; but who can love them? There is a fable of a prince doomed by a cruel enchanter to wear a loathsome, bestial form till some fair woman should redeem him by the transforming kiss of love. The fable is a parable of the experience of many a lost human soul.

The religion of Christ owes its peculiar power to its revealing a Divine Lover, the one Only Fair, the altogether Beautiful, who can love the unlovely back into perfectness. The love of Christ has been the dissolving power that has broken the spells and enchantments which held human souls in bondage and has given them power to rise to the beauty and freedom of the sons of God.

As Zeph walked homeward through the lonely stillness of the night, again and again the words thrilled through his soul, "*Christ loves you*"—and such tears as he had never wept before stood in his eyes, as he said wonderingly, "Me—me? Oh, is it possible? Can it be?" And Christ *died for him!* He had known it all these years, and never thanked him, never loved him. The rush of new emotion overpowered him; he entered his house, walked straight to the great family Bible that lay on a stand in the best room of the house; it was the very room where the

THE JOY OF HARVEST.

311

coffin of his wife had stood, where he had sat,
stony and despairing, during the funeral exercises. Zeph opened the Bible at random and
began turning the leaves, and his eye fell on
the words, " *Unto Him that* LOVED US and washed
us from our sins in his own blood and hath made
us to our God kings and priests, to him be
glory!" His heart responded with a strange
new joy—a thrill of hope that he, too, might
be washed from his sins.

Who can read the awful mysteries of a single
soul? We see human beings, hard, harsh, earthly, and apparently without an aspiration for any
thing high and holy; but let us never say that
there is not far down in the depths of any soul
a smothered aspiration, a dumb repressed desire
to be something higher and purer, to attain the
perfectness to which God calls it.

Zeph felt at this moment that Christ who so
loved him could purify him, could take away
his pride and willfulness; and he fell on his knees,
praying without words, but in the spirit of him
of old who cried, " If thou wilt, thou canst make
me clean." As he prayed a great peace fell upon
him, a rest and stillness of soul such as he had
never felt before; he lay down that night and
slept the sleep of a little child.

But when next day Zeph Higgins walked into
Deacon Dickenson's store and of his own accord

offered to put back the water-pipes that led to his spring, and to pay whatever cost and damage the Deacon might have incurred in throwing them out, there was then no manner of doubt that some higher power than that of man had been at work in his soul.

The Deacon himself was confounded, almost appalled, by the change that had come over his neighbor. He had been saying all his life that the grace of God could do anything and convert anybody, but he never expected to see a conversion like that. Instead of grasping eagerly at the offered reparation he felt a strange emotion within himself, a sort of choking in his throat; and now that he saw the brother with whom he had contended yielding so unconditionally, he began to question himself whether he had no wrong to confess on his side.

"Wal now, I expect I've ben wrong too," he said. "We ain't perfectly sanctified, none on us, and I know I hain't done quite right, and I hain't felt right. I got my back up, and I've said things I hadn't orter. Wal, we'll shake hands on't. I ain't perticklar 'bout them water-pipes now; we'll let bygones be bygones."

But Zeph had set his heart on reparation, and here was a place where the pertinacity of his nature had an honest mission; so by help of reference to one or two neighbors as umpires the whole loss was finally made good and the long-standing controversy with all its ill-feeling settled and buried forever out of sight.

The news of this wonderful change spread through all the town.

" I declar' for 't," said Liph Kingsley to Bill Larkins, " this ere's a reel thing, and it's time for me to be a-thinkin'. I've got a soul to be saved too, and I mean to quit drinkin' and seek the Lord."

" Poh!" said Bill, "you may say so and think so; but you won't do it. You'll never hold out."

" Don't you believe that; Christ will help you," said Zeph Higgins, who had overheard the conversation. " He has helped me; he can help you. He can save to the uttermost. There 'tis in the Bible—try it. We'll all stand by ye."

A voice like this from old Zeph Higgins impressed the neighbors as being almost as much of a miracle as if one of the gray cliffs of old Bluff Head had spoken; but his heart was full, and he was ready everywhere to testify to the love that had redeemed him. No exhorter in the weekly prayer-meeting spoke words of such power as he.

The few weeks that followed were marked in the history of the town. Everywhere the meetings for preaching and prayer were crowded. Glazier's bar-room was shut up for want of

custom, and Glazier himself renounced the sell-
ing of liquor and became one of the converts
of the revival. For a while every member of
the church in the village acted as if the wonderful things which they all professed to believe
were really true—as if there were an immortality of glory to be gained or lost by our life
here.

The distinction between the aristocracy of
Town Hill and the outlying democracy of the
farming people was merged for the time in a
sense of a higher and holier union. Colonel
Davenport and Judge Gridley were seen with
Doctor Cushing in the school-houses of the outlying districts, exhorting and praying, and the
farmers from the distant hills crowded in to the
Town Hill meetings. For some weeks the multi-
tude was of one heart and one soul. A loftier
and mightier influence overshadowed them, under whose power all meaner differences sunk
out of sight. Such seasons as these are like
warm showers that open leaf and flower, buds
that have been long forming. Everybody in
those days that attended Christian services had
more or less of good purposes, of indefinite
aspiration to be better, of intentions that related
to some future. The revival brought these out
in the form of an immediate practical purpose,
a definite, actual beginning in a new life.

"Well, Mother," said Hiel Jones, "I've made up my mind to be a Christian. I've counted the cost, and it will cost something, too. I was a-goin' up to Vermont to trade for a team o' hosses, and I can't make the trade I should 'a' made. If I jine the church I mean to live up to 't, and I can't make them sharp trades fellers do. I could beat 'em all out o' their boots," said Hiel, with rather a regretful twinkle in his eye, "but I won't; I'll do the right thing, ef I don't make so much by 't. Nabby and me's both agreed 'bout that. We shall jine the church together, and be married as soon as I get back from Vermont. I allers meant to git religion sometime—but somehow, lately, I've felt that *now* is the time."

On one bright autumnal Sabbath of that season the broad aisle of the old meeting-house was filled with candidates solemnly confessing their faith and purpose to lead the Christian life. There, standing side by side, were all ages, from the child to the gray-haired man. There stood Dolly with her two brothers, her heart thrilling with the sense of the holy rite in which she was joining; there Nabby and Hiel side by side; there all the sons of Zeph Higgins; and there, lastly, the gray, worn form of old Zeph himself. Although enrolled as a church member he had asked to stand up and take anew those vows of which he had never before understood the meaning or felt the spirit, and thus reunite himself with the church from which he had separated.

That day was a recompense to Dr. Cushing for many anxieties and sorrows. He now saw fully that though the old *régime* of New England had forever passed, yet there was still in the hands of her ministry that mighty power which Paul was not ashamed to carry to Rome as adequate to regenerate a world. He saw that intemperance and profanity and immorality could be subdued by the power of religious motive working in the hearts of individual men, taking away the desire to do evil, and that the Gospel of Christ is to-day, as it was of old and ever will be, the power of God and the wisdom of God to the salvation of every one that believeth.

CHAPTER XXXII.

IX years step softly, with invisible foot-steps, over the plain of life, bearing us on with an insensible progress. Six years of winter snows and spring thaws, of early blue-birds and pink May-flower buds under leafy banks, of anemone, crowfoot and violet in the fields, of apple-blossoms in the or-chards, and new green leaves in the forest; six years of dark-green summers in the rustling woods, of fire-lilies in the meadow-lots and scar-let lobelias by the water-brooks, of roses and lilies and tall phloxes in the gardens; six years of autumnal golden rod and aster, of dropping nuts and rainbow-tinted forests, of ripened grain and gathered corn, of harvest home and thanksgiv-ing proclamation and gathering of families about the home table to consider the loving-kindness of the Lord:—by such easy stages, such comings and goings, is our mortal pilgrimage marked off. When the golden rod and aster have bloomed for us sixty or seventy seasons, then we are near

317

the banks of the final river, we are coming to the time of leaving the flowers of earth for the flowers of Paradise.

The six years in Poganuc had brought their changes, not in external nature, for that remained quiet and beautiful as ever; the same wooded hills, with their sylvan shades and hidden treasures of fruits and flowers, the same brown, sparkling river, where pickerel and perch darted to and fro, and trout lurked in cool, shadowy hollows: but the old graveyard bore an added stone or two; mounds wet with bitter tears had grown green and flowery, and peaceable fruits of right-eousness had sprung up from harvests sown there in weeping.

As to the Parsonage and its inmates, six years had added a little sprinkle of silver to the Doctor's head, and a little new learning of the loving-kindness of the Lord to his heart. The fruits of the revival gathered into his church were as satisfactory as ordinary human weakness allows. The Doctor was even more firmly seated in the respect and affection of his parish than in old days, when the ministry was encompassed by the dignities and protections of law. Poganuc was a town where an almshouse was almost a super-fluous institution, and almsgiving made difficult by the fact that there were no poor people; for since the shutting of Glazier's bar-room, and the reformation of a few noted drunkards, there was scarce anybody not in the way of earning a decent and comfortable living. Such were our New England villages in the days when its people were of our own blood and race, and the pauper population of Europe had not as yet been landed upon our shores.

As to the characters of our little story, they, also, had moved on a stage in the journey of life.

Hiel Jones had become a thriving man; had bought a share in the stage-line that ran through the town, and owned the finest team of horses in the region. He and our friend Nabby were an edifying matrimonial firm, comfortably established at housekeeping in a trim, well-kept dwelling not far from the Parsonage, with lilac bushes over the front windows, and red peonies and yellow lilies in the door-yard.

A sturdy youngster of three years, who toddled about, upsetting matters generally, formed a large part of the end and aim of Nabby's existence. To say the truth, this young, bright-eyed, curly-pated slip of humanity was enough to furnish work for a dozen women, for he did mischief with a rapidity, ingenuity and energy that was perfectly astonishing. What small efforts the parents made in the direction of family government were utterly frustrated by the fond and idolatrous devotion of old Zeph, who evidently considered it the special privilege of a grandfather to spoil the rising generation.

Scarce a day passed that Zeph was not at the house, his pockets stuffed with apples, cakes or nuts for the boy. The old man bowed his grey head to the yoke of youth; he meekly did the infant's will; he was the boy's horse and cantered for him, he was a cock and crowed for him, he was a hen and cackled for him; he sacrificed dignity and consistency at those baby feet as the wise men of old laid down their gold, frankincense and myrrh.

Zeph had ripened like a winter apple. The hard, snarly astringency of his character had grown sweet and mild. His was a nature capable of a great and lasting change. When he surrendered his will to his God he surrendered once for all, and so the peace of God fell upon him and kept him. He was a consistent and most useful member of the church, and began to be known in the neighborhood by the semi-affectionate title of "Uncle Zeph," a sort of brevet rank which indicated a certain general confidence in his disposition to neighborly good offices.

The darling wish of his wife's heart had been accomplished in his eldest son Abner. He had sent him through college, sparing no labor and no hardship in himself to give the youth every

advantage. And Abner had proved an able
scholar; his college career had been even brilliant, and he had now returned to his native
place to pursue his theological studies under Dr.
Cushing.

It will be well remembered that in the former
days of New England there were no specific
theological institutions, but the young candidate
for the ministry took his studies under the care
of some pastor, who directed his preparatory
course and initiated him into his labors, and this
course of things once established was often continued from choice even after institutions of
learning were founded.

The Doctor had an almost paternal pride in
this offshoot that had grown up in his parish; he
taught him with enthusiasm; he took him in his
old chaise to the associations and ministerial
meetings about the State, and gave him every
opportunity to exercise his gifts in speaking.

It was a proud Sunday for old Zeph when his
boy preached his first sermon in the Doctor's
pulpit. The audience in the Poganuc meeting-
house, as we have indicated, was no mean one in
point of education, ability and culture, but every
one saw and commended the dignity and self-
possession with which the young candidate filled
the situation, and there was a universal approval
of his discourse from even the most critical of

his audience. But the face and figure of old Zeph as he leaned forward in his seat, following with breathless eagerness every word; his blue eyes kindling, the hard lines of his face relaxing into an expression of absorbed and breathless interest, would have made a study for a painter. Every point in the argument, the flash of every illustration, the response to every emotion, could have been read in his face as in an open book; and when after service the young candidate received the commendations of Colonel Davenport, Judge Belcher and Judge Gridley, Zeph's cup of happiness was full. Abner was an exception to the saying that a prophet hath no honor in his own country, for both classes in society vied with each other to do him honor. The farming population liked him for being one of themselves, the expression of what they felt themselves capable of being and becoming under similar advantages; while the more cultivated class really appreciated the talent and energy of the young man, and were the better pleased with it as having arisen in their own town.

So his course was all fair, until, as Fate would have it, he asked one thing too much of her— and thereof came a heart-ache.

Our little friend Dolly had shot up into a blooming and beautiful maiden—warm-hearted, enthusiastic, and whole-souled as we have seen her in her childhood. She was in everything the sympathetic response that parents love to find in a child. She entered with her whole soul into all her father's feelings and plans, and had felt and expressed such an honest, frank, and hearty friendliness to the young man, such an interest in his success, that the poor youth was beguiled into asking more than Dolly could give.

Modern young ladies, who count and catalogue their victims, would doubtless be amused to have seen Dolly's dismay at her unexpected and undesired conquest. The recoil was so positive and decided as to be beyond question, but Dolly's conscience was sorely distressed. She had meant nothing but the ordinary loving-kindness of a good and generous heart. She had wanted to make him happy, and had ended in making him apparently quite miserable; and Dolly was sincerely afflicted about it. What had she done? Had she done wrong? She never thought—never dreamed—of such a thing.

The fact was that Dolly had those large, earnest, persuasive eyes that are very dangerous, and sometimes seem to say more than they mean; and she had quick, sudden smiles, and twinkling dimples, and artless, honest ways, and so much general good-will and kindliness, that one might pardonably be deceived by her.

It is said that there are lakes whose waters
are so perfectly transparent that they deceive
the eye as to their depth. Dolly was like these
crystal waters; with all her impulsive frankness
there was a deep world within—penetralia that
had been yet uninvaded—and there she kept
her ideals. The man she *might* love was one of
the immortals, not in the least like a blushing
young theological student in a black coat, with
a hymn-book under his arm. Precisely what
he was she had never been near enough to see;
but she knew in a minute what he was *not*.
Therefore she had said "No" with a resolute energy that admitted of no hope, and yet with a
distress and self-reproach that was quite genuine.

This was Dolly's first real trouble.

CHAPTER XXXIII.

THE DOCTOR MAKES A DISCOVERY.

"WHY, wife," said the Doctor, pushing up his spectacles on his forehead and looking up from his completed sermon, "our little Dolly is really a grown-up young lady."

"Well, of course, what should she be?" rejoined Mrs. Cushing, with the decisive air which becomes the feminine partner on strictly feminine ground; "she's taller than I am, and she's a handsome girl, too."

"I don't think," said the Doctor, assuming a confidential tone, "that there's a girl in our meeting-house to be compared with her—there really is not."

"There is no great fault to be found with Dolly's looks," said Mrs. Cushing as she turned a stocking she had been darning. "Dolly always was pretty."

"Well, what do you think Higgins has been saying to me about her?" continued the Doctor.

"Some nonsense I suppose," said Mrs. Cush-

ing, "something he might as well have left un-
said, for all the good it will do."

"Now, my dear, Higgins is going to make
one of the leading ministers of the State. He
has a bright, strong, clear mind; he is a thor-
ough scholar and a fine speaker, and I have had
a letter from the church in Northboro' about
settling him there."

"All very well. I'm sure I'm glad of it, with
all my heart," said Mrs. Cushing; "but if he has
any thoughts of our Dolly the sooner he gets
them out of his head the better for him. Dolly
has felt very kindly to him, as she does to everybody; she has been interested in him simply
and only as a friend; but any suggestion of particular interest on his part would exceedingly
annoy her. You had better speak very decidedly
to him to this effect. You can say that I understand my daughter's mind, and that it will be
very painful to her to have anything more said
on the subject."

"Well, really, I'm sorry for Higgins," said
the Doctor, "he's such a good-hearted worthy
fellow, and I believe he's very deep in love."

"Perhaps," said Mrs. Cushing decidedly; "but
our Dolly can't marry every good-hearted worthy
fellow that comes in her way, if he is in love;
and I'm sure I'm in no hurry to give her away,—
she is the light and music of the house."

"So she is," said the Doctor; "I couldn't do without her; but I pity poor Higgins."

"Oh, you may spare your pity; he won't break his heart. Never fear. Men never die of that. There'll be girls enough in his parish, and he'll be married six months after he gets a place—ministers always are."

The Doctor made some few corrections in the end of his sermon without contradicting this unceremonious statement of his wife's.

"But," continued Mrs. Cushing, "the thing is a trial to Dolly; I think it would be quite as well if she should n't see any more of him for the present, and I have just got a letter from Deborah urging me to let her go to Boston for a visit. Mother says she is getting old, now, and that she shall never see Dolly unless the child comes to her. Here's the letter."

The Doctor took it, and we, looking over his shoulder, see the large, sharp, decided style of writing characteristic of Miss Debby Kittery:

"DEAR SISTER:

"Mother wants you to let us have Dolly to make a good, long visit. Mother is getting old now, and says she hasn't seen Dolly since she has grown up, and thinks we old folks will be the better for a little young life about us. You remember Cousin Jane Davies, that married John Dunbar and went over to England? Well, brother Israel Kittery has taken a fancy to her youngest son during his late visit to England, and is going to bring him to Boston and turn over his business to him and make him his heir. We are expecting them now by every ship, and have invited them to spend the Christmas Holidays with us. I understand this young Alfred Dunbar is a bright, quick-witted young slip, just graduated from Oxford, and one that finds favor in all eyes. He will help make it lively for Dolly, and if anything should come of it why it will be all the better. So if you will have Dolly ready to leave I will be up to visit you in December and bring her home with me. Mother sends a great deal of love,—her rheumatism has gone to her right arm now, which is about all the variety she is treated to; but she is always serene, as usual, and sends no end of loving messages.

"Your affectionate sister,
"Debby.

"P. S.—Don't worry about Dolly's dress. My pink brocade will cut over for her, and it is nearly as good as new. I'll bring it when I come."

On reading this letter the Doctor fell into a deep muse.

"Well, what do you think?" asked his wife.

"What? Who? I?" said the Doctor, with difficulty collecting himself from his reverie.

"Yes, *you,*" answered his wife incisively, with just the kind of a tone to wake one out of a nap.

The fact was that the good Doctor had a little habit of departing unceremoniously into some celestial region of thought in the midst of conversation, and the notion of Dolly's going to Boston had aroused quite a train of ideas connected with certain doctrinal discussions now going on there in relation to the Socinian controversy, so that his wife's voice came to him from afar off, as one hears in a dream.

To Mrs. Cushing, whose specific work lay here, and now, in the matters of this present world, this little peculiarity of her husband was at times a trifle annoying; so she added, " I do wish you would attend to what we were talking about. Don't you think it would be just the best thing in the world for Dolly to make this visit to Boston?"

" Oh, certainly I do—by all means," he said eagerly, with the air of a man just waked up who wants to show he hasn't been asleep. "Yes, Dolly had better go."

The Doctor mused for another moment, and then added, in a sort of soliloquy: " Boston is a city of sacred associations; it is consecrated ground; the graves of our fathers, of the saints and the martyrs are there. I shall like little Dolly to visit them."

This was not precisely the point of view in which the visit was contemplated in the mind of his wife; but the enthusiasm was a sincere one. Boston, to all New England, was the Jerusalem— the city of sacred and religious memories; they took pleasure in her stones, and favored the dust thereof.

CHAPTER XXXIV

"ONLY think, Hiel, Dolly's going to Boston," said Nabby, when they had seated themselves cosily with the infant Zeph between them at the supper-table.

"Ye don't say so, now!" said Hiel, with the proper expression of surprise.

"Yes, Miss Kittery, her Boston aunt, 's comin' next week, and I'm goin' in to do up her muslins for her. Yes, Dolly 's goin' to Boston."

"Good!" said Hiel. "I hope she'll get a husband there."

"That's jest all you men think of," answered Nabby. "Dolly ain't one o' that kind; she ain't. lookin' out for fellers—though there's plenty would be glad to have her. She ain't one o' that sort."

"Wal," said Hiel, "she's too good-lookin' to be let alone; she'll *hev* to hev somebody."

"Oh, there's enough after her," said Nabby. "There was that Virginny fellow in Judge Belcher's office, waitin' on her home from meet-

330

in' and wanting to be her beau; she wouldn't have nothin' to say to him. Then there was that academy teacher used to walk home with her, and carry her books and go with her to singin' school; but Dolly didn't want him. And there's Abner—he jest worships the ground she treads on; and she's jest good friends with him. She's good friends with 'em all round, but come to case in hand she don't want any on 'em."

"Wal, there ain't nothin' but the doctrine o' 'lection for such gals," said Hiel. "When the one they's decreed to marry comes along then their time comes, jest as yours and mine did, Nabby."

The conversation was here interrupted by the infant Zeph, who had improved the absorbed state of his parents' minds to carry out a plan he had been some time meditating, of upsetting the molasses pitcher. This was done with such celerity that before they could make a move both his fat hands were triumphantly spatted into the brown river, and he gave a crow of victory.

"There! clean table-cloth this very night! Did I ever see such a young un!" cried Nabby, as she caught him away from the table. "Father thinks he's perfection. I should like to have him have the care of him once," she added, bustling and brightening and laughing as she scolded; while Hiel, making perfectly sincere but ill-directed efforts to scrape up the molasses with a spoon, succeeded only in distributing it pretty equally over the table-cloth.

"Well, now, if there ain't a pair of you!" said Nabby, when she returned to the table. "If that ain't jest like a man!"

"Wal, what would ye hev me—like a girl, or a dog, or what?" asked Hiel, as he stood, with his hands in his pockets, surveying the scene. "I did my best; but I ain't used to managing molasses and babies together; that's a fact."

"It's lucky Mother went out to tea," said Nabby, as she whisked off the tablecloth, wiped the table, re-clothed it with a clean one, and laid the supper dishes back in a twinkling. "Now, Hiel, we'll try again; and be sure and put things where *he* can't get 'em; he does beat all for mischief!"

And the infant phenomenon, who had had his face washed and his apron changed in the interim, looked up confidingly in the face of each parent and crowed out a confident laugh.

"Don't let's tell Mother," said Nabby; "she's always sayin' we don't govern him; and I'm sure she spoils him more than we do; but if she'd been here she wouldn't get over it for a week."

In fact, the presence of Mother Jones in the family was the only drawback on Nabby's domestic felicity, that good lady's virtues, as we have

seen, being much on the plaintive and elegiac
order. There is indeed a class of elderly relatives
who, their work in life being now over, have
nothing to do but sit and pass criticisms on the
manner in which younger pilgrims are bearing
the heat and burden of the day.

Although Nabby was confessedly one of the
most capable and energetic of housekeepers,
though everything in her domestic domains
fairly shone and glittered with neatness, though
her cake always rose even, though her bread
was the whitest, her biscuits the lightest, and
her doughnuts absolute perfection, yet Mother
Jones generally sat mildly swaying in her
rocking-chair and declaring herself consumed
by care—and averring that she had "*everything*
on her mind." " I don't *do* much, but I feel
the care of everything," the old lady would remark in a quavering voice. "Young folks is so
thoughtless; they don't feel care as I do."

At first Nabby was a little provoked at this
state of things; but Hiel only laughed it off.

" Oh, let her talk. Mother *likes* to feel care;
she wants something to worry about; she'd be
as forlorn as a hen without a nest-egg if she
hadn't that. Don't you trouble your head,
Nabby, so long as I don't."

For all that, Nabby congratulated herself that
Mother Jones was not at the tea-table, for the

nurture and admonition of young Zeph was
one of her most fruitful and weighty sources
of care. She was always declaring that "children was sech an awful responsibility, that she
wondered that folks dared to git married!" She
laid down precepts, strict even to ferocity, as
to the early necessity of prompt, energetic
government, and of breaking children's wills;
and then gave master Zeph everything he cried
for, and indulged all his whims with the most
abject and prostrate submission.

"I know I hadn't orter," she would say, when
confronted with this patent inconsistency; "but
then I ain't his mother. I ain't got the responsibility; and the fact is he *will* have things and
I *hev* to let him. His parents orter break his
will, but they don't; it's a great care to me;"
and Mother Jones would end by giving him the
sugar-bowl to play with, and except for the immutable laws of nature she would doubtless
have given him the moon or any part of the
solar system that he had cried for.

Nevertheless, let it not be surmised that Mother
Jones, notwithstanding the minor key in which
she habitually indulged, was in the least unhappy.
There are natures to whom the "unleavened bread
and bitter herbs" of life are an agreeable and
strengthening diet, and Mother Jones took real
pleasure in everything that went to show that

this earth was a vale of tears. A funeral was
a most enlivening topic for her, and she never
allowed an opportunity to pass within riding distance without giving it her presence, and dwelling on all the details of the state of the " corpse"
and the minutiæ of the laying-out for weeks
after, so that her presence at table between her
blooming son and daughter answered all the
moral purposes of the skeleton which the ancient
Egyptians kept at their feasts. Mother Jones
also, in a literal sense, "*enjoyed* poor health" and
petted her coughs and her rheumatisms, and was
particularly discomposed with any attempt to
show her that she was getting better. Yet when
strictly questioned the good lady always admitted, though with a mournful shake of the
head, that she had everything to be thankful
for—that Hiel was a good son, and Nabby was
a good daughter, and 'since Hiel had jined the
church and hed prayers in his family, she hoped
he'd hold on to the end—though it really worried
her to see how light and triflin' he was.'

In fact Hiel, though maintaining on the whole
a fairly consistent walk and profession, was undoubtedly a very gleesome church member, and
about as near Mother Jones's idea of a saint as
a bobolink on a clover-top. There was a worldly
twinkle in his eye, and the lines of his cheery
face grew rather broad than long, and his moth-

er's most lugubrious suggestions would often set
him off in a story that would upset even the old
lady's gravity and bring upon her pangs of re-
pentance. For the spiritual danger and besetting
sin that Mother Jones more especially guarded
against was an "undue levity;" but when she
remembered that Dr. Cushing himself and all
the neighboring clergymen, on an occasion of a
"ministers' meeting" when she had been helping
in the family, had vied with each other in telling
good stories, and shaken their sides with roars
of heartiest laughter, she was somewhat consoled
about Hiel. She confessed it was a mystery to
her, however, ' how folks could hev the heart
to be a-laughin' and tellin' stories in sich a dying
world.'

CHAPTER XXXV.

MISS DEBBY ARRIVES.

"TO Dr. Cushing's, Ma'am?"

This question met the ear of Miss Debby Kittery just after she had deposited her umbrella, with a smart, decisive thump, by her side, and settled herself and her bandbox on the back seat of the creaking, tetering old stage on the way to Poganuc.

Miss Debby opened her eyes, surveyed the questioner with a well-bred stare, and answered, with a definite air, " Yes, sir."

"Oh, yis; thought so," said Hiel Jones. " Miss Kittery, I s'pose; the Doctor's folks is expecting ye. Folks all well in Boston, I s'pose?"

Miss Debby in her heart thought Hiel Jones very presuming and familiar, and endeavored to convey by her behavior and manner that such was her opinion; but the effort was quite a vain one, for the remotest conception of any such possibility in his case was so far from Hiel's mind that there was not there even the material to make it of. The look of dignified astonishment with which the good lady responded to his ques-

337

tion as to the "folks in Boston" was wholly lost on him.

The first sentence in the Declaration of Independence, that all men are "created equal," had so far become incarnate in Hiel that he never yet had seen the human being whom he did not feel competent to address on equal terms, and, when exalted to his high seat on the stage-box, could not look down upon with a species of patronage. Even the *haute noblesse* of Poganuc allowed Hiel's familiarities and laughed at his jokes ; he was one of their institutions; and what was tolerance and acceptance on the part of the aristocracy became adulation on the part of those nearer his own rank of life. And so when Miss Debby Kittery made him short answers and turned away her head, Hiel merely commented to himself, "Don't seem sociable. Poor old lady! Tired, I s'pose; roads *is* pretty rough," and, gathering up his reins, dashed off cheerfully.

At the first stage where he stopped to change horses he deemed it his duty to cheer the loneliness of the old lady by a little more conversation, and so, after offering to bring her a tumbler of water, he resumed:

"Ye hain't ben to Poganuc very often;—hain't seen Dolly since she's grow'd up?"

"Are you speaking of *Miss* Cushing, sir?" asked Miss Debby, in tones of pointed rebuke.

"Yis—wal, we allers call her 'Dolly' t' our house," said Hiel. "We've know'd her sence she was *that* high. My wife used to live to the Doctor's—she thinks all the world of Dolly."

Miss Debby thought of the verse in the Church Catechism in which the catechumen defines it as his duty to 'order himself lowly and reverently to all his betters.' Evidently Hiel had never heard of this precept. Perhaps if he had, the inquiry as to who *are* betters, as presented to a shrewd and thoughtful mind, might lead to embarrassing results.

So, as he seemed an utterly hopeless case, and as after all he appeared so bright, and anxious to oblige, Miss Debby surrendered at discretion, and during the last half of the way found herself laughing heartily at some of Hiel's stories and feeling some interest in the general summary of Poganuc news which he threw in gratis.

"Yis, the Doctor's folks is all well. Doctor's had lots o' things sent in this year, Thanksgiving time—turkeys and chickens and eggs and lard—every kind o' thing you can think of. Everybody sent—Town Hill folks, and folks out seven miles round. Everybody likes the Doctor; they'd orter, too! There ain't sech a minister nowhere. The way he explains the doctrines and sets 'em home—I tell ye, there ain't no mistake about *him;* he's a hull team, now, and our folks knows it. Orter 'a' ben here a week ago, when the Doctor had his wood-spell. Tell ye, if the sleds didn't come in! Why, his back-yard's a perfect mountain o' wood—best sort too, good oak and hickory, makes good solid coals—enough to keep him a year round. Wal, folks *orter* do it. He's faithful to them, they'd orter do wal by him."

"Isn't there an Episcopal church in your town?" asked Miss Debby."

"Oh, yis, there is a little church. Squire Lewis he started it 'bout six years ago, and there was consid'able many signed off to it. But our Poganuc folks somehow ain't made for 'Piscopals. A 'Piscopal church in our town is jest like a hill o' potatoes planted under a big apple-tree; the tree got a-growin' afore they did, and don't give 'em no chance. There was my wife's father, he signed off, 'cause of a quarrel he hed with his own church; but he's come back agin, and so have all his boys, and Nabby, and jined the Doctor's church. Fact is, our folks sort o' hanker arter the old meetin'-house."

"Who is the rector of the Episcopal church?"

"Oh, that's Sim Coan; nice, lively young feller, Sim is; but can't hold a candle to the Doctor. Sim he ain't 'fraid of nobody—preaches up the 'Piscopal doctrine sharp, and stands up for his side; and he's all the feasts and fasts and anthems and things at his tongue's end; and his folks likes him fust rate. But the church don't grow much; jest holds its own, that's all."

These varied items of intelligence, temporal and spiritual, were poured into Miss Debby's ear at sundry periods when horses were to be changed, or in the interval of waiting for dinner at the sleepy old country tavern; and by the time she reached Poganuc she had conceived quite a friendly feeling towards Hiel and unbent her frigid demeanor to that degree that Hiel told Nabby "the old lady reely got quite sociable and warmed up afore she got there."

Dolly was somewhat puzzled and almost alarmed on her first introduction to her aunt, who took possession of her in a summary manner, turning her round and surveying her, and giving her opinion of her with a distinct and decisive air, as if the damsel had been an article of purchase sent home to be looked over.

"So this is my niece Dolly, is it?" she said. "Well, come kiss your old aunty; upon my word, you are taller than your mother." Then holding her at arm's length and surveying her, with her head on one side, she added, "There's a good deal of Pierrepont blood in her, sister; that is the Pierrepont nose—I should know it anywhere. Her way of carrying herself is Pierrepont. Blushing!" she added, as Dolly grew crimson under this survey; "that's a family trick. I remember when I went to dancing school the first time, my face was crimson as my sash. She'll get the better of that as she gets older, as I have. Sit down by your aunty, child. I think I shall like you. That's right, sit up straight and hold your shoulders back— the girls of this generation are getting round-shouldered."

Though Dolly was somewhat confused and confounded by this abrupt mode of procedure, yet there was after all something quaint and original about her aunt's manner that amused her, and an honest sincerity in her face that won her regard. Miss Debby was one of those human beings who carry with them the apology for their own existence. It took but a glance to see that she was one of those forces of nature which move always in straight lines and which must be turned out for if one wishes to avoid a collision. All Miss Debby's opinions had been made up, catalogued, and arranged, at a very early period of life, and she had no thought of change. She moved in a region of certainties, and always took her own opinions for granted with a calm supremacy altogether above reason. Yet there was all the while about her a twinkle of humorous consciousness, a vein of original drollery, which gave piquancy to the brusqueness of her manner and prevented people from taking offence.

So this first evening Dolly stared, laughed, blushed, wondered, had half a mind to be provoked, but ended in a hearty liking of her new relative and most agreeable anticipations of her Boston visit.

CHAPTER XXXVI.

PREPARATIONS FOR SEEING LIFE.

HE getting ready for Dolly's journey began to be the engrossing topic of the little household.

Miss Simpkins, the Poganuc dress-maker, had a permanent corner in the sitting-room, and discoursed *ex cathedra* on "piping-cord" and "ruffling cut on the bias," and Dolly and Mrs. Cushing and Miss Deborah obediently ran up breadths, hemmed, stitched and gathered at her word of command.

The general course of society in those days as to dress and outward adornment did not run with the unchecked and impetuous current that it now does. The matter of dress has become in our day a yoke and a burden, and many a good house-mother is having the springs of her exist-ence sapped by responsibilities connected with pinking and frilling and quilling, and an army of devouring cares as to hemming, stitching and embroidery, for which even the "consolations of religion" provide no panacea.

In the simple Puritan days, while they had
344

before their eyes the query of Sacred Writ,
" Can a maid forget her ornaments?"—they felt
that there was no call to assist the maid in her
meditations on this subject. Little girls were
assiduously taught that to be neat and clean was
the main beauty. Good mothers who had pretty
daughters were very reticent of and remarks that
might lead in the direction of personal vanity;
any extra amount of time spent at the toilet, any
apparent anxiety about individual adornment,
met a persistent discouragement.

Never in all her life before had Dolly heard
so much discourse on subjects connected with
personal appearance, and, to say the truth, she
did not at all enter into it with the abandon and
zeal of a girl of our modern days, and found the
fitting and trying on and altering rather a tribulation to be conscientiously endured. She gathered, hemmed, stitched and sewed, however, and
submitted herself to the trying-on process with
resignation.

" The child don't seem to think much of dress,"
said Miss Debby, when alone with her sister.
" What is she thinking of, with those great eyes
of hers?"

" Oh, of things she is planning," said her
mother; " of books she is reading, of things her
father reads to her, of ways she can help me—
in short, of anything but herself."

"She is very pretty," said Miss Debby, "and is sure to be very attractive."

"Yes," answered her mother, "but Dolly hasn't the smallest notion of anything like co-quetry. Now, she has been a good deal admired here, and there have been one or two that would evidently have been glad to go farther; but Dolly cuts everything of that kind short at once. She is very pleasant, very kind, very friendly, up to a certain point, but the moment she is made love to—everything is changed."

"Well," said Miss Deborah, "I am glad I came after her. There's everything, with a girl like Dolly, in putting her into proper society. When a girl comes to her years one should put her in the way of a suitable connection at once."

"As to that," said Mrs. Cushing, "I always felt that things of that kind must be left to Providence."

"I believe, however, your husband preaches that we must 'use the means,' doesn't he? One must put children in proper society, to give Providence a chance."

"Well, Debby, you have your schemes, but I forwarn you Dolly is one who goes her own path. She seems very sweet, very gentle, very yielding, but she has a little quiet way of her own of looking at things and deciding for herself; she always knows her own mind very definitely, too."

"Good!" said Miss Debby, taking a long and considerate pinch of snuff. "We shall see."

Miss Debby had unbounded confidence in her own powers of management. She looked upon Dolly as a very creditably educated young person so far, but did not in the least doubt her own ability to add a few finishing touches here and there, which should turn her out a perfected specimen.

On Sunday morning Miss Debby arose with the spirit of a confessor. For her brother-in-law the good lady had the sincerest respect and friendship, but on this particular day she felt bound to give her patronage and support to the little church where, in her view, the truly appointed minister dispensed the teaching of the true church.

The Doctor lifted his glasses and soberly smiled as he saw her compact energetic figure walking across the green to the little church. Dolly's cheeks flamed up; she was indignant; to her it looked like a slight upon her father, and Dolly, as we have seen, had a very active spirit of partisanship.

"Well, I must say I wonder at her doing so," she commented. "Does she not think *we* are Christians?"

"She has a right to her own faith, my child," said the Doctor.

"Yes, but what would she think of me, when I am in Boston, if I should go off to some other church than hers?"

"My dear, I hope you will give her no such occasion," said Mrs. Cushing. "Your conscience requires no such course of you; hers does."

"Well, it seems to me that Aunty has a very narrow and bigoted way of looking at things," said Dolly.

"Your aunt is an old lady—very decided in all her opinions—not in the least likely to be changed by anything you or I or anybody can say to her. It is best to take her as she is."

"Besides," said the Doctor, "she has as much right to think I am in the wrong as I have to think she is. Let every one be fully persuaded in his own mind."

.   .   .   .

"I was very glad, my dear, *you* answered Dolly as you did," said Mrs. Cushing to her husband that night when they were alone. "She has such an intense feeling about all that relates to you, and the Episcopal party have been so often opposed to you, that she will need some care and caution now she is going where everything is to be changed. She will have to see that there can be truth and goodness in both forms of worship."

"Oh, certainly; I will indoctrinate Dolly," said the Doctor. "Yes, I will set the whole thing before her. She has a good clear mind. I can make her understand."

CHAPTER XXXVII.

LAST WORDS.

T last all the preparations were made, and Dolly's modest wardrobe packed to the very last article, so that her bureau drawers looked mournfully empty. It was a little hair trunk, with "D. C." embossed in brass nails upon one end, that contained all this young lady's armor—a very different affair from the Saratoga trunks of our modern belles. The pink brocade with its bunches of rose-buds; some tuckers of choice old lace that had figured in her mother's bridal toilet; a few bits of ribbon; a white India muslin dress, embroidered by her own hands;—these were the stock in trade of a young damsel of her times, and, strange as it may appear, young ladies then were stated by good authority to have been just as pretty and bewitching as now, when their trunks are several times as large.

Dolly's place and Aunt Debby's had been properly set down on Hiel's stage-book for the next morning at six o'clock; and now remained only an evening of last words.

350

So Dolly sits by her father in his study, where
from infancy she has retreated for pleasant quiet
hours, where even the books she never read
seem to her like familiar friends from the
number of times she has pondered the titles
upon their backs. And now, though she wants
to go, and feels the fluttering eagerness of the
young bird, who has wings to use and would
like to try the free air, yet the first flight from
the nest is a little fearful. Boston is a long
way off—three long days—and Dolly has never
been farther from Poganuc than she has ridden
by her father's side in the old chaise; so that
the very journey has as much importance in
her eyes as fifty years later a modern young
lady will attach to a voyage to England.

" My daughter," said the Doctor, " I know you
will have a pleasant time; I hope, a profitable
one. Your aunt is a good woman. I have great
confidence in her affection for you; your own
mother could not feel more sincere desire for
your happiness. And your grandmother is an
eminently godly woman. Of course, while with
them you will attend the services of the Episcopal
Church; for that you have my cordial consent
and willingness. The liturgy of the church is
full of devout feelings, and the Thirty-nine
Articles (with some few slight exceptions) are a
very excellent statement of truth. In adopting

the spirit and language of the prayers in the service you cannot go amiss; very excellent Christians have been nourished and brought up upon them. So have no hesitation about uniting in all Christian exercises with your relatives in Boston."

"Oh, Papa, I am almost sorry I am going," said Dolly, impulsively. "My home has been always so happy, I feel almost afraid to leave it. It seems as if I ought not to leave you and Mother alone."

The Doctor smiled and stroked her hair gently in an absent way. "We shall miss you, dear child, of course; you are the last bird in the nest, but your mother and I are quite sure it is for the best."

And then the conversation wandered back over many a pleasant field of the past—over walks and talks and happy hours long gone; over the plans and hopes and wishes for her brothers that Dolly had felt proud to be old enough to share; until the good man's voice sometimes would grow husky as he spoke and Dolly's long eye-lashes were wet and tearful. It was the kind of pleasant little summer rain of tears that comes so easily to young eyes that have never known what real sorrow is.

And when Dolly after her conference came to bid her mother good-night, she fell upon her neck and wept for reasons she could scarce explain herself.

"I should like to know what you've been saying to Dolly," said Mrs. Cushing to the Doctor, suddenly appearing at the study-door.

"Saying to Dolly?" exclaimed the Doctor, looking up dreamily, "why, nothing particular."

"Well, you've made her cry. I declare! you men have no kind of idea how to talk to a girl."

The Doctor at first looked amazed, and then an amused expression passed slowly over his face. He drew his wife down beside him and passing his arm around her said significantly,

"There *was* a girl, once, who thought I knew how to talk to her—but that is a good many years ago."

Mrs. Cushing laughed, and blushed, and said, "Oh, nonsense!"

But the Doctor looked triumphant.

"As to Dolly," he said, "never fear. She's a tender-hearted little thing, and made herself cry thinking that we should be lonesome, and a dozen other little pretty kindly things that set her tears going. She's a precious child, and we shall miss her. I have settled her mind as to the church question."

CHAPTER XXXVIII.

MY DEAR PARENTS: Here I am in Boston at last, and take the very first quiet opportunity to write to you. Hiel Jones said he would call and tell you immediately about how we got through the first day. He was very kind and attentive to us all day, taking care at every stopping-place to get the bricks heated, so that our feet were kept quite warm, and in everything he was so thoughtful and obliging that Aunt Deborah in time quite forgave him for presuming on his rights as a human being to keep up a free conversation with us at intervals, which he did with his usual cheerful goodwill.

It amuses me all the time to talk with Aunty. All her thoughts are of a century back, and she is so unconscious and positive about them that it is really entertaining. All this talk about the " lower classes," and the dangers to be apprehended from them; of " first families" and their ways and laws and opinions; and of the impropriety of being too familiar with common people,

354

amuses me. She seems to me like a woman in a book—one of the old-world people one reads of in Scott's novels. She is very kind to me; no mother could be kinder—but all in a sort of taking-possession way. She tells me where to sit, and what to do, and what to wear, and seems to feel a comfortable sense that she has me now all to herself. It amuses me to think how little she knows of what I really am inside.

We stopped the first night at a gloomy little tavern, and our room was so cold that Aunty and I puffed at each other like two goblins, a cloud coming out of our mouths every time we opened them. They made a fire in the chimney, but the chimney had swallows' nests in it and smoked; so we had to open our windows to let out the smoke, which did not improve matters.

The next night we slept at Worcester, and thought we would try not having a fire in our room; so it grew colder and colder all night, and in the morning we had to break the ice in our pitchers. My fingers felt like so many icicles, and my hair snapped with the electricity. But Aunty kept up good cheer and made me laugh through it all with her odd sayings. She is very droll and has most original ways of taking things, and is so active and courageous nothing comes amiss to her.

Our third and last day was in a driving snow-storm, and the stage was upon runners. I could see nothing all day but white drifts and eddies of snow-feathers filling the air; but at sunset all cleared away and the sun came out just as we were coming into Boston. My heart beat quite fast when I saw the dome of the State House and thought of all the noble, good men that had lived and died for our country in that brave old city. My eyes were full of tears, but I didn't say a word to Aunty, for she doesn't feel about any of these things as I do. I daresay she thinks it a great pity that the old Church and King times cannot come round again.

It was quite dark when we got home to Grandmamma's, and a lovely, real home it seems to me. Dear Grandmamma was so glad to see me, and she held me in her arms and cried and said I was just my mother over again; and that pleased me, for I like to hear that I look like Mother. Mamma knows just how the old parlor looks, with Grandmamma's rocking-chair by the fire and her table of books by her side. The house and everything about it is like a story-book, the furniture is old and dark and quaint, and the pictures on the wall are all of old-time people—aunts and cousins and uncles and grand-fathers—looking down sociably at us in the flickering fire-light.

It was all nice and sweet and good. By and

by Uncle Israel came in and I was introduced
to him, and our new English cousin, Alfred
Dunbar. They both seemed glad to see me,
and we had a very cheerful, pleasant evening.
Uncle Israel is a charming old gentleman, full
of talk and stories of by-gone times, and Cousin
Alfred is not stiff and critical as Englishmen
often are when they come to our country. He
likes America, and says he comes here to make
it his country, and so far he is delighted with
all he has seen. He seems to be one of those
who have the gift of seeing the best side of
everything. I think it is as great a gift as any
we read of in fairy stories.

Well, altogether we had a very pleasant evening, and at nine o'clock the servants came in,
and Grandmamma read prayers out of the great
prayer-book by her side. It was very sweet
to hear her trembling voice commending us all
to God's care before we lay down to rest.
Grandmamma is really altogether lovely. I feel
as if it was a blessing to be in the house with
her. I am so sleepy that I must leave this letter to be finished to-morrow.

December 24th.

I have not written a word to-day, because
Aunty said that we had come home so late
that it would be all we could do to get the
house trimmed for Christmas; and the minute

breakfast was done there was a whole cart-load
of greens discharged into the hall, and we set
to work to adorn everything. I made garlands
and wreaths and crosses, and all sorts of pretty
things, and Cousin Alfred put them up, and
Aunty said that really, "for a blue Presbyterian
girl," I showed wonderful skill and insight in
the matter.

Cousin Alfred seemed puzzled, and asked me
privately if our family were "Dissenters." I
explained to him how in our country the tables
were turned and it is the Episcopalians that are
the dissenters; and he was quite interested and
wanted to know all about it. So I told him
that you could tell much better than I could,
and he said he was coming some day to see his
relations in the country, and inquire all about
these things. He seems to be studying the facts
in our country philosophically, and when I told
him how I meant to visit the Copp's Hill Cem-
etery and the other graveyards where our fathers
are buried, he said he should like to go with
me. He is not at all trifling and worldly, like
a great many young men, but seems to *think* a
great deal and to want to know everything about
the country, and I know Papa would be interested
to talk with him.

Between us, you've no idea how like a bower
we have made the old house look. Aunty prides

herself on keeping the old English customs, and had the Yule log brought in and laid with all ceremony, and we had all the old Christmas dishes for supper in the evening, and grew very merry indeed. And indeed we have made it so late that, if I am to sleep at all to-night, I must close this letter which I want to have ready to be posted to-morrow morning.

Dear parents, I know you will be glad that I am happy and enjoying everything, but I never forget you, and think of you every moment.

Your affectionate   DOLLY.

CHAPTER XXXIX.

DOLLY'S SECOND LETTER.

MY DEAR PARENTS: We had such a glorious Christmas morning—clear, clean white snow lying on the earth and on all, even the little branches of the trees. You know, Mamma, the great square garden back of the house. Every little tree there was glittering like fairy frost work. We all hung our stockings up the night before, and at breakfast examined our presents. I had lovely things—a beautiful prayer-book bound in purple velvet from Grandmamma, and a charming necklace of pearls from Uncle Israel, and a scarlet cloak trimmed with lace from Aunt Deborah, and a beautiful Chinese fan from cousin Alfred. Aunty has been putting up the usual Christmas bundle for you; so you will all share my prosperity.

I was waked in the morning by the old North chimes, which played all sorts of psalm tunes and seemed to fill the air with beautiful thoughts. It was very sweet to me to think of what it was all about. It is not necessary to believe that our Saviour really was born this very day of all others; but that he was born on *some* day we all know. So when we walked to church together, and the church was like one green bower, and the organ played, and the choir sung, it seemed as if all there was in me was stirred. I never heard the *Te Deum* before, and how glorious, how wonderful it is! It took me up to the very gates of heaven. I felt as if I was hearing the angels sing; and when I thought of the prophets, the apostles, the martyrs, and the holy church of Christ throughout the world, I felt that I was one with them, and was happy to be one drop in that great ocean of joy. For though I was only a little one I felt *in* it, and *with* it, and a part of it, and all the joy and glory was mine. I trembled with happiness.

When the communion service came I went with Grandmamma and knelt at the altar. It seemed as if Christ himself was there giving me the bread and the wine. I never felt so near to Him. After church I went home. I was so full that I could not speak. No one else seemed to feel as I did—they were all used to it—but it was all new and wonderful to me, and made heavenly things so real that I felt almost averse to coming back to every day life. I wanted to go alone to my room and dwell on it. There was quite a company invited to dinner, and I did not feel like joining them, but I knew Aunty wanted me to make myself agreeable, and so I tried my best, and after a while took my part in the conversation, as gay as the rest of them. Only once in a while some of those noble words I had been hearing came back to me with a sudden thrill, and would bring tears to my eyes even while I was gayest.

Cousin Alfred noticed that I was feeling very much about something, and in the evening when we were alone for a few minutes he asked me about it, and then I told him all how the service affected me, and made me feel. He looked a little surprised at first, and then he seemed thoughtful; and when I said, "I should think those who hear and say such glorious things at church, ought to live the very noblest lives, to be perfect Christians," he said, "Cousin, I am sorry to say, it is not so with me. We hear these things from childhood; we hear them Sunday after Sunday, in all sorts of moods, and I'm afraid many of us form a habit of not really thinking how much they mean. I wish I could hear our service as you have done, for the first time, and that it would seem as real and earnest to me as it does to you."

We talked a good deal after this; he has a deep, thoughtful mind, and I wish you, my dear Father, could talk with him. I know you will like him. Is n't it pleasant to find relations that one can like and esteem so much? Cousin Alfred is like a brother to me already, and to-morrow we are going out to explore the antiquuities of Boston. He seems as much interested in them as I do.

Dear Parents, this Christmas puts me in mind of the time years ago when they dressed the little church in Poganuc, and I ran away, over to the church, and got asleep under a great cedar-bush, listening to the Christmas music. It affected me then just as it has done now. Is it not beautiful to think we are singing words that Christians have been singing for more than a thousand years! It gives you the feeling of being in a great army—one of a great host; and for a poor little insignificant thing like me it is a joyful feeling.

You ought to see how delighted Aunt Deborah is that I take so kindly to the prayer-book and the service. She gives me little approving nods now and then, and taps me on the shoulder in a patronizing way and says there is good blood in my veins, for all I was brought up a Presbyterian! This is all very well, but when she goes to unchurching all our churches and saying there are no ordained ministers in the United States except the few in Episcopal pulpits, I am dreadfully tempted to run a tilt with her, though

I know it would do no earthly good. I believe I should do it, however, if Cousin Alfred did not take up the argument on our side, and combat her so much better than I could that I am content to let her alone. She tells him that he is no Englishman and no churchman, but a very radical; and he tells her that he came to America to learn to use his common sense and get rid of old rubbish!

For all this they are excellent friends, and dear old Grandmamma always takes our part because she is so afraid Aunt Debby will hurt my feelings, though Aunty says that in her heart Grandmamma is a regular old Tory.

I asked Grandma about this one day, when we were alone, and she said she always loved and honored the king and royal family, and was grieved when they stopped praying for them in the churches. If she was a Tory she was so from love, and it is quite charming to hear her talk about the old times.

It seems to me no great change ever comes on this earth without grieving some good people.

But it is past midnight and I must not sit up writing any longer. Dear parents, I wish you a happy Christmas!

Your loving   DOLLY.

CHAPTER XL.

EAR OLD FELLOW: Here I am in America—in Boston—and every day I spend here makes me more and more satisfied with my change of situation. The very air here is free and inspiring, full of new hope and life. The old world with all its restraints and bounds, its musty prejudices, its time-honored inconveniences and hindrances, is a thing gone by; it is blue in the dim distance, and I see before me a free, generous, noble country that offers everything equally to all. I like Massachusetts; I like Boston; and more and more I feel that I am a fortunate fellow to have been selected by my uncle for this lot.

He is all that is kind and generous and fatherly to me, and I should be an ungrateful cur if I did not give him the devotion of a son. He is so amiable and reasonable that this is not at all a hard task.

We are spending our Christmas holidays with his mother and sister; after that he will go to housekeeping in his own house. He wants me to get married with all convenient dispatch, but I am one that cannot enter into the holy state simply to furnish a housekeeper to my uncle or to place a well-dressed, well-mannered woman at the head of my own table.

You at home called me fastidious and romantic. Well, I am so to this degree, that I never shall marry unless I see the woman I cannot live without. The feast of matrimony may be well appointed, the oxen and fatlings be killed, and all things ready, but I never shall accept unless some divine power "*compels*" me to come in;— and up to this day I have felt no such call.

Mark me, I say, *up to this day;* for I am by no means certain I shall say as much a month hence. To be frank with you, there is spending the Christmas holidays under the same roof with me a very charming girl whom I am instructed by my Aunt Deborah to call "Cousin Dolly."

Now, in point of fact, this assumption of relationship is the most transparent moonshine. I am, I believe, second or third cousin to my "Uncle Israel," who is real uncle to this Miss Dolly. Of course my cousinship to her must be of a still more remote and impalpable nature; but if it is agreed that we call each other "cousin," certainly it is not *I* that am going to object to the position and its immunities—oh, no! A cousin stands on a vantage-ground; all sorts of delightful freedoms and privileges are permitted to him!

I "take the good the gods provide" me, and so Cousin Dolly and I have become the best of friends, and we have been busy making wreaths and crosses and Christmas decorations under the superintendence of Aunt Deborah, in the most edifying and amicable way. This Aunt Deborah is the conventional upright, downright, good, opinionated, honest, sincere old Englishwoman, of whom there are dozens at every turn in the old country, but who here in America have the interest that appertains to the relics of a past age. But she is vigorously determined that in her domains the old customs shall be in full force, and every rule of Christmas-keeping observed.

Of course I put up mistletoe in all the proper places, and I found my new cousin, having grown up as a New England Congregational minister's daughter, knew nothing of its peculiar privileges and peculiarities, so that when the kissing began I saw a bright flush of amazement and almost resentment pass over her face; though when it was explained to be an old Christmas custom she laughed and gave way with a good grace. But I observed my young lady warily inspecting the trimmings of the room, and quietly avoiding all the little green traps thereafter.

It is quite evident that, though she has all the gentleness of a dove, she has some of the wisdom of the serpent, and possesses very definite opinions as to what she likes and does not like. She impresses me as having, behind an air of softness and timidity, a very positive and decided character. There is a sort of reserved force in her; and one must study her to become fully acquainted with her. Thus far I hope I have not lost ground.

I find she is an enthusiast for her country, for her religion, for everything high and noble; and not one of the mere dolls that have no capability for anything but ribbons and laces. She has promised to show me the antiquities of Boston and put me in the way of knowing all that a good American ought to know; you see our time for the holidays is very agreeably planned out in advance.

And now, my dear old fellow, I see you shake your head and say, What is to come of all this?

Wait and see. If it *should* so happen that I should succeed in pleasing this little American princess—if, having gained her ear as Cousin, I should succeed in proving to her that I am no cousin at all, but want to be more than cousin or brother or the whole world together to her—if all this should come to pass, why—there have stranger things happened in this world of ours.

But I am running before my time. Miss Dolly is yet an unknown quantity and there may be a long algebraic problem to be done before I can know what may be; and so, good-night for the present. Yours ever truly,

ALFRED DUNBAR.

CHAPTER XLI.

FINALE.

FTER reading the preceding letters, there is no one who has cared to follow Dolly's fortunes thus far that is not ready to declare the end of the story. One sees how the Christmas holidays stretched on and on; how Aunt and Grandmamma importuned Dolly to stay longer; how Dolly staid, and how she and Cousin Alfred walked and talked and studied New England history, and visited all the shrines in Boston and Cambridge and the region round about; how Aunt Debby plumed herself on the interesting state of things evidently growing up, but wisely said nothing to either party; how at last when spring came, and April brought back the mayflower buds, and Dolly felt that she could stay no longer but *must* go home to her parents, "Cousin Alfred" declared that he could not think of her taking a three days' journey alone, that he must go with her and protect her, and improve the opportunity to make the acquaintance of his relations in the country.

All this came to pass, and one fine evening, just at sunset, Hiel drove into Poganuc in glory, and deposited Dolly and her little hair trunk and her handsome attendant at the Parsonage door.

There was a bluebird singing on the top of the tall buttonwood tree opposite, just as he used to sing years before; and, as to Hiel, he returned home even better content with himself than ordinarily.

"There now, Nabby! didn't I tell ye what would happen when Dolly went to Boston? Wal, I've just set her down to the Doctor's with as fine a young sprig as you'd wish to see, who came all the way from Boston with her. I tell *you*, that air young man's eyes is *sot ;* he knows what he's come to Poganuc fer, ef no one else don't."

"Dear me!" exclaimed Nabby and Mother Jones, both rushing to the window simultaneously with the vain hope of getting a glimpse.

"Oh, there's no use lookin'!" said Hiel; "they're gone in long ago. Doctor and Mis' Cushing was standin' in the door-way when I come up, and mighty glad they was to see her, and him too, and shook hands with him. Oh, thet air's a fixed-up thing, you may depend."

"Dear me, what is he?" queried Mother Jones. "Do you know, Hiel?"

"Of course I know," said Hiel; "he's a merchant in the Injy trade up there to Boston. I expect he makes lots o' money."

"Dear me! I hope they won't set their hearts on worldly prosperity," said Mother Jones in a lugubrious tone; "this 'ere's a dyin' world."

"For all that, Mother," said Hiel as they sat down to the tea-table, "you enjoy a cup o' hot tea as well as any woman livin', and why shouldn't the parson's folks be glad o' their good things?"

"Wal, I don' know," answered Mother Jones, "but it allers kind o' scares me when everything seems to be goin' jest right fer folks. Ye know the hymn says:

> 'We should suspect some danger nigh
> When we possess delight.'

I remember poor Bill Parmerlee fell down dead the very week he was married!"

"Well, Nabby and I neither of us fell down dead when *we* was married," said Hiel, "and nobody else that ever I heerd on, so we won't weep and wail if Dolly Cushing *hez* got a rich, handsome feller, and is goin' to live in Boston."

But, after all, Dolly and Alfred Dunbar were not yet engaged. No decisive word had been spoken between them; though it seemed now as if but a word were wanting.

It was after a week of happy visiting, when he had made himself most charming to all in the house, when Dolly and he had together explored every walk and glen and waterfall around Poganuc, that at last the young man found voice to ask the Doctor for what he wanted; and, armed with the parental approval, to put the decisive question to Dolly. Her answer is not set down. But it is on record that in the month of June there was a wedding at Poganuc which furnished the town with things to talk about for weeks.

It was a radiant June morning, when the elms of Poganuc were all alive with birds, when the daisies were white in the meadows, and the bobolink on the apple-tree was outdoing himself, that Hiel drove up to the door of the Parsonage to take Dolly and her husband their first day's journey towards their new home. There were the usual smiles and tears and kissing and crying, and then Hiel shut the stage-door, mounted his box, and drove away in triumph. It was noticed that he had ornamented his horses with a sprig of lilac blossoms over each ear, and wore a great bouquet in his button-hole.

And so our Dolly goes to her new life, and, save in memories of her childhood, is to

be no longer one of the good people of Poganuc.

. . . .

Years have passed since then. Dolly has held
her place among the matronage of Boston; her
sons have graduated at Harvard, and her daughters have recalled to memory the bright eyes
and youthful bloom of their mother.

As to Poganuc, all whom we knew there have
passed away; all the Town-Hill aristocracy and
the laboring farmers of the outskirts have gone,
one by one, to the peaceful sleep of the Poganuc graveyard. There was laid the powdered
head, stately form, and keen blue eye of Colonel Davenport; there came in time the once
active brain and ready tongue of Judge Belcher;
there, the bright eyes and genial smile of Judge
Gridley; there, the stalwart form of Tim Hawkins, the gray, worn frame of Zeph Higgins.
Even Hiel's cheery face and vigorous arm had
its time of waxing old and passing away, and
was borne in to lie quiet under the daisies.
The pastor and his wife sleep there peacefully
with their folded flock around them.

> " Kinsman and townsman are laid side by side,
> Yet none have saluted, and none have replied."

A village of white stones stands the only witness of the persons of our story. Even the old
meeting-house is dissolved and gone.

Generation passeth, generation cometh, saith
the wise man, but the earth abideth forever.
The hills of Poganuc are still beautiful in their
summer woodland dress. The Poganuc river still
winds at their feet with gentle murmur. The
lake, in its steel-blue girdle of pines, still reflects
the heavens as a mirror; its silent forest shores
are full of life and wooded beauty. The elms
that overarch the streets of the central village
have spread their branches wider, and form a
beautiful walk where other feet than those we
wot of are treading. As other daisies have
sprung in the meadows, and other bobolinks and
bluebirds sing in the tree-tops, so other men
and women have replaced those here written of,
and the story of life still goes on from day to
day among the POGANUC PEOPLE.

THE END.

TRADE PUBLICATIONS

OF

FORDS, HOWARD, & HULBERT,

No. 27 Park Place, New York.

———o———

TO BE HAD OF BOOKSELLERS, OR WILL BE MAILED, POST-PAID, ON RECEIPT OF PRICE.

———o———

MAY 1st, 1878.

BRYANT, WILLIAM CULLEN.

A LIBRARY OF POETRY AND SONG: Being Choice Selections from the Best Poets, English, Scotch, Irish and American, including Translations from the Greek, Latin, German, Spanish, Italian, etc., with an Introduction in the form of a Treatise on the History and Functions of the Poetical Art, from the pen of the Editor. 832 pp., 8vo. *Illustrated* with a Steel Portrait of Mr. Bryant, 26 Autographic Fac-Similes of Celebrated Poets, and 16 Full-page Wood Engravings. Cloth, $5; Cloth Gilt, $6; Turkey Morocco, $10.

" Selections which nearly cover the entire historical period over which English poetry extends . . . matter suited to every conceivable taste and variety of feeling and culture. We know of no similar collection in the English language which, in copiousness and felicity of selection and arrangement, can at all compare with it."—*New York Times.*

" Mr. Bryant's introduction to the volume is a most beautiful and comprehensive critical essay on poets and poetry, from the days of 'the father of English poetry' to the present time."—*Albany Evening Journal.*

DAVIS, MRS. S. M.

LIFE AND TIMES OF SIR PHILIP SIDNEY. A Memorial of one whose name is a Synonym for every Manly Virtue. *Illustrated* with 3 Steel Plates: Portrait of Sidney; View of Penshurst Castle; Fac-Simile of Sidney's Manuscript. Stamped in ink and gold, with Sidney's Coat of Arms. 12mo. Cloth, beveled, $1.50.

" There are few more attractive figures in the glorious company of English heroes than Sidney, the soldier, courtier, scholar—the accepted type of an English gentleman . . . yet, except in encyclopedias and kindred works, there is scarcely any satisfactory memoir of him accessible to the general reader, and the author of this book has done a good service in presenting a clear and well-written narrative."—*Philadelphia Inquirer.*

" A book well deserving the beautiful printing and binding into which the Fords have put it."—*N.Y. Evening Mail.*

" Worthy of place as an English Classic."—*Pittsburgh Commercial.*

FAMOUS FICTION.

A LIBRARY OF FAMOUS FICTION, or World's Story Book. Containing the Nine Standard Masterpieces of Imaginative Literature : " Pilgrim's Progress;" "Robinson Crusoe;" " Elizabeth, or the Exiles of Siberia;" " Undine;" "Vicar of Wakefield;" "Paul and Virginia;" "Picciola;" "Vathek;" "Tales from the Arabian Nights." 1,066 pp., 8vo. 34 Full-page Wood Engravings. Cloth, beveled, $4.

GOODWIN, REV. T. A.

THE MODE OF MAN'S IMMORTALITY ; or, The When, Where, and How of the Future Life. By the Author of "The Perfect Man." (*Third edition.*) 12mo. Cloth, $1.25.

" It is the product of his brain, for it is a book with an idea."—*Dover Morning Star.*

" The fact that this little treatise has reached a second edition is sufficient evidence that it finds appreciation among those who derive pleasure in speculation concerning the future existence."—*Boston Post.*

" Combats with energy and freshness of thought the idea of a resurrection of the material body that is laid in the grave. . . . A good book to arouse men to read the scriptures afresh, and to think."—*Christian Union.*

PATTON, JACOB HARRIS, A.M.

A CONCISE HISTORY OF THE AMERICAN PEOPLE, from the Discoveries of the Continent to 1876 ; giving a clear Account of their Political, Military, Moral, Industrial, and Commercial Life. *Illustrated* with Stuart's Portrait of Washington, Maps and Charts ; and containing Marginal Dates, Statistical References, and a full Analytical Index. 1,018 pp. 8vo. Cloth, $3.00 ; Half Russia, $5.00.

" Mr. Patton's style is deserving of unqualified praise. It is pure, simple, strong, free from mannerism, and singularly easy and graceful. We anticipate for the work a cordial reception and extensive popularity among those who know how to prize the best books."—*North American Review.*

" A very satisfactory account of the history of the country from its first discovery ; not so full as to be umanageable from its numerous details, nor so short as to be merely a dry detail of facts and dates."—*Cleveland Herald.*

" With evident integrity of purpose, as well as with rare sagacity, the author has steered clear of the errors of a partisan, and has given us the story of the last few years very much as it will be read by an impartial posterity."—*N.Y. Evangelist.*

" Our wonder is that so much of American history could be comprised in one octavo volume ; at the same time, it is very graphically written, in a clear unostentatious style ; our frequent use of it convinces us of its great accuracy."—*N.Y. Observer.*

RAYMOND, ROSSITER W.

BRAVE HEARTS. An American Novel. Illustrations by Darley, Stephens, Beard, and Kendrick. 12mo. Cloth, $1.00.

" A successful experiment. It is a tale of two regions—alternations between the quiet scenes of New England and the rough, boisterous and dangerous life of an extempore Californian."—*Philadelphia Evening Herald.*

" A really good American novel. . . . The purpose of the book is indicated by its title. It is a representation of *courage*, in various forms of individual character."—*Boston Globe.*

Fords, Howard, & Hulbert—Trade Books.

STOWE, Mrs. HARRIET B.

MY WIFE AND I: Or, Harry Henderson's History. A Novel. *Illustrated.* 12mo. Cloth, $1.50.

"Always bright, piquant, and entertaining, with an occasional touch of tenderness, strong because subtle, keen in sarcasm, full of womanly logic directed against unwomanly tendencies."—*Boston Journal.*

WE AND OUR NEIGHBORS: The Records of an Unfashionable Street. A Novel. *Illustrated.* 12mo. Cloth, $1.50.

"Written in Mrs. Stowe's genial, hearty style, with the sparkle of fun, wit and humor, and the touches of deep pathos which characterize her work."—*Worcester Spy.*

BETTY'S BRIGHT IDEA: and Other Tales. Comprising "Betty's Bright Idea," "Deacon Pitkin's Farm," and "The First Christmas in New England." *Illustrated.* 12mo. Cloth, 75 cts.

"They are charming tales."—*Springfield Union.*

"There are tears between the lines, and smiles—bits of sunshine in an April sky—such as Mrs. Stowe knows how to paint."—*Chicago Inter-Ocean.*

POGANUC PEOPLE: Their Loves and Lives. A Novel. *Illustrated.* 12mo. Cloth, $1.50. (*Just out.*)

In the style of early New England scene and character, in which Mrs. Stowe is so inimitable. As "Oldtown Folks" was said to be founded on Dr. Stowe's childhood memories, so this is drawn from some of the author's own reminiscences, and has all the brightness of genuine portraiture.

BIBLE HEROINES: Narrative Biographies of Prominent Hebrew Women in the Patriarchal, National and Christian Eras. Imperial Octavo. *Spirited frontispiece,* "Deborah the Prophetess." Elegantly bound, red burnished edges. $2.

"The fine penetration, quick insight, sympathetic nature, and glowing narrative, which have marked Mrs. Stowe's previous works are found in these pages, and the whole work is one which readily captivates equally the cultivated and the religiously fervent nature."—*Boston Commonwealth.*

FOOTSTEPS OF THE MASTER: Studies in the Life of Christ. With Illustrations and Illuminated Titles. 12mo. Cloth, $1.50.

"A very sweet book of wholesome religious thought."—*N.Y. Evening Post.*

"A congenial field for the exercise of her choice literary gifts and poetic tastes, her ripe religious experience, and her fervent Christian faith. A book of exceptional beauty and substantial worth."—*Congregationalist* (Boston).

Fords, Howard, & Hulbert *publish, by subscription, a list of attractive Illustrated Standard Works, which afford remunerative employment to Canvassers of the right kind. These publications are of high literary and artistic character, and command ready sales.*

☞ CORRESPONDENCE IS INVITED.